The House in Morocco

Also by Rosalind Brackenbury

Novels
A Day to Remember to Forget
A Virtual Image
Into Egypt
A Superstitious Age
The Caelocanth
The Woman in the Tower
Sense and Sensuality
Crossing The Water
The Circus at the End of the World
Seas Outside The Reef

Poetry
Telling Each Other It Is Possible
Making for the Secret Places
Coming Home the Long Way Round The Mountain
The Beautiful Routes of the West

Short Stories
Between Man and Woman Keys

Novella
Septembre (French edition only, translated by Elizabeth Janvier)

Rosalind Brackenbury

The House in Morocco

The Toby Press

First Edition 2003

The Toby Press *LLC*
www.tobypress.com

ISBN 1 902881 76 1, *hardcover*

A CIP catalogue record for this title
is available from the British Library

Typeset in Garamond by Jerusalem Typesetting

Printed and bound in the United States by
Thomson-Shore Inc., Michigan

For Miranda, Sam and Stephanie

Contents

"The marvel of a house is not that it shelters or warms a man, nor that its walls belong to him. It is that it leaves its trace on the language."

Antoine de Saint-Exupery: *Wind, Sand and Stars 1939*

Prologue

*M*ogador. It was in a place called Mogador. That was the old name for the town, when the French controlled that part of Morocco. Morocco was divided into the Spanish and the French sectors. Tangiers was an international city, then.

It was in 1936. I was twenty years old, imagine, so much younger than you are now. Such a long time ago. Didn't I tell you this before? My uncle, Uncle Hajji, was the British consul in Rabat. He wrote to ask for my cousin Lucy to join him for six months, to help him to entertain. Lucy was going to marry Michael, so she didn't want to go. But I was free. I was thrilled at the idea. So he got Marion instead of Lucy, and Michael got Lucy, and that was the way it all turned out.

I remember taking the train with my mother to Tilbury. She came to see me off. From there I took the steamship around Spain, through the Bay of Biscay, to Tangiers. People were terribly sick in the Bay, and a man gave me champagne; he said it was the best cure. On the ship I danced with a young man who wanted to come down to Rabat with me. He was terribly keen. But I wanted to go alone. In Tangiers, Uncle Hajji met me with a Daimler and asked me to drive. He hated driving, *he said. We were coming through the Spanish Protectorate when we had a flat tyre. A wild place, it was. He didn't know how to change a wheel, so I said I would. I had my good skirt on, one I'd bought at Debenham's just before I left, so I took it off and got down on my knees. Imagine, an English girl in her petticoat, changing a wheel in the dust. Wild country for as far as you could see. I'll never forget that.*

In Rabat we had dances. Uncle Hajji loved dancing. We used to roll up the carpet and put chalk on the floor and wind up the gramophone to dance. All sorts of people came, Moroccans, Europeans. There was a young man, a Moroccan, studying law. His name was Abdel. He took me to the town that was once Mogador.

I remember the wife of the French consul stood on the beach and shouted at a Zeppelin that went over. Sales boches! she shouted. Sales boches! It was a strange time, as if we were waiting for something to happen. But nobody ever said, what.

Part 1
Sarah

Chapter one
The Blue Door

The eyes follow her all the way from the bus station and past the spice market, through the gate called the Bab Doukala and into the Medina, the heart of the town. The eyes of the town, from the high-up windows in whitewashed walls, from behind the nearly closed blue doors.

She has a bag, a suitcase, and a portable typewriter in its case. All these things she manages to carry without looking burdened; she brought them with her in the bus from Marrakesh. Men help her with them as she gets down. She's watched, by men on street corners, men who pass close to her in the street.

"Sarah," she'll say, if anyone asks her, *"Je m'appelle Sarah."* In the open, frank way of the western world, maybe holding out a hand to shake another's.

Why is she here, they may be thinking, where is she from and why is she, a woman, travelling alone?

The smells, she notices, are of smoke, fish, dung. Above all there is the smell of the sea. The line of it, a darkness beyond the yellow lights of the town.

She has notebooks, a camera. A few old photographs in a folder. Clippings from magazines in French and English, typed quotations from books. Photocopied articles from the library at the Institut du Monde Arabe in Paris, from the sociology department at the university in Marrakesh. A thin book bought in Tangiers. She believes in reason rather than chaos, in being able to discover the causes of things: she hopes for it, even though her own life so far has not given grounds for it. She walks past the men calling out "Taxi!" her long stride across puddles and craters in the road, she follows the lights, the fires, walks in the near-darkness carrying all her own burdens because she wants to, the sky above her the colour of a plum.

At the first hotel she finds, the Hotel Sahara, a man wrapped in a blanket gets up from the narrow bench where he has been lying, to let her in. He shows her the room, the bed, a cold night ahead in the Hotel Sahara. She pulls a wool scarf over her head and lies down fully dressed. Nothing is unpacked. She's been travelling since just after dawn. The bed's single damp sheet smells of mildew and she hunches into herself, holds herself tight and eventually sleeps, her hands folded between her thighs in blue jeans, her shoulders protecting her, her hair across the pillow. The cold holds her still. The voice of the muezzin hauls her up four-hourly out of dreams.

In the morning she'll find the man whose address she has from Marrakesh, who will find her somewhere permanent to stay. "I trust you will take care of her. *Je te fais confiance, que tu t'occupes bien d'elle.*" Like a precious object, or a lost child, to be labelled and led away; to be passed from hand to hand invisibly, across Morocco.

*   *   *

Blue-white-blue. In the morning, sky, walls, painted doors and shutters. The sky dark as an iris when she wakes close to midday. The blue of new-painted railings, deep delphinium. Essaouira. The city's name has the sound of the wind. It hisses through the sand dunes. There is the long calligraphy of wind on sand. The open hand of the long beach and the closed fist of the fortified tower. At one end of the town, the Atlantic beats up against rocks and the walls of the ramparts, called La Skala. At the other, it unfolds in gentle fan shapes on the sand. She walks from one to the other, discovering the town's boundaries, before she goes down to find the *café* on the beach and the man to whom her letter is addressed.

*   *   *

The blue door in the high wall inside the Medina opened and a man let her in. Sarah saw darkness behind him, and very blue eyes in a tanned face.

"*Entrez,*" he said to her, standing back to let her pass. She was here for a reason, she wanted to say, but the reason had not quite caught up with her, it was travelling somewhere behind, like lost luggage to be delivered the next day. The man who stood in the street with her, *Monsieur* Haj, whom she'd found at the *café* on the beach, he had taken her letter—Arabic on one side, French on the other—read it and smiled. He followed her inside, bowing.

The door closed slowly behind her with a wheeze. The blue-eyed man led her up a white stairway. Going into the house was like going into a small church, white and vaulted and clean. There was a well at the centre so you could look down all the way from the top floor to the ground. She saw that there were no true angles to this house, but a gentle merging of vertical and horizontal that curved where angles might have been. They came out on to the roof. The light was extraordinary. It was the time of early evening when everything began to be transformed, distance seemed near and the edges of everything were very sharp. The sunset began changing everything from the horizon in.

"You can have the room on the roof when it is ready. I will ask *Monsieur* Nick. It is he who owns this house. I am sure he will say yes. I am sure he will like you. We have no guests at present. There is perhaps a week's work to do up here. The builders are very slow. But while they finish, you can live downstairs. There are many rooms, you will see. You want heating, you said? Heating, *bien sûr*, there is a wood fire, fires in the rooms, you can light a fire up here if you want, you can have fire everywhere."

"And tables? I need a table. I'm here to write."

"Table? Of course, table. Table and heat."

"*Je m'appelle Yann.*" His hand on his heart.

"Sarah," she said. "Are you French?"

"*Oui, Madame. Enchanté.*" He bowed over her hand.

Who was she, this American woman (for he'd caught her accent), who'd walked in here this calmly? He guessed her age, probably younger than his own, late thirties or a young forty. She threw back her hair and fixed him with a grey-green look, then she followed him into the house talking her accented French as if they'd known each other forever. He looked at her eyes, her legs, took in breasts and neck. He was used to looking at women this way. But she outstared him, made him a little embarrassed. She walked away from him and leaned against the white parapet on the rooftop, looked out across the darkened city, its domes and roofs and minarets, as if she owned it already. In spite of the accent, she reminded him of Nick—that Anglo-Saxon arrogance that intrigued him even as he resented it. He stood back at the staircase head to let her go first down the tight white curve of the stair. Someone had left a bucket of cement and a flat trowel on the floor, and he pushed them aside with his foot.

"*Bon.* Now, we have seen up here, let us go down and meet Nick. He is *le patron.*"

She went down, her hand on the curve of the wall—the rectangular eliminated by coats and coats of whitewash, years of being smoothed by human hands—her feet feeling their way. Behind her she heard him puffing slightly, and the slap of his leather slippers on stone.

The man he called Nick—Neek—looked up at her from the chair where he lounged, one ankle hooked across the other knee, a moccasin dangling from a naked foot.

"Well, Yann seems to have taken a fancy to you. How much can you afford? I gather you are desperate for a bit of warmth? Nobody realizes how chilly Moroccan winters can be, do they?"

He smoked Winstons, leaning brown elbows on the table beside the pack, his white shirtsleeves rolled back. He spoke with an easy, lazy drawl she recognized from British movies and thought of as old-fashioned. He stared at her and raised an eyebrow.

"Yann says you need a table. Yann, have we done anything about a table yet?"

"Omar's gone out to look for one." What was the relationship between these two? Were they master and servant? Friends? Business associates? She couldn't guess.

Nick jiggled the table in front of him, a thick knotty polished wood inlaid with mother of pearl. "Trouble is, all the pretty ones are so rickety. Well, you won't need one tonight, will you? You aren't that keen to start work? Why don't you fetch your luggage, though? You might as well move in straight away. Where were you staying? The Sahara? Oh, God."

He lit another cigarette from the stub of the one he'd just finished and looked at her through clouds of smoke.

"Sit down, Sarah. I can call you Sarah? I'm Nick, as Yann says, I am kind of *le patron*, but then so is he, only he hates responsibility so I do all the work. Welcome to the Villa Sadia. It's nice to have a guest. I should tell you the form: you can have coffee and bread for breakfast and eat with us in the evening. Midday, we all fend for ourselves. We go down to the port and eat sardines, like one big happy family. I'll tell them to give you a special price. That suit you? Tell me, what do you write?"

She sat down on an ornate and uncomfortable chair in the alcove, the curtains behind her open on the purplish night. "I'm here to do a series of articles on Moroccan women. I've been in Marrakesh. A friend told me to come here. So I came." It was at least half true.

"Moroccan women, eh. You'll have your work cut out."

"I guess I'm used to it."

There was something edgy about her, he thought, self-composed, but like a racehorse waiting in the stalls to run. He guessed at her age, education, background. Boston, maybe, she had almost English R's. Posh America, definitely, not the boondocks. A good women's college—Smith or Vassar perhaps. Sarah. Sarah who? Oh, they could fill in the details later. She might amuse them. Anyway, it would be better than just being a houseful of men. He saw she wasn't going to be a nuisance.

"Well, has Yann shown you your room? You can always move up to the one on the roof when it's done, if you want to be away from it all. Show her the one next to mine, Yann, will you, it's quieter on that side, she won't hear the worst of the racket the builders make. So. We'll meet at dinner."

*   *   *

Yann said, "If you should need anything, ask me. And if anybody bothers you, tell them you are a guest of Nick."

"Okay. Thanks."

"And if you need anything—?" He ran a hand across his unshaven chin and lounged in the doorway of her room.

"I can't think of a thing I could need. Here I am with a room of my own and a view of the ocean, three meals a day and a table on its way."

She was already opening her long-handled bag where it lay on the white embroidered bedspread, spilling its contents, making a dent in the smoothness. Damn, her other bag was still at the appalling Hotel Sahara up the street. But if she was going to be treated like a queen, with people running after her finding antique tables, perhaps she could get someone to go and pick it up.

"You know," he says, "I am glad you are here. I am glad that you are a writer." His eyes on her, as she moved about. "I think it could be helpful to me. I have stories in my head that I never write down. One day, I will write them. Perhaps you will help me. Who knows?"

She longed for him to go. No more talk, for God's sake, please.

"You want me to go now. You want to be alone, *n'est-ce pas?*"

"Yes."

She set her small typewriter on the floor where the table would be, where she would have her view. White room, blue ceramic pots, white curtains and bedspread, blue flowers in a gouache hung on the wall above the bed. A blue door in a white wall. And the man with blue sailor's eyes—good-looking, though a mess, she conceded—lounging in the doorway, watching her move in. In this town that used, long ago, to be called Mogador. She took out a small, creased black and white photograph of a young woman standing between two men in blinding sun under a palm tree, whose shadow sliced across the face of the younger man; and she tucked it into the corner of the blue flowers. In her room, which was perfect for her, just perfect, she walked about, placing things, thinking, while across the city the muezzin called out again on what was beginning to be a familiar slide of notes. Beyond the white curtains the sky was now sloe-black, dusted with stars.

* * *

It was so good to have arrived here, after the long, slow bus journey from Marrakesh. Incredible, this city on the Atlantic like some long white liner only just moored to land. She'd left early, after saying a whispered goodbye to her friend Suzanne in the dawn kitchen of the house in the suburbs of Marrakesh, and then taken a cab down to the bus station. Suzanne had said: I'll drive you. But the household was asleep. So she'd left on her own, hung out for hours in the central bus station, waiting for the bus to Essaouira. The bus had been full, women holding chickens upside down by their feet, men dozing. On the way here she'd been lulled to sleep by the chant of Arabic on the radio, shaken awake again by the lurch of the wheels over stones, the sudden stops and starts. Occasionally the bus stopped with no warning, to let someone off who just walked off into the landscape, no sign of a dwelling anywhere, or pick up someone else who'd materialized equally strangely out of a terrain of rocks and sky. There was a pit stop for mint tea drinking and buying cakes and oranges. A boy cleaned men's shoes for them, with spit and lemon juice. The smells of dung and lemons, the smells of Morocco. Then they'd all climbed on board again and lurched off down the winding road between the strange, stunted trees and rocks, where goats scrambled and seemed in the dusk to be trying to climb the trees.

At dinner that first night, she sat at the long dark wood refectory table with five men. Yann sat at one end, Nick at the other, with Omar, a young Moroccan, next to him. Jake, Nick's teenage nephew sat on his other side, and then Ramon, the round-faced young Spaniard who had, she was told, come from Spain to do the plumbing. Yann was next to her, wearing a black burnous fastened on one shoulder with a golden brooch. He was sleek-haired, younger for having shaved. He played with his wine glass, a big square emerald on the middle finger of his right hand, and glanced sideways at her from time to time. Sarah looked straight ahead and drank her wine.

"The house was a brothel, you know. Terribly famous among seafaring men. Half the French navy used to come here. It was owned by a woman called Madame Sadia. She never exactly let on that it was a brothel. She just had wonderful parties. Lobster, champagne, the lot. The officers used to love it. The feasting used to go on here, on this floor, then the bedrooms were upstairs where you're sleeping, Sarah—and down below she used to let it to fishermen, so if you can imagine, a million fishermen downstairs sleeping among their stinking gear, and the champagne drinking going on here, and then upstairs, the sex. God knows what happened on the roof. Omar, is there any more of this Toulal? It's not bad. Well, I bought this place from Sadia." Nick put his elbows on the table and grinned.

"What happened to her?" All this sounded to her like the nineteenth century, not the end of the twentieth.

"She was the most beautiful woman in Morocco, you know. That was her official title. She's old, now. Lives in an apartment in Agadir. Everyone thought she was rich, but maybe she spent all her money having a good time. She was still a hell of a flirt, when I knew her. Stunning looking, even as an old woman. Brothels aren't legal here, so she just had to carry it off as a place where all the best parties happened. Anybody objected, she just seduced him. If he had money, she married him. It worked pretty well."

"Sounds practical. Was she really the most beautiful woman in Morocco?"

"Well, if anyone really thinks they are, and gets the publicity organized, they are, wouldn't you say? She certainly had what it took. If you want to write about Moroccan women, you could start with her. She was a businesswoman. Hard bargainer. I think she took a slight fancy to me. But then I'm a hard bargainer too."

He smiled his secretive smile and looked down the table at her to judge his effect. She thought: I'm sure you are.

Omar, who'd brought in all the food and then sat to eat with them said, "Yes, she was the most beautiful woman in Morocco. The king came here once, people say. She had a child of the king. Then she could say that she was of the royal household, she gave herself the royal name."

He was slim, with a shock of hair. His small brown hands gestured as he spoke: royal, they said, beautiful, the king, a child of the king.

Nick said, "Well, you may be embroidering a bit there. She had some tall stories. But then, who's to say that tall stories are never true?"

Omar got up to clear the bowls away and to bring the salad and the *tajines*. He touched people's arms, their shoulders, as he served them like a mother. Nick sat there like the king himself, enjoying his own table. Yann broke off pieces of the round flat bread. He leaned towards her and she smelled smoke and garlic on his breath.

"Buried treasure. Treasure at the bottom of the sea. What could be more fascinating? Do you have any idea of how much there is down there? There is a whole world of treasure, out of sight, under the sea. I have been a diver, I have seen it, I have brought it up with my own hands. You're from America? Do you know the Florida Keys? I lived there for five years, in Key West; I worked as a diver for a man whose obsession was to bring up the treasure. The treasure from the Atocha, that was the big one. I will show you on a chart. I have charts in my room. That is what I must write about one day, that dream. Because once you have done it, you can't stop. When you are down there you are alone, with just your hands, your own heart. All you can hear is the beat of your own heart. And it goes on, and on, and on. You are a writer. It is like that, to be a writer. *Non?* You keep searching for something, you are alone with it, you search, sometimes you find a clue, but you must go on. On until you find the treasure. *N'est-ce pas?*"

"Yes, it's a bit like that." And here she was, after just one day alone, up close with all these unknown lives, these men who wanted to show her, tell her who they were. She drew back, wanting to protect what she had, her small decision to live life on her own terms.

"And you are a woman. Forgive me, but how can a woman live like that? How can you be alone at the bottom of the sea? You have husband, children, you like pretty things, other things, you cannot have this mentality."

"You can," she said. "It just leads to complications, that's all."

"Ah?" He looked up from his hunched position, both arms on the table. "So you, too, are alone at the bottom of the sea?"

"Sometimes."

"You are very discreet."

"Well, we don't know each other."

"Ah, but we will," he said, draining his wine glass. "We will, I am sure of that." How ironic, that she should find herself in a house full of foreign men, when she'd just broken up with the man in her life. She was proof, she thought, against any kind of advances, like someone who'd been vaccinated.

Omar lifted the lid of the *tajine* and fingers went in among the lamb and raisins and onions. She copied the others, digging out each mouthful with three fingers drawn together to make a scoop.

Yann said, "You eat like a Moroccan already."

"Can you tell me something? Have you ever heard of a man called El Saouiri?"

"Well, that just means the man from Essaouira. Anybody here could be called that."

"I guess so."

"Why do you ask?"

"It's just an old story I want to find out about while I'm here."

"He has another name?"

"Abdel something."

"Do you know how many men there are in Morocco called Abdel? It means, come from God, next to God, something like that." Yann drank and smoked incessantly and by the end of dinner was mumbling. "You'll have to excuse me. I am very tired. But we will see each other in the morning? Come to my room, I will show you the books, the charts. My room is on the roof. I have to go now, I have a *rendezvous*. But allow me to say that I am very, very glad that you have come. I think you will find all the stories you need here. I think you will help me to write. And maybe I will help you too."

"Okay, goodnight. *A demain*." She watched him stumble in his Moroccan slippers, his long robe tangling about him, as he went out.

Nick said, "He drinks too much. Stupid idiot. Watch out for him, Sarah, he doesn't mean it, he's just very French, but you need to tell him where to get off, if you see what I mean."

"I can look after myself, you know."

"Yeah, that's what we all think, isn't it? Well, I don't want to interfere. Just don't say I didn't warn you."

Suzanne, as she'd seen her out of the sleeping house, had said: "Take care, Sarah. I mean, it can be hard here, being a woman on her own."

"Hey, I can look after myself, you know that."

Suzanne hadn't answered, but looked at her seriously. There was a moment in which their different experiences of life informed them—Suzanne's as the wife of a Moroccan professor, hers as the maverick journalist who picked men up and dropped them this easily. Who had left her latest lover asleep upstairs, for Suzanne to deal with.

"What do you want me to do with him?"

"Make him leave, when he gets up. It was coming to an end

17

anyway. I'm just sorry it was here. And thank you, thank you both. Tell Cherif goodbye for me. I'll call, if I can."

"Come back soon. And take care. I mean it. I know this country, Sarah."

* * *

When she went up in the morning to hang out her laundry, the whitewashed rooftop was dazzling in the morning light. Huge gulls bombed down to land on the chimney pots. From the roof of the next house, behind the slope of the chimney, four little children were shouting in Arabic, punctuated by the wail: *Donne-moi un dirham, donne-moi un dirham!*

She showed them her armful of wet underwear. Then she found pins in a bag tucked behind one of the chimneys and began pinning them like small sails in the wind. Anything she dropped would be blown away. She held the stuff in her teeth and felt the wind pull it.

"*Bonjour.* The women here would do that for you." He stepped out from his lookout room. She thought, so that is why you wanted me to have a room on the roof, so that we'd be neighbours.

"I don't like asking other people to do my laundry."

"You are such a *femme indépendente*."

"Well, yes. I've had to be."

"Do you want to see my room?" It was so obviously guileless, that she simply said, "Okay, if you like."

It was like a little hut built on the roof. It had a bed tucked in under the window, which looked straight out over the ocean. There was a fireplace built in the wall, and the shelves above it held battered books, printed ones and notebooks, and folded up maps and sea charts stained with water. The brown stubs of his cigarettes filled both ashtrays and saucers. She leaned to look at the books. Stevenson. Camus. Daniel Defoe.

"I like this room," he said, "because it's like a lookout post. Like the princess's room in a fairy tale, from which she looks out for her lover coming back across the sea."

"But that makes you the princess."

"Ah, yes, but you see, from here I can look out to see myself approaching. I can look out for my own return."

She thought, so he knows that about himself; interesting. A man whose feminine side stands here, waiting, as in a fairy story, for the ships to come in. He stood in the alcove where the bed was, smoking a cigarette and looking out, avoiding her. From here you could see the island and the purplish, deeper water beyond.

"It's a sailor's room," he said.

"It's true, it feels like a boat."

She liked him more this morning, clean-shaven and not smelling of wine and stale smoke. As she'd told Nick, she could look after herself; she was not about to be lured anywhere by the obviousness of a sex-obsessed French sailor. The room was small, but untidy. His clothes were thrown everywhere, as if he had torn them off in a hurry. He stood close, wearing a stained, cotton *d'jellaba* and his Moroccan slippers of scuffed yellow leather.

"Have you always been a sailor?"

"For as long as I can remember. I was in the navy, in France, when I was young. Recently, I've been crewing for people. Rich women, mostly, with yachts."

He grinned at her.

"And the diving was before that?"

"Yes, the diving finished when my contract ended with Bob Heller, the treasure man. I've been wanting to get back to it ever since. But Nick wanted to buy this house and wanted someone to help him with it. We had the idea of a house to which we'd invite all our friends. But now he has the idea of a hotel. I am not interested in the idea of a hotel. I do not like tourism, money, all that. I am not a businessman. So I think I will not stay."

"Have you been friends with Nick for long?"

"For a long time. Once, I was in love with his sister."

"And you never married?"

"Either I have been married many times or not at all, I cannot tell which. I have lived with, loved, many women. But I cannot tell you which I was married to."

"Oh." What else could she say? It sounded like a strangely convenient case of amnesia.

"Sarah."

"Yes? What?"

"I am drawn to you. I cannot tell what it is. Perhaps it is that you also know what it is to be alone with something, alone at the bottom of the sea." He gripped her arm below the elbow and she tried to back away, but since the room was so small, had to stand her ground.

"No. Yann, just forget it. I'm not interested."

"I'm sorry. I know, I am too intense. But it is not what you think. Yes, you are also a beautiful woman. But what I want is to warn you. Here, this place, it can be too much for people. It can harm you, if you are sensitive, that is. Just, to be careful, that's all that I want to say."

For the second time in twenty-four hours she was saying it, "I can look after myself, you know."

What was there to be so careful about, for God's sake?

But he looked straight back with his blue stare, letting go of her arm, "You know, Sarah, that is not true of any of us. That is one of the lies of our age. That is what we pretend. But none of us can look after himself, not really, that is what I think. So, I look after you. Do not be insulted. We are friends, no?" And he held out his hand, which after a moment's hesitation she shook, as if completing a deal.

Going down the stairway, she came face to face with a woman sloshing soapy water on the floor with a bucket and mop. The woman wore a bright red scarf on her head and pants rolled up to the knee, with a blue, embroidered dress over the top. A gold chain lay on her prominent collarbones. She blocked the way, her bucket at Sarah's feet. Her face was beautifully angular, her eyes alarming.

"*Bonjour*, Madame," she said, and stuck out a hand.

"*Bonjour.*"

"*Je m'appelle Aisha. Comme la femme du prophète.* The wife of the prophet Mohammed."

"I'm Sarah. How are you?" She shook hands. Aisha's hand was thin and strong.

"Sarah. Arabic name. You are tourist, Sarah?"

"I'm a writer. *Ecrivain*."

"Oh, a writer. Let me tell you, madame, I am the one who has lived longest in this house. I tell you this because"—she spat on the floor a tiny dollop of spit—"these men will not tell you the truth. I worked for Madame Sadia. She said, Aisha, this is your house after I am gone. But these men will not listen. They lie all the time. Where is that *voyou*, that Yann? Is he still in his bed? Does he tell you to come to his bed?"

"He's up there. No, he hasn't."

"You beware, Madame. You beware these men. They are shit, all of them. You hear me?"

"Yes. Thanks for the warning. Okay. Now, may I go down?"

"Bien sûr. Passez, Madame Sarah."

She shifted her bucket so that Sarah could squeeze past her. She was small but stood very upright, her head held high.

"You take care, Madame," she said.

Three warnings. And yet, every time she walked back down the street beside the high red wall and felt in her pocket for the key to that blue door and slipped it into the lock, it was with a feeling of privilege. The house had opened to her and offered her its sanctuary, once, magically and suddenly; and now every day it opened to her again.

*   *   *

You went in off the street and the dust underfoot changed suddenly to cleaned stone. There was usually somebody sitting in the inner room at the bottom of the well, Omar or his friend, Ibrahim, who brought his little black dog with him, or Yann drinking coffee with Nick. You would hear the low rumble of men's voices about the house. There was a small table, a tray with glasses of tea, the puppy curled on a square of folded carpet, an ashtray with stubs in it, smoke curling upward even when the men had gone.

You went on up the white curving stairs. Food smells drifted from the kitchen, cumin, lemon, hot oil. Aisha would be in there, or Omar. New wood cracked in the lit fire. Sometimes there was music, Yann's choice of flamenco or Italian opera, Nick's of modern jazz, or Jake in his room, playing rap with the door open. Sometimes there was silence and you knew that everybody was out.

You came to the floor where Madame Sadia had held her parties. The long refectory table stood empty in the daytime beneath the old gilt mirrors with their pitted surfaces and the portrait of Mohammed v. The metal chairs stood along the table's sides, awaiting guests. There was the big candlestick and a book of Yann's thrown down—Camus' *L'Etranger*, or a book on marine archaeology—and Nick's cigarettes, the remains of coffee in a bowl, some cassettes of World Music left by Jake. If you went up to the next floor there were the tiled, cool bedrooms where the most beautiful woman in Morocco had received her French officers and where her own room looked out over the red wall and beyond the row of palm trees in the Riad, to the ocean. Following the curve of the stair and its steep way up to the roof terrace, you came to the place where laundered sheets hung in their white stiffness in the mornings and the whitewashed walls made you blink; where Yann kept his lookout over the ocean waiting for himself to come back.

From this place on the roof, you could look down beyond the fishing port and the quay where they went down at lunchtime to eat sardines and watch the Atlantic battering at the sides of the town. You could turn your back on it, lean against the bumpy white wall and look back over the town itself, the red-walled Medina, with its rooftops hung with washing and carpets and its television aerials. Up here it was a city of white roofs and little jutting towers and the shadows of seagulls cruising down. The wind knocked flowerpots sideways and tore at the laundry so that towels and underwear flew away over the edge. It was like standing on a ship's deck, a place only just tethered to land. Up here at night you could watch everything turn mauve and the stars appear, and the wind came in out of darkness tasting of salt.

She was in love with it, this house built by a long-dead Portuguese merchant, its solid stone, arched and graceful, and the well at the centre like the space inside a ribcage with room for heart and entrails. It was love for an atmosphere, a sense of safety: a reminder of home for the soul as well as for the body. From the street you could see only peeling white walls, blue shutters, high-up windows. Like most houses in this country, it was secret, until you were given the key and could easily let yourself in, as she did now. As she was to in her dreams, over and over again, long after she no longer had the key and anyway the locks were changed.

Chapter two

The Geography of Love

After just a few days, the rest of her journey began to seem so long ago. It was only two weeks since she and Bill had arrived in Tangiers, less than a week since they'd been in Marrakesh. The fight they'd had there had been strangely short and simple, almost a relief. Looking back, she saw it had been building ever since they left New York. Travelling, these things came out into the open more quickly, like diseases caught when you were already tired, they rampaged through you, had their own momentum. The strange thing was, that it had turned out to be about Islamic fundamentalism, not sex or money or the lack of it, or one of them having a stomach upset or any of the more normal things you can fight about in a foreign land. She'd known he wasn't thrilled with Tangiers, even though they did sleep in the most uncomfortable hotel ever (his choice), one which William Burroughs had apparently lived in for years. Burroughs must have been stoned all the time, or too excited about Arab boys, she said, to notice. But Bill thought it was great. It was the real thing, he said, it was what they as spoiled Americans needed to experience.

Squalor? said Sarah ironically, opening her suitcase and looking for a sweater to wear in bed. No, just the way the rest of the world lived. No heating, cockroaches and uncomfortable iron beds. Bill liked these things, they assuaged his conscience. He'd been reared in too much comfort, he said, and so had she. Sarah went down to ask the two old queens downstairs for spare blankets and they passed their bottle of Bourbon back and forth until both were in a better mood.

In Marrakesh, they'd stayed with her old college friend, Suzanne and her husband Cherif, whom she'd met in Aix-en-Provence when they were both students. They had five children and lived in a new suburb of Marrakesh, where Cherif taught engineering at the University. It was in Suzanne's spare bedroom, in the grey, small hours broken open too soon by roosters and the cry of the muezzin, that Bill and Sarah had their fight.

"I can't stay here," Bill said, pulling the single blanket tighter around his shoulders, "Morocco just isn't on the front line, as far as fundamentalism's concerned. It's just too much like Europe."

Bill wanted to be a war correspondent but had not yet found his war. He'd spent the evening talking to Cherif and evidently Cherif hadn't been interested enough in what Americans thought were Arab predicaments. That first evening, he'd been shocked to see Cherif and a colleague from the University lie down together on the couch to watch TV. An antique American soap called "Santa Barbara" was on, dubbed into Arabic, and the two men lay in a cosy heap like puppies watching it, while two of the children, twin boys of ten, lay on the floor. No one seemed to want to discuss fundamentalism and its dangers. When Cherif's friend got up to go, the two men kissed and hugged more warmly than most lovers, Bill said, and he'd had to look away. For all his interest in Arab affairs, he still found their habits upsetting.

"You mean," Sarah said, "It's not oppressive enough to be interesting? You want more repression? Or is it that you're afraid of them hugging in public?"

"No, nothing to do with hugging, don't be ridiculous. No, it's just that we've only got so much time to research, and there's a whole scene going on elsewhere, you know, in the Mid-East—here, Iran, Iraq, Saudi—and frankly, the public back home's only interested in Arabs if they're doing something violent. Fundamentalism's where it's at. It's what people are worried about. So that's what I have to go after."

It was at that moment that Sarah looked at him from the sudden distance of an ex-lover.

"I can't believe it. You want to go where people are cutting each other's hands off for petty theft, stoning each other for adultery? You're just not interested in a moderate, European-style Arab state? You have to go for the blood?"

"It's not that, it's the military angle. There is going to be a war, not too far ahead. And it's not going to be with a moderate Arab state. Or one that's nowhere near any oil. When it happens, I want to be there."

Bill had his contacts at the Pentagon and was close to the military, back home. "I'm a journalist. So are you. You know what I mean. You don't have to come."

"Well, I'm going to stay here, then go to Essaouira, work on my book, have a vacation and be glad I don't find people being mutilated on every street corner."

It was then that the whole thing escalated in the way that fights do. From lying reasonably comfortably beside him listening to roosters and calls to prayer and savouring the new strangeness of yet another foreign city; from liking the shape of his body and the way his ears grew close to his head and the way he stroked her back, she was suddenly upright, gone, a stranger glaring down at the other hostile stranger he had in a minute become.

"Okay," he said, "Then I guess this is goodbye. Have a good time. See you back in the States."

And he put his head right under the blanket. Sarah flung on her clothes, zipped up her bag, thrust her feet into her shoes and went downstairs in the pre-dawn spreading light, to watch palm trees emerge as cut-outs against a greenish winter sky, and the city of Marrakesh warm to its early-morning salmon pink.

* * *

It was strange how once you'd split up with someone this dramatically, everything about them in retrospect seemed simply wrong. It was such a relief to be alone again, to have your own thoughts, do everything when you wanted to and not have to consult anybody or worry about his feelings for you, the world, his dinner, the country in which you were travelling. Sarah loved her room in the house as she'd loved her first bedroom as a teenager, as she'd loved the first room she had had to herself after her divorce. You longed to be together with people, and then you were so, so happy to be alone. To be in a house where the men were nothing to do with you. To be free, yet not out there where you had to fight for things and survive. It was like waking from a dream each morning, and discovering that it was true. It was hers, Nick had said, for as long as she wanted; it was an incredible gift.

And what of the woman in the photograph that was already curled with the damp from the sea air, that she'd tucked into the corner of the blue flower gouache? She wasn't sure what she wanted to discover, here. The question had been in her mind for the last couple of years, since her mother's slow illness had ended in death. Marion Flood, who had been Marion Henderson, had died of forgetting. That was how Sarah had seen it. Memory left you, and with it, life. Only life was slower to go than memory, which drew out like a long, low tide and left the land it had covered naked and littered with apparently meaningless things. At her mother's bedside in the Boston nursing home, the best that her mother's careful insurance policies could provide, Sarah had sat and listened as the scattered words emerged, as she pressed the few photographs she could find into Marion's hands.

She should have started earlier. But how could you know when someone was going to start forgetting? Perhaps it was Alzheimer's, perhaps not. You forget what you can't bear to remember, Sarah thought. Once she'd found the photograph, with the palm trees, the gash of shadow, the sunlight bleaching everything out of the shadow's reach, the young man gazing so adoringly at her mother—of course she wanted to know the story. Sometimes, you left things so nearly too late, that when you got to them there was only a sketch left, a faded line, a few words, a name. Mogador, Marion had said, that was the place they called Mogador.

Sarah, looking on a present-day map, had found Essaouira, the town on the west coast of Morocco, which had once been called Mogador. The rest of the plan had gradually taken place around it: a vacation, a project she'd cajoled from her editor, a series of free-lance articles for other papers on the troubled subject of women in Moroccan society, finally, perhaps the book she had in mind. Then Bill had said that it was exactly what he needed to do, travel in the Arab world, check out a few things. The journey, which was really two separate journeys, his and hers, had begun. And had bifurcated already, as it had to. This was her own journey now.

She'd brought the books with her, to discover what was going on in 1936. That was when Marion was here, in that turbulent time of nationalism and near-revolution, twenty years before Independence. Marion's uncle, the one they called Hajji, had been the British consul in Rabat, and Marion had come out from England to spend a year with him. How much had he told her?

Ah, not any more. I'm tired, darling. See you tomorrow? Are we going home?

Uncle Hajji, as British consul in Rabat, had been involved in the complex pre-war negotiations between the French and the Moroccan resistance. But how much, if anything, would he have told his niece? Did Marion know that the young law student she danced with most evenings was an associate of Allal el Fassi, one of the co-founders of the Moroccan Action Committee and their newspaper, *L'Action du Peuple...*?

And what had happened to him, the intense young man in

the photograph who was later to be known as El Saouiri, the man from Essaouira?

Sarah had approached her mother with all this, before her death, when Marion was already struggling with memory. Her mind would come on and switch off again like a faulty electric light. Memory, Sarah thought, was the one thing you needed, to make sense of your life, and it was leaving her. It was all so long ago, she kept saying. Names, places, feelings came back to her in sudden flashes and then let her go. Sarah, at her bedside, waited for the fragments to come, wished she could bear to leave her in peace. Yet there was something Marion wanted to tell her, she felt it in her mother's hand in hers, the pulse of some urgency.

> *Are you still there?*
> *Yes, I'm here. It's all right.*
> *I don't know what I did, Sarah, if I did something wrong.*
> *I don't think you did anything wrong.*

Perhaps the British consul was supposed to be impartial, not a close friend of the king. Mohammed v refused French demands to make Morocco into a colony. It was at a time when the Franco-British alliance was supposed to be so solid. Perhaps Uncle Harold, called Hajji for his knowledge of the Arab world, had overstepped some mark. His eccentricities had long been tolerated by the Foreign Office because of his brilliance, his linguistic abilities and his swift grasp of what went on around him. Perhaps now his niece Marion had been targeted as a result. Who knew? It was all, as her mother said, so long ago. But there was a story here: as a journalist she couldn't let go of that teasing loose end, and as a daughter she wanted the truth of her mother's life. The Marion in this photograph was very different from the Cape Cod matron Sarah had known for her adult life, and from the rather conventional young woman who had travelled to America with her small daughter in the first place, to marry Boston money and forget about the past.

First of all, had the plot the nationalists hatched been incubated under Uncle Hajji's roof? Second, how much had Marion known? Third, had she been close friends with, loved, had an affair with, the young man in question? And fourth, most interesting of all, what had happened? Sarah imagined a rich mix of politics and sex under the diplomatic roof; her own mother perhaps an unwitting pawn at its centre. She knew Marion had been sent home in some sort of disgrace. She knew that the young student lawyer had ended up in jail, most probably because of his associates, but not helped by his connection with a young white woman. And what was the nature of the disgrace? Indiscretion, in a diplomatic household? Sex? Even pregnancy? What exactly had Marion and the young man done?

She would have to ask someone. Someone in this town would know the story, at least the political part of it. It was only fifty years ago, after all, and it would have been told, as scandal always was, over and over, *de bouche à l'oreille as* the French said, in these same streets. But who would remember? Who would know?

* * *

So, she had her notes from the sociology department in Marrakesh and from the Institut du Monde Arabe in Paris, to which she and Bill had walked from their hotel near the Jardin des Plantes, that first day. Before Africa. Before this. Paris in cold rain, a tall glass building reflecting the rainy sky, and the Seine thick as if choked with silt, running close by. Inside, the photocopy room, the smell of chemicals, and Arab men—Algerian, Moroccan?—quietly there to assist. In her room, she spread out these materials, to begin writing. Was it that day that she and Bill, like rivers flowing in opposite directions, had begun to part? Did it matter, that they had ever been together in the place called love? Geography, she thought. Love is geographical perhaps, it has its own weather and climate, and you can leave it behind.

That first sight from the train window as they came down from Tangiers: buildings flowing across the red land like Arab calligraphy, a fluency of form she had never seen or imagined. The walls blank, with no windows. That first clue. How did you get beyond stereotypes when everything was hidden the way women were, veiled, meant to be unseen? How could you begin to understand a country you were not supposed to decipher, read its fluid texts?

Bill, in that hotel room, reading a magazine on the bed while she stood to look out of the window at the street below. Bill in Tangiers, wanting things to be dangerous. Bill going off, perhaps to be shot or imprisoned, to fulfil his fantasy of the Arab world, to court the violence and strangeness he imagined. Bill—William Jackson, native of New York—not seeing those fluent walls, their messages, only hearing what he had picked up at the Pentagon. Or so it seemed to Sarah, increasingly disappointed by his attitudes. Perhaps this would be her last thought of him. Perhaps she would easily let him go, as she'd walked out that easily to find the bus station and the bus west, to Essaouira.

She hadn't told him the El Saouiri story at first; imagining his sardonic humour turned on it, his easy dissection. Upper-class English girl going for a bit of local colour, going native; that was what he'd say. So your mother had a fling here, did she? Well, good for her. Proves that all English women aren't quite the iron lady. But it doesn't *matter*, Sarah. When she did tell him, he was mild and curious; she had misjudged him. As she had to misjudge him in the end, to get away.

Strange, how as soon as you noticed you didn't love somebody, you realized you didn't even like them. Up till then, his body had comforted her. Sometimes. And he'd stood, with his physical size and his ideas, between her and the uneasy world.

Chapter three

A Berber Princess

N ick stood at the centre of the house, directing operations in his white shirt and dark glasses, waving a hand with a cigarette in it to show where a door was to be cut in a wall, where a ceiling was to be pulled down, where a room would go. His plan was to turn the old house into a hotel; but the speed and continuity of the external change he kept going made it feel as if he were about to change the whole world. One day thirty workmen were hammering and drilling and dragging buckets of cement; the next there was silence because the mayor had ordered everyone to stop work. Then there were consultations, visits from elegant men in dark *d'jellaba*s and pointed leather slippers, tea in glasses on little tin trays and the next day it all began again.

In the early morning, the long cry went out across the town for the first call to prayer, an hour or so later the first hammer blows sounded and Sarah woke to rubble falling and the shouts of working men. In her room with the rickety thuya wood table split with damp and the white curtains blowing open on a view of walls and far-down sea, she sat and listened to the shudder of falling masonry and the whine of the drill. The house was being stripped back to its skeleton.

"Well, how's your story going? Finding out anything about Moroccan women? You should interview Aisha. She'd tell you a thing or two. Sorry I can't stop to chat just now."

In the evenings he'd be there, leaning against the big stone fireplace, a drink in one hand, as if he was waiting for her conversation. She came downstairs, ready to talk to someone, even glad to see him.

"Sarah? What have you been up to today?"

She spent her evenings with these men, each one apparently alone: Yann, Nick, and the younger ones, Jake and Ramon. She didn't even have to ask herself if she liked them; they were just here. In spite of Nick's warning, Yann seemed essentially harmless. And Nick himself—who was Nick? His smooth English charm erased his tracks completely, his arrogance possibly just covering shyness after all. His company was strangely restful. What effect she had on them, she couldn't know, but wondered. They told her their stories, entertaining her, laying themselves before her; they, the men, before her, the only woman. The only woman in the house who was not Aisha, who kept her fierce and sardonic distance.

While Yann's stories were all about sunken galleons and lost treasure, Nick's were about corpses and unlikely couplings. He told them deadpan, leaving pauses for amusement and shock while his eyes darted sideways at his audience to assess the effect. He wrote scripts for movies, and Sarah wondered if anyone would ever dare to put them on.

"But Nick, you can't have that sort of thing happening!"

"I promise you," he said, and grinned at her, "There they were, stuck in the car between the dashboard and the seat and he was stuck in her, you know, the way dogs get stuck, and they had to be medically separated. Once the car door was unjammed, that was. Then there was all the money he owed her husband. It cost him a fortune in legal fees. And medical ones as well. You can't get uncoupled on the National Health."

His green eyes flickered at her as he smiled his down-curved smile.

"Bigamy, of course. That's the solution. Perfectly normal. The only problem is, here at least, you have to keep them both in the style to which they've become accustomed. Polygamy's getting expensive, that's the only reason people are giving it up."

"Men, you mean."

"Well, of course, men. It's no good having feminist ideas here, Sarah, it simply doesn't work."

The night he told her about the poison, she'd been in the kitchen with Yann all evening, drinking wine and making onion soup. Somehow having confronted him directly had made him safe. 'La Bohème' soared and sobbed around them from the cassette recorder.

"Sarah, come and keep me company in the kitchen!" Yann had called from where he stood examining the contents of the refrigerator.

"Do you know how to make onion soup? I have a sudden longing for some French onion soup. Wait, I'll bring the music in too."

Omar was making up the fire, on his knees before the great fireplace. Then he stood on a chair to light the candles in the iron chandelier that swung from the ceiling. She went into the kitchen with Yann.

"Sure, I can cook most things, I did it for years. You have some garlic?"

"Of course. What else? Onions, oil, white wine?"

"Do you really not know how to make it? I thought all French men knew how to cook."

"All French men know how to eat, that's all. And I've always been a sailor. Sailors don't cook much. So who did you cook for, for all this time?"

"I cooked every day. Once upon a time."

"You don't give much away, do you?"

"Well, neither do you. Apart from being the flying Dutchman all your life."

"Okay, that makes two of us. I'll open a bottle of wine and we can drink some too, that will be nice."

On the cassette recorder Mimi was dying in the snow and all the frozen artists burned their manuscripts for a scrap of warmth. It was Yann's favourite opera, he said. Here, the leaping driftwood fire burned in the great fireplace while she and Yann sliced onions small, hands close together wielding knives, his blue eyes snapping away at her over the chopping board. Sarah pulled faces at him, mocked his lust, smiled when he scowled back.

Omar came and looked and went away. Sarah tipped the chopped onions and garlic into the hot oil in the pressure cooker and stirred them until they were soft and golden. Yann stood close behind her, watching. Her wooden spoon went round and round and she felt him behind her, making it hard to move anything except her slowly stirring hand. Damn him, she wouldn't react. She tipped in a little flour, stirred, added salt and pepper, then splashed in some wine so that everything fizzed. Then she fastened the lid down on the pressure cooker and waited till the valve whizzed round on its own.

"Sit down now and relax."

He handed her a glass of wine and pushed her gently on to a stool in the corner where the strings of onions hung.

"You sit there and read the paper and I'll do the vegetables."

"I can cut up vegetables too, you know."

"No, you've done enough. My turn. Sit and read the paper and relax and just keep me company."

He handed her his copy of *Libération* stained with onion juice and oil and she sat and pretended to read. He was too tall for the sink. Bent over in his striped sweater, he looked a little laborious and weary. He sliced carrots and potatoes for the *tajine* and hummed Puccini out of tune. The grand emotions of opera filled the kitchen. The other room behind them was in darkness, with candles. The fire jumped and sparked and spat red on to the stone floor. They were burning rotten timbers as well as driftwood and there was a smell of burned paint. She watched Yann from behind the paper.

"There."

He turned and showed her the vegetables all cut thin and washed. His hair flopped forward over his forehead and with one hand he pushed it back. He leaned back against the sink and folded his arms, the vegetables put to one side.

She said, "Have you read this thing about Romania?"

"Not yet, I haven't read any of it, I've been too busy. It's good, isn't it, working with somebody else in a kitchen? I like it."

"I do, too."

"Tell me, have you ever been married, Sarah?"

"Yes, but I'm not any more. It was a long time ago."

"Was your husband like you?"

"No, not at all. Except that he was American."

"Ah, American. I see. Me, I have always been a bachelor."

He opened the fridge, found olives in a little pottery bowl, handed it to her quite formally. Their hands touched for a second. Then the cassette ended and there was silence except for the sound of the fire. Somebody came up the stairs, perhaps Nick, perhaps Omar. Yann's hand shook slightly as he reached into the olive bowl for a soft black olive.

"I've lived with quite a few women, though."

"Yes, you said. You said you didn't know which of them you'd been married to."

"I did? I think the truth is that I have never been married."

She said, "What else are you putting in your *tajine*? If we don't put it on to cook now, it won't be ready in time."

"I don't know. Perhaps I'll leave the rest to Omar. He is a better cook. All Moroccan men can cook, even if all French men do not."

"You give up easily, don't you?"

He pushed the vegetables around on the chopping board and left them in a little mound.

"Anyway, I'm not eating with you tonight."

"Why the cooking, then?"

"Oh, the soup. I'll have some probably when I come in. I am going to see my daughter."

"Your daughter?"

37

"Yes, I have a daughter."

He shrugged on his battered leather jacket and turned to go, an unlit cigarette between his lips. She sat on the stool for a minute. Then she turned off the soup, let the air escape from the valve in a long hissing stream, and went to sit by the fire with the paper. Omar went into the kitchen without speaking and took over the cooking of the *tajine*.

* * *

Nick said, "She poisoned him, last time."

"Last time what?"

"Last time he tried getting off with someone else."

They sat at dinner, Nick and Sarah, at the small table set beside the fire. The young men—Ramon, Jake and Omar—had gone out together to pick up girls. Before he went, Omar had spiced the onion soup with cumin and coriander so that it tasted thoroughly Moroccan, not French at all. There was one big candlestick at the centre of the round table and they peered at each other round it.

"I don't believe you. Nick, you're making it up."

"No, it's true, he got weaker and weaker and finally he had to go to hospital in France. They couldn't find anything wrong with him so they sent him back here. I thought he had cancer. He turned up looking terrible. Then he promised to marry her and after that I think it was more or less all right."

Sarah said, "I didn't know."

"Didn't know what?"

"Any of it. That he had a relationship with Aisha. That they were practically married. That they had a daughter. He told me he was a bachelor."

"He always says that. I suppose, technically he is. But not according to Aisha, he isn't. Yes, I imagine it's probably more convenient at times to forget about Aisha and Souad. I think she used belladonna that time. Lots of women here do, you know, it's quite traditional. They go off and get a recipe from some old woman and make sure that their husbands can't get it up with anyone else. Or they make them so weak that they'd agree to anything. What else can they do? They have no rights in law. It's really quite an effective way of keeping things under control. Works a lot better than some of the things people do in so-called civilized countries. I'd never get involved with a Moroccan woman. I'd be much too scared."

"Jesus."

"Yes," said Nick, "here jealousy is a fact of life. D'you know, the last time Yann was away, the canaries kicked the bucket? Apparently there's a particularly effective spell that involves cutting off birds' heads. I came down one morning and found the canaries had their heads cut off. I don't know if it worked, but he certainly came back. Then there was something about putting chameleons in the yoghurt, you can do that too."

"D'you believe it, Nick?"

"D'you mean, do I believe it happens or do I believe that it works? Both, really. I'd be an idiot not to, living here. I was pretty careful about drinking coffee here at that time, I can tell you. I didn't want to get his by mistake. And another thing, you can take a man's knickers away and do some fairly alarming things to him. So I sent my stuff to the laundry, just to be on the safe side."

"And he really got ill as a result of all of this?"

"Well, he went yellow and his shit went yellow and he shook all the time. They thought he might have jaundice, and he couldn't get out of bed. Then I suppose she let up, because he gradually got better. There was a time when a woman came to stay here, someone whose yacht he'd sailed, and her knickers kept disappearing. She was pissed off because they were rather expensive French ones and you can only buy horrible ones here. I don't know what happened to her exactly, but she left pretty abruptly."

"Perhaps she went back to France to stock up on underwear."

Nick just looked at her with his innocent smile and ladled more soup. "Perhaps. This is good soup, who made it?"

"I did. But it tastes this good because Omar put in the spices."

"More wine, Sarah? Yes, the day of the canaries was pretty hide-

ous. I hope that doesn't happen again. I bought budgies the next time,
I don't know if that makes any difference. They still seem okay."

He offered his protection again. Like royalty, thinking he had
no limits. She remembered how Yann had said: "If anyone bothers
you, say you are a guest of Nick." The house was like a kingdom, and
he its self-made king. A king was what, as an American, you were
not supposed to want.

*   *   *

Sarah heard from below in the street the cry that sounded like "Gabi!
Gabi!" from the man selling Javel disinfectant from a cart. His voice
was like a bird's, sharp and regular. "Gabi! Gabi!"

In the cage where there had been one solitary male bird, there
were now two more. Nick had been off to the market early and come
back with a subdued green pair of budgerigars who now perched in a
corner of their cage and looked in fear at their noisier companion.

Nick sat down opposite her and hooked his leg over the chair
arm. She dipped bread into her coffee and looked at him across the
breakfast tray, the blue plates and bowls, the bread and honey, and
the coffee in its silver pot. He spread butter on a very small piece
of bread.

"Wash your knickers yourself, and don't get shut in the kitchen
with Yann, that's my advice."

"But, a baby, how can he have a baby with someone and simply
pretend he hasn't?"

"I guess it's their affair, not ours."

"Until we get poisoned coffee."

He picked up her bowl and tasted it seriously.

"I think this is okay."

*   *   *

That morning Sarah met Aisha standing on the stairs giving directions
to the two Berber girls who were washing the steps.

"*Bonjour*, Aisha."

"*Bonjour, Madame* Sarah. How are you today?"

"Fine. How are you?"

"*Ça va bien. Très bien. Comme toujours. Très, très bien.*" Whatever Aisha said, her tone was still unfriendly. She stood aside to let Sarah pass; the stairs were narrow and they met once again among buckets and mops. Every day, those two, Myriam and Kiltoun, washed the stairs after the builders had been up and down them treading mud and cement. They had their dresses tucked up high and wore purple and scarlet footless tights, they laughed and talked in Berber and sloshed water about. They wore brief scarves on their heads and had their sleeves rolled back to the elbow. Aisha this morning was wearing a black scarf with her brilliant dress, and gold shoes. Her eyes were rimmed with kohl. She said, "I was not here for breakfast this morning."

"I know, I noticed."

"I was with Yann. "

"Oh, were you?"

"Somebody else made the coffee this morning?"

"Yes."

"And was it good?"

"Very good."

"And you slept well?"

"Very well. And you, Aisha?"

"Very, very well."

"Good."

"Tonight I will bring my daughter. You want to see my daughter? She is a princess, a Berber princess."

"I'd love to see her. What is her name?"

"Her name is Souad."

It was like a game, Sarah thought: you say this, I say that. Polite, ultra-polite, insulting-polite. Hidden agenda, hidden threat. They were both speaking French, neither one at home in her own language, that could be it: the language of the colonizers, of law, of order. Aisha flashed her black eyes at her and never smiled, but drew down her lips in scorn. She looked capable of poisoning anybody. But when she said the word "Souad" something happened, her tone changed, she spoke the name with love.

* * *

The baby gazed at the fire and the firelight was reflected in her eyes. She stood upright on Yann's knee where he danced her up and down like a stiff little doll. Her face was solemn, her small head with its combed quiff of black hair held upright by Yann's fingers at the back of her neck. He bounced her, trying to amuse her, but her attention was held by the movement of the flames.

Aisha stood behind his chair, her hands moved slightly as if she wanted to take the baby back. But there was no need. She stood there in her brilliant dress, her face sad; her attention which had been all on the baby was no longer needed, for Yann had the baby, and Souad, in spite of both, of them was fixated on the flames. They were at the centre of the room, a little group, he in his big chair before the fireplace holding his child like a doll. All the others came and sat round him, their eyes on the baby. When Aisha had brought her in she'd been crying and restless till she saw the great ring of lit candles in the chandelier and her eyes sparkled up at them and the movement of the fire. A last sob came and then she was silent. Yann took credit for her silence.

"Look, with me she is happy, she is fine."

He held her firm, one hand at her nape, one at her feet. Aisha said, "Take off her shoes, she is too hot. Undo her coat."

The baby was all wrapped up for the winter night outside and now her face was steaming red above her coat.

Yann took no notice. Aisha had brought her to show them and Yann had taken her. Nobody said anything. They were a family before the fire, a rather stiff and uncertain-looking family, but real, at least for now.

Sarah moved closer, put out a hand. Souad's tiny finger curled around hers, she gripped it like a bird. "She's lovely, Aisha. *Elle est belle, ta fille.*"

Aisha looked relieved. "She is a princess, like the old princesses. A Berber princess."

The young men, Jake and Ramon, went down on their knees before her, cooed and clucked. Jake, the teenager, took her and rubbed his nose against her cheek, kissed her wet neck, but she cried and went straight back to Yann. She only wanted to look at the fire, it was what held her still. When Yann turned her and held her against his shoulder, her face to his leather jacket, she began to yell. Sarah felt that strange generalized discomfort of hearing babies yell, when you don't know what to do for them, yet they pluck some string inside.

Aisha urged him, "Give her to me, give her to me."

He had moved her, shut the fire off from her, that was all. Aisha rummaged and found a pacifier in her pocket and pushed it into the squared red mouth, but the baby spat it out. Sarah thought she looked too hot, and anyway, weren't pacifiers a bad idea? She nearly offered to take her; longed to take some of her clothes off and hold her still, not jiggling up and down.

Yann said, "She was fine, now look what you have done, you have disturbed her."

Aisha walked up and down with her, shaking and rocking her. Against her shoulder the baby's head was red through her black hair and her neck wet with crying, she moved her face from side to side seeking what she wanted.

Yann frowned as he looked into the fire. Aisha walked the baby and fussed her and crooned at her and the baby yelled and yelled. The young men started talking about going out. Sarah, standing by the big fireplace, saw all the discord in this little scene as if it had been staged just to show them all how bad for each other these two parents were.

"I'll take her home. *Elle est malade.* She is ill, you can see that. You should not have made me bring her."

Yann said, "She's not ill, she's fine."

"She has had a bad cold, can't you hear it, when she cries, in her chest? She should not be out on such a cold night."

"She was all right with me, she liked it."

"But Yann, look what you have done to her!"

"Don't talk nonsense." He did not move.

"Say goodnight, *habibti, embrasse papa.*"

The wet red face of the child brushed his cheek as she was dangled down to him. Suddenly her black eyes caught and held the movement of the fire again and she was quiet. Her face went quiet and entranced again and two little flames appeared in her eyes. Sarah smiled at her, held out a hand.

"You see?" Yann held her face briefly to his with a hand that was bigger than her whole head, and then let her go.

"A princess, a Berber princess."

"Bonsoir, Aisha."

"Bonne nuit."

"Bonsoir." They were leaving, Aisha with her child.

Yann didn't get up to see her out but let her go with the child, both of them wrapped up tight against the cold. He stayed slumped in his chair and gazed into the fire. Then he got up and left the room to go upstairs alone, without speaking. They heard the shuffle of his *babouches* upon the stone stairs and then the creak of the door to the roof—open, and then shut again. The young men raised their eyebrows and shrugged and waved their fingers to Sarah. "Want to come? We're going for a beer, at the *café.*"

"No, thanks. I'm going to bed."

She felt saddened. Aisha had wanted to show them her family, man, wife, baby; and it hadn't worked, it hadn't worked at all.

Chapter four
Gold

In the morning, she woke to the thud of the sledgehammer. She went downstairs, wearing jeans and a sweater and thick socks against the cold. There was a hole in the kitchen wall and rubble in a heap just where only a couple of days ago she had sat with Yann drinking wine. A cold draught blew through. A pickaxe was pulling at the remaining masonry, so that the hole grew bigger by the minute and there were shouts from the men working on the other side of the wall. The fireplace was full of cold ash and charred ends of wood.

Nick had bought the house next door and there was to be a new door to join it to this one. She picked her way through stones and dust to get her coffee and took the little tray back into the untouched part of the house. In the birdcage in the window there were two live budgies and one dead one lying with its claw feet turned upwards, its feathers ruffled but unmarked. The coffee she sipped was strong and grainy. Aisha came through from the kitchen wearing her scarlet dress and watched her drink it.

"It's good? You want more coffee, Sarah?"

"No thanks. This is fine. Look, one of the birds is dead."

"*Oui*. I told Nick it was no good having three."

"Do you think the others killed it?"

"I don't know. Perhaps. It happens." Aisha shrugged.

It happens. Nick came in, his white shirtsleeves rolled, a white sweater hung over his shoulders, clean jeans. He perched on a chair, took a piece of bread from Sarah's plate and chewed it.

"Nick, one of the birds is dead."

"Oh, God, so it is." He crouched in front of the cage that was built like a miniature palace with domes and arches for the birds. The original male bird sat on his perch, his neck feathers ruffled, and stared out. One of the little green ones was hunched in a far corner and the other, the dead one, was just a sad little heap of feathers and two wire feet sticking up. Nick opened the cage door, put in a hand and lifted out the corpse. It lay in his open palm as he held it out towards her and with one finger he gently turned the head this way and that and then stroked the breast feathers flat. She saw how his hands were small and strong, his fingers blunt, and how he touched the bird sadly, tenderly.

"No mark on him, look."

"Was it a him or a her?" She put out a finger, to touch.

"No way of telling, is there, when they're this young? I bought them as a pair. Perhaps it died of fright. Probably it's a male and the other male killed it or frightened it to death. What a pity. Still, at least it's got its head on." He smiled at her with his deprecating downward look.

"Well, that's something."

"Perhaps now the other two will nest. Ibrahim's making some nesting boxes for them. He told me I have to have them or the birds won't mate."

"I expect he's right. They'll need a bit of privacy."

"As if there wasn't enough going on, without having to make private bedrooms for birds."

"Nick, d'you want some coffee? Here, have some of mine."

"I've had mine, thanks. I've been up for hours. Is this noise bothering you? I thought they might as well get on with it, instead of waiting for all the permits to come through. I'm having the mayor to tea today to cheer him up about the whole thing."

He took the dead bird and went away with it in the palm of his curved hand

Outside in the street the seller of disinfectant went past again on his return journey. "Gabi! Gabi!" The male bird jumped down from his perch and began to strut about in front of the female, if female she was. She stayed in her corner, refusing to look.

Shivering, wanting the sun, Sarah went up to the roof terrace to read about the household of the prophet Mohammed in the sixth century. He was very liberal, apparently. So what had happened in between? She sat with her back against the whitewashed chimney-stack, her legs stretched out in front of her, sun warming her through wool. She'd read about five pages when Yann came out of his room, a *d'jellaba* over his nightshirt, his feet in his scuffed yellow babouche slippers.

"Hey, you never told me you had a child with Aisha." She put the book down, stared up at his shape against the sun.

"*Bonjour*, Sarah. What a beautiful day."

He leaned on the white parapet and lit a cigarette. Smoke rose. The morning trembled out there over the rooftops.

"Didn't I? I thought you knew."

"Where does she live? Where does Aisha live?"

"Aisha lives with her mother and so does the baby."

"Why didn't you tell me you had a family?"

He turned and looked away over the roofs, out towards the sea. At the question his eyes had closed down their blue shutters. Now he had to look out at the horizon as if nothing else would do.

"I'm a sailor," he said, "I've spent my life sailing round the world. I'm not much good on dry land."

"I know. The Flying Dutchman. You said."

"Well, everything is not always easy to explain."

Sarah stood up, stretched, came to join him at the parapet.

47

This close, he smelled of sleep and stale tobacco, and she drew back, leaned her elbows a way away from him on the white wall. Down on the quay she saw the men getting out the plastic topped tables for lunch, starting up the charcoal fires. The areca palms stood like fake trees against the sky. The tide was in and the water stood close up against the walls, choppy and red-stained today with mud from the rivers inland. The horizon showed a dark rim like the edge of an iris on a blue eye.

Yann said, "I wanted this house as a place to invite friends back to, all the people I've stayed with all over the world. I wanted it to be an open house. So that I could go to sea and come back and have a home. But it seems, as soon as I set foot on land, I am trapped."

"You mean, you got Aisha pregnant?"

"It seems rather that she got me pregnant."

He stubbed out his cigarette on the wall top and looked back at her.

"Do you know, Sarah, there are two things which are driving me mad? One, those boats they're building down there. I can hardly bear to watch them. They'll be finished soon and then they'll go to sea. And the other thing, when I hear you typing, I'm mad with envy. I've all these stories in my head, you've not heard a fraction of them yet, they'd amaze you. I've got to write them one day. But when? You've got to help me, Sarah."

"I hardly dare speak to you now, for fear of getting poisoned or worse. You should have told me about Aisha."

The blue shutters closed again. "You have nothing to be afraid of. I want nothing. I simply ask you this as a fellow artist. Believe me."

"Well, if it's all there, I'm sure you'll write it. And I'm sure if you want to enough, you'll get back to sea. And you probably won't let anyone stop you."

"Are you? How are you so sure? If you want something enough, does it just happen? What star sign are you? I believe in the stars."

"Taurus. What are you?"

"Taurus too. There, you see? Dangerous people, Taureans."

"Why dangerous?"

"Feet on the earth and head in the clouds. I need the ordinary ... that is, the ordinary things of life. Coffee, a sunny morning, buying myself a newspaper or a packet of cigarettes, sitting down with a new book. You know? These things can make me happy. You know what I think sin is? Taking things for granted."

"And people?"

I'm not going to let him off this one, Sarah thought.

He ignored the question. The blue gaze went seaward again.

"You can never be really lost if you can wake up in the morning and think—ah, a good cup of coffee, that's all I want. You can live through the little things. But then, there's still all the rest."

He nodded his head to include the ocean, the blue air, the vast sunny morning. The gulls flapped overhead. He lit another Gitane and leaned against the parapet beside her. She saw grey in the blond of his hair, the roughness of skin tanned after years at sea.

"Yes, like babies, like families."

"Sarah, please. Please drop it? You know, I've always more or less followed what my body wanted to do, until now. If I needed rest and solitude I'd hole up somewhere. If I felt like going to sea, that's what I did. But now—ouah!"

He faced her, his back turned to the ocean. "Tell me. Sarah. How do you do it? How do you live?"

"Like you. Sunny mornings and the next cup of coffee." She yawned. His and Aisha's life was really not her concern. "And curiosity. I guess I'm always curious about what happens next."

He said, "It's my dreams that undo me, you know. Hunting for treasure. All that time on the seabed, searching. It's all still there, tons of it, on the floors of all the oceans of the world. Only a tiny percentage has been found. Gold. What men have died for. Ingots, doubloons. And yet, you know, even while you're down there that it's really the story of the treasure hunt that matters, not the stuff itself. It's all that drowned history. Finding it is amazing. I've got

49

some things I've brought up: jewels, little gadgets, seamen's things. The most beautiful was a little astrolabe. Imagine! The things people used, I love most. I'll show you. But it's also disappointing. You know that isn't really it."

"What is it?" She was really interested now; he'd drawn her in.

"Somehow, the process not the thing. It's confusing. The lives that are spent for it, the conflicts there are, the dangers. The whole thing. When I was in Key West there were a bunch of us who got obsessed with it. It's like an addiction. You spend your whole day thinking about it, when you're not doing it. The guy I worked for, his daughter and son-in-law got drowned. He ran out of money, and we were working the wrong place, then a clue came up all the way over in Spain, in some library, that we were looking in the wrong place for the Atocha. We were forty miles out. We moved right down near the Marquesas and started again. The first clue we got that there was anything down there was through the magnetic equipment. It was the cannons that did it, the brass cannons. We were mad with joy. It was so exciting. Then gradually we got it, bit by precious bit. The ship was crammed with gold and silver. It was greed that sank that ship. Every single sailor had been smuggling, we reckoned she was carrying nearly twice her tonnage in precious metal alone. I'll have to get back there sometime, there's so much more, I'm convinced of it. We only touched the surface."

"Where are the Marquesas?"

"Near Key West. You know it, last island in the Florida Keys? The wreck was about twenty miles out. You know, I have a theory about certain places. There are places in the world that everything passes through. Like the eye of a needle, drawing a long thread. Gold, precious things, migrations of people, ideas. Are you interested, Sarah? I'm not interrupting you?"

"No, no, go on." She couldn't be angry with him anymore. Up here, it was like being above everything, floating, flying—a world in which large movements took place. She stood against the low wall beside him, looking out. Too bad if Aisha were to find them here. She would take what came.

"Key West is one. This place, here, is another. It's right on the trade routes, the old caravans used to come up from black Africa with slaves and gold, and trade them with the Portuguese, and it would all go through the port here, up the Mediterranean and eventually across the Atlantic to the New World. We're all connected up through these highways across the sea, across the desert. Always have been. This goes way back. And of course people follow wealth and ideas come with people. So these invisible tracks, through these places that are like magnets, are the tracks of thought, of ideas. Everything passes through them. They are like the trackways of termites. We're the termites, you and I. We are on this track, and we don't know why exactly, but we are in the vanguard of something because of the geography, the configurations of it. For the people who can be drawn into the vanguard of change, these places are magnets. Why are you here, for example? You don't know. Any more than I knew why I went to Key West, why I left France in the first place. *Mais, pourquoi je suis ici, maintenant?* Why I am here now. That's why I can talk to you, Sarah. That's why I have to talk to you. That's why anything else—conventions, fears—is ridiculous. *Non? Tu comprends? Tu comprends ça?*"

"It's an interesting idea." She was thinking, everyone in this house has his own version of reality. But perhaps everyone in this house was really living in a dream.

"It's not just an idea, it's a reality." It was as if he'd read her mind. Dream or reality, perhaps it was simply a matter of choice.

"When I was in Florida I met up with people from all over the world," he continued. "We were completely international. Like here, like this house. Why? The old alchemists knew it, why men have a desire for gold. The world now is full of base metal. Base metal—greed—dominates us. Gold is something else; the desire for gold is not just greed. It is for transformation. That is what we are looking for, Sarah. That is what I think."

Transformation. But how?

The door from the stairs opened and Aisha came out on to the roof in her scarlet dress with her black scarf and her outdoor cloak on. She looked straight past Sarah, at Yann. Her eyes were like wet coal.

"Yann, telephone. Somebody wants you." She spoke in French. She stared steadily at him. He pushed a hand through his hair that had dried out and ruffled in the sun.

"I'll be down in a minute."

"Yann, telephone," she said as if she had not heard.

"I said I'll be down in a minute!"

Sarah held her notebook and pencil as if they excused her. There was no point in saying anything.

Yann said to her in English, "Do not be scared. Be courageous."

Aisha looked back at him with scorn in her stare. Then, shuffling his large feet in their yellow *babouches*, he went to the stair well. She stood aside to let him pass. With a final glance flashed at Sarah, she turned to follow him down, and shut the door behind them both.

*   *   *

The tendency towards safety and the tendency towards danger. In an unknown place, the signs are mixed; you don't know which is which. In Tangiers, that city the colour of old teeth where cold winds came down alleyways and men hooded in black walked close to the walls, she had first thought this. Bill had been fascinated by an idea: that of reporting back to safe democratic America the way danger worked in the world. Sarah had always thought that danger is inside us, we carry it like human bombs, wherever we may go. Courting it was an absurdity, one she had never enjoyed even when she was young and it was fashionable to scare oneself with living at the edge, driving fast, taking drugs, whatever it might be.

They had both read Paul Bowles. Which of them would be Kit, which Port? In Bowles' hero, Sarah recognized the urge to self-destruction. She watched her lover develop his thesis. Yes, even at that point, she'd wanted to draw back. Bill hoped to be transformed by violence, in what he called the real world. In bed, she didn't want him inside her, not with what he was thinking. Was that in Paris? She remembered a *café* on the Quai du Louvre, in the rain. He, the healthy American, her compatriot, exporting his American expectations intact into another world.

"Why Essaouira?" He'd asked her this already, and then because she had thought she was still in love with him, his adventurousness, his boyish simplicities, she told him.

"That was where my mother went in the thirties. It was called Mogador then. Something happened there, with a man, the one in the photo I think."

"I thought you said, Rabat. That she was with the consulate in Rabat."

"I think that Essaouira was where he took her, to be alone."

"Can't have been too easy, a Moroccan with a white woman in those days."

"I think something bad happened. There were rumours, apparently. She was sent home."

"She wouldn't tell you?"

"She either didn't remember or pretended not to, at first. But it did start coming back to her. It was either politics or sex, or both. Probably both. But I was too late, really. It was just before she died."

"Didn't she ever talk about it before? I mean, it's weird to have done something like travel to North Africa and never mention it, isn't it?"

"Not if you're English. I mean, Americans are just so much more open about their lives. We go round telling everybody everything. There were a million things she never talked about. Her previous life, period. Everything that happened to her before she moved to the States. Her life with my father. I don't know, perhaps she thought Charlie would be upset by it. Perhaps she just decided to live in the present."

But there was something; his mention of North Africa reminded her. The Africa stone. It sat on her mother's desk, first in the house in Boston, then in Provincetown, when she and Charlie moved there after he'd retired. A round, black, polished lump of stone. As a child she'd called it the Africa stone, because it was black. Now, she saw it could have come with Marion from Morocco. But that was all, apart from the photographs. And when she'd had to go through everything in the house, with her half-brother Tom to help her, she'd not seen it. In all the papers and photographs and objects that had been packed away in the drawers and closets of her mother's life, there was nothing that could tell her any more.

"Weird, I'd say," was Bill's opinion. "I guess she had something to be ashamed of."

"Or maybe it just didn't seem important any more. Perhaps when I'm eighty I won't think of telling anyone I travelled to Morocco with you?"

Marion Henderson. In England, where she was born, known as Marion. In Morocco, Marianne. Her daughter Sarah, born in England after her father Ted's early death, moved with her to Boston when she was three, when Marion became Mrs. Charles Flood. Charles Flood, the handsome American stepfather whom Sarah had loved was with a shipping line and had made money after the war. Sarah, in Tangiers, in Marrakesh, had often thought of her mother, of her unlikely journey. Her widowhood, at an age much younger than Sarah was now. Her life, and the men who had vanished, the ones Sarah had never even seen: Ted Henderson, Abdel Jadid. Sarah had taken the photograph from an old album, on her last visit to the old house, after her mother had gone to the nursing home. In its place was left a pale rectangle on a yellow-brown page. It was her private research. The public research could be going on outside, while on the inside this private question grew, perhaps to meet it. Perhaps there would be only one real question, in the end. It would be about memory; what we choose to let go of, what we have to remember.

Chapter five

Aisha Gandisha

Aziz was there for the first time that night when they played music. But they hardly met. Later, she tried to remember the details of how he was. A laugh, a glance? A warm handshake. *Bonjour, je m'appelle Aziz.*

Omar built the fire up high after dinner and people came in to warm themselves at the only fireplace in town. Yann, Jake and Omar had brought visiting friends: there was Malik from the carpet shop, Hafid from the *café* on the Place Moulay Hassan, and Aziz from the windsurf base. Nick had invited his architect friend, Mustafa, who had dinner with them. Aisha came in wrapped in her black cloak and brought with her Kiltoun and Myriam, the two young Berber women who were always cleaning the stairs. They came through together from the kitchen where they had left their outer clothes. They were wearing bright blue and purple dresses and thin trousers underneath. Aisha tonight was in deep blue with a gold necklace and earrings and little high-heeled black velvet slippers.

"*Bonsoir*, Sarah." Aisha flickered a small smile at her: challenge, rather than friendliness.

"*Bonsoir* Aisha." Sarah wished, on seeing her that she had changed into something more glamorous than pants and a shirt.

Aisha ignored Yann, who was sitting in his usual chair in his black burnous, a yellow slipper dangling from one bare calloused foot. She picked up a tambourine from the table. Omar was strumming on the guitar. She shook the little tambourine as if she were shaking it dry, then picked up the rhythm he was trying for and quickened it with her beat. The little bells jingled and Omar looked up and smiled. Mustafa joined in with the drum, Malik picked up a metal tray, the rhythm hung somewhere between western rock and Berber, all the fingers in the room tapped in time, on trays, knees, matchboxes, table tops. Aisha moved out into the centre of the room, the two young Berber women watching and clapping. She tied the belt of her dress just below her buttocks so that their shape was emphasized. She smoothed down her belly with her hands. She lifted her head and shook her breasts, clearing a space around herself and moving inside it, circling her pelvis as if she were slowly fucking an invisible lover. Her gaze went way beyond them, beyond the walls of this house even; it was somewhere else.

Yann sat beside Sarah at the fireside, watching, his eyes invisible behind dark glasses. Ramon stood a little in the background. He was twisting his hands. The faces of the white men were suddenly full of a wistful sexual longing, like grief, or loss. Sarah sat close to the hearth and watched every movement and suddenly Aisha grinned across at her. This, her glance said, is the power of women. This is what we can do. Sarah! Pay attention, watch!

Then Nick moved into the circle with her. She gestured to him with one hand, to come nearer. He bowed, giving her formal acceptance. He began to dance with her, moving his hips in tune with hers, close but not touching; he faced her, moving his pelvis ever closer. He looked full into her face and kept his arms outstretched, his body formal and aware and his face expressionless. They circled, moving around each other, inches apart. The drum and the tambourine beat quickened and Omar struck chords from the guitar and the two of them circled each other like cats. All the Moroccans present were leaning forward, tapping to the music, close and attentive. For them it was entertainment and for the moment Nick had joined them, playing the same game. Then he stopped suddenly, released himself and blushed. Everyone began to clap. Nick stood apart again. Aisha acknowledged him with a slow smile. Somebody passed her a cigarette and a glass and she stood there drinking her wine. Yann lit another cigarette and his foot in its yellow slipper tapped up and down, his expression invisible behind his dark glasses.

Then Aisha and Omar began a song together in Arabic, which made them both laugh. It was called 'Bake your bread and wake up your husband'; this was the chorus and everybody joined in. Sarah, laughing, clapping, exchanged a glance with the man called Aziz. All the Moroccans present began to laugh at the verses in between. Omar laughed so much that tears ran down his cheeks, he was doubled up as if in pain. The Berber girls giggled and wiped their eyes.

He was there that evening, but she was hardly aware of him. She remembered a broad face, a smile across the clapping, laughing crowd, a handshake at the end of the evening. A warm hand. She did remember that. What he remembered, he would say later, was a movement like a cloud, of light hair. A glance that passed across him like a shadow, there and then gone. Her voice, when she sang.

Yann passed her a joint when the singing was over. He'd taken off his glasses and she saw from his dilated eyes that he was stoned. All through the singing, he'd sat still, clapping the rhythm with his palms and fingertips coming together neatly, as a child claps.

"You sing well, Sarah."

"I enjoy it."

"You know, I don't understand you."

"What do you mean?"

"*Eh bien*, you seem to have a certain sensuality. You enjoy eating, music, I can hear it in your voice. I don't understand. What do you do with it? And how is it that you and I manage to have a purely asexual relationship?"

She said, "I told you, don't you remember? And the poisoned coffee's kind of off-putting, too." Speaking French to him, she found it easy to be open. It was a language made for flirting, for coming on.

"I'd love to make love to you. Or rather, perhaps I'd like to be close and stroke your head as you go to sleep and say, it's all right, Sarah, you can go to sleep, it's safe, I'll watch over you. Just to be gentle and close."

He drew on the shaggy end of the joint and its bitter smell came to her, sharp as memory.

"It's not possible, Yann."

In America, she would have mocked him: what are you talking about? But here, this evening, in French, with the joint passing back and forth between them, she picked up his elegiac mood and felt it herself—a certain regret.

"No, maybe not, but it is what I would like. You need it, don't you? I don't mean sex necessarily, but someone."

"Yann, I—" Suddenly she could hardly speak for tears coming.

"I think of sex probably because I am French. I'm very French in that way."

She began to laugh. But the laughter was at the edge of something else. She wanted either to move much closer or go right away. Her head ached, her eyes stung, and her body wanted to move on its own, without her consent.

She said, "What about you?"

"What about me? You are changing the subject."

"Well, you hide all the time. Half the time you just aren't there at all."

"Ah, well, maybe I'll tell you about that some other time, not now. *D'accord*, Sarah? But shall I tell you the story of Aisha Gandisha? Do you know about her?"

"No?"

"Well, she's a very beautiful woman who walks about on the ramparts here. She seduces men, young men that is. All the men in this town wish to meet her and are also afraid to. Because when she makes love to you, she sucks your brains dry. You become crazy. You want nothing but her."

"So, she's an addiction. Like alcohol." The story was putting her back in charge; she couldn't take it seriously.

"In a way, yes. But she is also poetry. She is also all that you could ever want."

"All that men want, you mean."

"Yes. And there are men in this town who have slept with her. You can see them. They have become crazy. There is one man, have you seen him, the man who feeds seagulls down by the port in the early morning. He is one of them. They say he was an intelligent man, now he is crazy."

Yann waved his hand around his head, to indicate craziness.

"And now he feeds seagulls?"

"Yes. *C'est fou, non?*"

Aisha stood over them; she wanted a key, she wanted to leave, she wanted a word with him. She frowned at Sarah.

Sarah said, "Your dancing was wonderful."

Aisha said nothing but looked down at her with her most scornful expression. Yann got up to see her to the door in her black cloak and when he came back he went to sit alone in an armchair in the corner, not speaking to anyone.

Yann's words, "I don't mean sex necessarily, but someone…"

They touched her in a place she had tried to forget: the expressions on the faces of the men, the music, the longings evoked that evening. The ancient dance of Nick and Aisha that spoke of the power of sex. The sweet, harsh taste of the herb running through her body, making her weak.

Where was she in all this, a woman sitting apart? Apart had been a relief, until now. Nobody asking, or at least nobody really wanting to know. She'd felt the freedom of it, alone, a woman who could look after herself, whatever Yann and Nick thought. She was up in her room reading, doing her research into Moroccan women, reading in French about Islamic inheritance laws. An observer, who might change the situation she saw around her, but who could not be changed herself.

Tonight, all the notes she'd been taking from books, the instructions from her editor in New York, the pamphlets and articles she'd brought from Paris and Marrakesh, seemed reduced by the presence of Aisha. How could she be researching Aisha, when she didn't even know herself?

She went to her room and leaned on the sill of the open window, smoking. Then she sat on the bed. She felt young, younger than she had for years; and light, lightweight. It was the lost feeling of youth, the sense of being nothing, knowing nothing. It was the scared feeling of being alone, not the strength, not the self-reliance she'd been cultivating for the last few years since her divorce, even in her relationship with Bill. It was the self of before marriage, before other men, before Bill, before managing life. She remembered sitting on a bed in a hotel in Paris when she was nineteen, feeling floored by life. Now, twenty-five years later, here it was again.

"Sarah, I don't understand. What do you do with it?" The unthought words of a stoned, drunk Frenchman. She let the tears come. After all, nobody could see her, nobody would know.

That night, she dreamed of a funeral. She didn't know who was being buried and didn't feel sad, only curious. There was a procession behind the coffin and Aisha was there, wearing her black cloak over the dress she'd worn that evening. She woke thinking about who might be being buried. In the European graveyard on the outskirts of town, the graves were cracked open, set crooked in shallow earth. She'd seen the small headstones of European children, whole families, dead from living in a country where they didn't belong. Was it there? Or was it the Muslim graveyard, within the city gates, to which crowds of people in white processed, leaving no one unmourned or alone?

She lay on her back and watched the sway of the curtains in the light wind from the sea. The shutters were open, the night sky was paler than the window frame, and she could hear the far-down ocean. She got up to lean again in the window, looking out. It was high tide and the waves were beating at the sea wall. There were still some stars in the sky and it was pale, an hour before dawn.

Her ex-husband, Dave, had been among the mourners. And Charlie Flood, who had married her mother, and her young half-brother, Tom, they were both there in the dream. Long, oh, long ago. It was her own funeral. She was the one. She went back to bed and drew the clean white sheet over her. She'd been at her own funeral, and nobody was sad, only expectant.

What was it that had to die, then, before another thing could live? She slowed her breathing, listened to the breath of the ocean, on and on and on. Slept again.

Abdel, his name was. Abdel Jadid. How can I have forgotten? Sarah, it is terrible to begin to forget. It was so long ago. In Mogador, in the town which once was called Mogador. I was in Rabat and he took me to see his home, in Mogador. Cold stone, the smell of it, that is what I remember.

How can you smell cold stone?

It is like putting your face down a well. Memory is at the bottom of a well. You send down a bucket and some of it comes up, a little at a time, to the light.

Part II
Aziz

Chapter six

Playing with the Atlantic

He was stacking windsurfing equipment when she got there, rolling the big sails that were bright and thin as butterflies' wings and storing them in a corner. He was barefoot and wearing a wet suit, a cigarette in his mouth. Other men in wet suits padded around and somebody was pouring water from a hose. To Sarah they all had the compact look of insects, zipped up tight.

"*Bonjour*, Aziz."

"*Bonjour*, Sarah."

He took the cigarette from his mouth and threw it into a pool of water. He took her hand with his wet one.

"Omar said you might be able to lend me a table. I mean, a place to write. It's so noisy at the house at the moment."

"Sure. No problem."

He smiled at her, the American woman with her awkward, forward manner. His hair dripped wet from the sea and he rubbed it with a small towel. He saw her move through sunlight towards him in her thin sweater and dark flapping skirt against her thighs, her bare feet covered in sand. Her shoes in her hand, her bag pulling down one shoulder. Her head, with her light hair in the breeze wrapping her skull. So eager, so unsure, he saw, so swift in her movement towards him.

"Where would you like it?"

"Maybe just outside the door? In the shade?"

He picked up the table from his office and carried it outside, holding it on his head with its legs in the air.

She followed with the chair.

"You're sure you don't need it?"

"No, I don't need it. Is here all right?"

He stood beneath the wings of sails, pink, green and yellow, in the shade they created. A bike lay against the white wall. There was a hand painted word on the wall: *Buvette.* The sea was far out and the wind had dropped.

"Not much wind today." She spoke French with him, and noticed in his own speech the slow buzz of his accent.

"No, it's not really worth going out. We'll have to do something else for a day or two. All my clients will be complaining, they think it is me who makes the wind. There, is that all right. *Ça va comme ça?*"

He arranged the table and chair for her, with care. She sat down and took out her notebook.

He said, "People will think I have a secretary. Make yourself at home, won't you. *Fais comme chez toi.* There's water inside, a toilet, a shower if you want. I'm going to take a shower and get changed and then think what to do with these people who can't amuse themselves unless the wind is blowing. See you later."

A bientôt. It was somehow reassuring. He went off barefoot on the concrete, leaving her to her table, her white rectangle of paper. Inside the little building there were men's voices and sounds of gushing water, where his clients were showering. Men walked back and forth and came out to squint at the sea through sunlight, to test the air for wind. It was a place, she saw, where men came down to play with the ocean. Their giant toys were all stacked and tidied. Aziz went off on his bike to get some *café* au lait from the *café*, and came back again. Tall, black, Habib worked around the base, hosing down the floor. The wind scoured the beach, dusting it with sand. Nobody spoke for hours at a time. That was the way it was, here, once the clients were gone. She sat there at the tin table, her pen moving across the page, as the shadows moved round with the sun.

After what seemed like a long time she stood and leaned against the white wall and stretched in the sun. He came out wearing jeans and a sweatshirt. He stood close behind her, their shadows one.

"*Comment ça va*? How's it going?"

"Good. You've provided me with exactly what I needed."

"You can come here any time. Even if I'm not here, Habib will look after you".

*   *   *

She walked down to the ocean to swim. It seemed a long way from the base to the first small waves, going down alone through all that space, across the hot dry blowing sand and then the wet soft sand of low tide. She waded in, gasped at the sudden cold, then floated on the gentle swell of it. The sky was chalk-blue and the line of the beach was a long way away. In the distance were the *café* and the low white square of the windsurf base and the little bright sails and the small black figures of men. It was all dusty as if brushed with white pollen. It was all far away. She lay on her back and floated, her head back and hair streaming.

"Where are you going for lunch?" He asked her as she towelled her mop of light hair dry, watching her as it turned from dark honey to glittering fairness in the sun.

She rubbed the ends, then threw it back still damp over her shoulders and fastened it with elastic, so that her face was bare, still dusted white with salt.

"To the quay, as usual."

It was late; everybody else would have eaten and gone. But the charcoal fires would still be lit and there'd probably be some fish left and the white tables would still be there into the afternoon.

"I may see you there. Otherwise, see you tonight, maybe. I may call at the house."

She noticed how he said 'may' and 'maybe,' not as if there were any doubt in his own intention but rather in recognition that anything could intervene between present and future. There was a gap here, a possibility that he had to state.

"*Ouacha.*" She rolled her towel around her swimsuit, picked up the string bag with her writing pad in it and smiled at him because his own smile, its warmth, was so catching. He had a face made of curves, she thought, and light.

"*Ouacha!*" he laughed back.

"See you later, Aziz. *A tout à l'heure.*"

"*A tout à l'heure. Bon appetit.*"

It was as easy as that. Yet as she walked away from him down the long dazzling expanse of the beach, past the lunchtime football game, past the veiled women sitting in twos and threes, she felt a longing to turn round, see him again, wave to him; be sure that he was there. But she made herself walk without turning once, as if it were some kind of test.

At the quay, she went to sit alone at the table in the sunlight and wait while Topniveau's younger brother grilled sardines. The midday sun warmed goose bumps from her arms, dried her hanging hair. She broke off bread and ate it, drank water from a plastic bottle and felt the salt dry on her face. The smoke from the fires still thickened the air. The sea at the harbour wall came in quietly now that the tide had changed. The fish men were acting out their pantomime for a few tourists, waving their fish and live crabs as if they were conjurers. But it was a little half-hearted, because lunchtime was nearly past. The man in the brown *d'jellaba* who came round every day trying to sell grasses against the evil eye was still there, placing his little dried bundles on the plastic. There were still the old women who begged: wrinkled grandmothers wrapped to the eyes with only a hand coming out for money.

"*Ça va*, Sarah?"

The man the French had nicknamed Topniveau came with the plateful of salad, chopped onions and tomatoes with cumin and oil. He slid the blackened fish from the grill on to a plate.

He sat down beside her, handed her a wedge of lemon.

"*Ça va, bien.*"

"So you are alone today?"

"Yes, only you're never really very alone here, are you?"

He laughed.

"Never very alone, no. You have many friends."

Aloneness, she thought, was not much of a concept here. Wherever you went, you were seen. People moved about together, close. Only a foreigner could come here, as she had, imagining that she could be alone.

She looked out across the square and beyond it to the Riad and the sea wall. The trees were still, the dark areca palms that looked as if they were made from a kit, the elephantine palms.

Topniveau said, "You are waiting for someone?"

"Not really, no."

"You could learn Arabic while you eat your lunch. Shall I teach you? What about five words a day? Do you know any? *Tu comprends un peu l'arabe?*"

"*Un shwiya*," she replied. Meaning, a little.

"*Schwiya!* You want to learn more?"

"*Ouacha.*"

"*Ouacha?*" He laughed again and his teeth were like the battlements on the ruined fort. He looked old, although he was probably younger than she was.

It must be the sugar. But his eyes were bright and young.

That day, the first day she went to the windsurf base, he taught her to say in Arabic: "I will return." *H'dinerja.*

* * *

It was the first of a series of days, the beginning of a certain time. In the morning, after breakfast, she walked out of the house, through the gateway in the red wall, along the town wall that edged the municipal gardens, past the Riad, past the Chalet de la Plage and in a straight line along the sea wall to the windsurf base. All the twisted streets and complex alleyways of the town gave way, when you walked out through the gates, to the simplicity of this route. She carried her swimsuit, a towel and her notebook in a string shopping bag, the kind people took to the market to fill with vegetables. To the right, on the widening strip of beach were the games of football; the glistening pitch grew as the tide went out, the game quickened as more people came to join in. On the concrete pathway between the road and the sea, old women sat with their backs to the sea, folded in upon themselves. The young women sat very close to each other and whispered and giggled behind their hands. On the hard sand of the beach the young men ran, dribbling the ball with naked feet. There were men standing in ones and twos looking out to sea. Sometimes they called out to her. *Heh, bonjour!* and she'd reply, *Bonjour!* going straight ahead. The ruined fort out along the beach shimmered like a mirage. There were the giant sand dunes and all that open space. And just before you came to the openness of the far beach, there was the base, its flimsy little building perched on concrete.

There was the red Renault that Aziz drove; its doors left open like a bug about to fly away. There were the blue doors of the base. She saw Habib in swimming trunks carting equipment about. Then she saw Aziz himself, grimacing as he listened on the telephone to some client.

They shook hands. He held hers for a minute, their hands the same size.

"It's hot today, wouldn't you rather be inside? You can use my office."

There was the table and chair and a bottle of Sidi Harazem water on the table, and a roll of Scotch tape. His watch was hanging on a hook. In one corner there were big, stacked plastic bags for putting all the windsurf equipment away. Nothing else. It was the barest, simplest place to come to. She sat down, leaving the door open so that she could see him moving about outside. From time to time he put his head round the door and smiled. Writing grew under her fingers like knitting done without a pattern. She was writing about today, not the history of this place. It would be a journal, a poem. Somehow he nurtured it just by being there, just by moving about and not talking and getting on with his own work, letting her be.

He would have said to anyone who asked, *"Eh bien, elle ne me gêne pas.* She's no trouble."

The truth was, he liked her being there, sitting outside his little place day after day, writing in her notebooks. What was she writing? He didn't ask. But when he came up from the ocean and saw her sitting there, his heart warmed, he felt expansive towards her. She was like a cold creature thawing out in the sun.

The wind moved back to the north again and in a day the sea was darker and choppy. All the blue shutters and doors of the town banged open and shut.

"Thank God there's some real wind," said Aziz when she arrived. "There's a limit to the amount of tidying up I can do. These guys all want their money's worth and they start complaining if there isn't any wind, even for a day or two. They've paid for their vacations so they've paid for wind, and if there isn't any, there's trouble. You can't imagine how often I hear it—'Aziz, why isn't there any wind, when is the wind going to change, do you think there will be wind tomorrow?' But I suppose it is natural. I suppose they can't help it."

He kissed her on both cheeks, slow and deliberate, one, two and then three, in the French fashion. They leaned against the white wall together, smoking. He was in his wet suit, about to go out to sea.

He said, "I should be more tolerant. They wanted one particular thing, they're disappointed. But I don't think you can live like that. You only want one thing—you miss all the rest. Don't you think so? For them, if there is no wind there is nothing at all to do."

"I can't imagine thinking there was nothing to do here."

It was so easy, being with him. They chatted, or they said nothing. She thought he was the easiest man to be with she had ever known; he had no edges, no rough places, he flowed around her.

"Well, you and I, we would find something. Everything is

worthwhile in the end. Everything and everybody. You have to want what is, *n'est-ce pas?*"

He finished his cigarette and pulled up the zip of his wet suit so that he was sealed in. He, who so rarely talked about himself, enjoyed telling her what he thought, who he was. She listened to him, as if he were interesting. He began to rehearse what he thought to himself, imagining saying it to her. She would hear him, she would understand.

* * *

He stepped away to pull the boards and sails away down the beach with Habib. The two of them stood at the edge of the water. The sails bucked and flattened in the new wind. She watched them, slightly bow-legged Aziz and tall broad Habib, black against the sea. The sails were green and pink against the dark sea, and against the island as they went out. For a moment each of them was up there, triumphant and upright, riding the top of the wave; then they were dashed down again to struggle in a collapse of limbs and sails that looked like shipwreck. She laughed, watching their wet heads emerge.

They ran up out of the sea in a long disciplined trot, like men running in the desert. The sun burned hotter every minute. Omar came bouncing down on a bike, one free arm waving to her. His T-shirt said 'Fun Works—What Else?'

She waved back.

Two men who had been jumping up and down in the sea came out and skipped on the sand as if over an invisible rope. A woman walked past in a lapis-blue dress. On the beach a man wriggled out of his clothes to swim. He threw his clothes away from him quickly in the abrupt way she'd noticed men often have, as if they can't get them off quick enough. He waded into the sea, dived and came up like a seal, gleaming in the sun. Omar came out of the base in a wet suit, a surfboard under his arm. He walked into the water backwards, waving. The sea took them all and threw them about—an arm, a black head, splinters of a person. The sound of the wind was everywhere, all through everything.

"There isn't too much noise for you?" Aziz came out of the sea each time with his hair wet and curly. "Look, it's always curly, but I don't usually have ringlets!" He ran his hand through it and laughed at himself, splashing drops on to the concrete.

The windows of the town, far away, were like eyes looking out over the red wall. At the *café*, umbrellas went up and twirled around in the wind. Further along, at the Chalet de la Plage, there were striped awnings up. The sea splashed up the wall in great spurts. Close by, a couple walked past, he in a light beige suit, she in a pale *d'jellaba*, an intimate distance between them, closer than walking embraced. She was with Aziz, watching from inside his world, when she saw them pass. Out near the island now there was a long unfurling of white on rocks. It was like seeing the world from a vantage point, a safety people call home.

"I'm going to eat now." She packed up her things. It was nearly one.

"*Bon*. I have to make some phone calls. See you later? *A tout à l'heure.*"

They all saw her come and go—Habib, Omar and the others as she went daily to the table in Aziz's office. It became a routine, if pleasure can have routines. It was what she woke to in the mornings, and relished in advance. She left the house at about the same time every day, and didn't care who saw her, or what they might say.

"*Je m'installe?*" was what she'd said to Aziz, and he had said, "*Fais comme chez toi*. Make yourself at home."

Mostly, they talked about the wind. Aziz gave her a surfboard that he tied to her wrist fastened with Velcro 'so that you don't get lost'. She took the long waves as they came in and slid with them all the way to the shore. Sometimes he was there, smiling through water, shaking the drops from his hair.

She sat outside the base afterwards on the burning concrete, hands hooked over knees, just waiting now. Just as there was no point in going anywhere but along the straight route past the Chalet to the base, there was no point in worrying about what anyone else thought. Sometimes you are so absorbed in what you are doing

73

and it seems so entirely normal that you feel you are invisible. That was how it was, during those days, for however many weeks it was, and the scattered writing in her notebook was like the tracks of it, footprints in sand.

He came to the house some evenings, talked business with Nick or played chess with Omar. Sometimes he drank a glass of wine at the low table beside the fire. When Aziz came into the house, she saw that some calm came with him; he sat quite quietly and observed what was going on. Sometimes he spoke Arabic with Omar in the kitchen, sometimes he was downstairs with Yann and Nick, leaning on the table and speaking French. At other times he sat in the corner, one leg hooked over the chair arm, his head tipped back, apparently just listening. She waited for him to be there, even if he went to talk to one of the others, even if he was not apparently there for her. The dog came to him to be stroked, the black bitch who belonged to someone else. When he played chess with Omar at the table with the big carved chessmen set out on it and the single candlestick, his moves were swift against Omar's and he won in minutes. She sat across the room, reading, writing, and from her cover, watched the movements of his hands as he picked up the knight, the queen, placed the piece with a deliberate movement, marched his white pawns across the board, then sat back, waiting for Omar. When he sat back, his hands went behind his head, rubbed the base of his neck as his spine stretched, and she felt it in him, the stiffness from hours braced upon the board with the sail tugging him across waves. She felt his spine as if it were under her hands. She would remember the back of his neck, the slight hunch of his shoulders, their breadth compared to the rest of him.

Omar said, "Nobody beats me at chess. Only you, Aziz." They were friends, in a way no American men would be friends, unless they were gay. There was something like adoration in Omar's glance, and the surprising, easy physicality of Moroccan men together, holding hands, touching each other in passing, standing linked. It touched her, she loved to see it: the formality of the chess set, the ranks of the carved wood pieces, the two men leaning into it, then drawing back; the flow of their bodies towards each other afterwards, hands reaching, no boundaries, no edge. Then he'd come to her, and he'd be quite formal with her, because Omar was there, but his eyes and his smile would be for her, and the formal cheek-kisses would be warm, telling her of an intention beyond what he could show in public.

"The trouble about growing up in France is that I don't really fit in either here or there. In France I seem to have Moroccan reactions to things, here I seem to have French ones. People get surprised at me wherever I am."

"Is that a problem?"

In the house, a certain shyness seemed to touch them both, because someone might come in, or because he was not on his home ground, she wasn't sure. When Nick and the others were there, he was so quiet as to be almost invisible. When Omar was the only other person, he was Omar's friend. With her alone, he was veiled in propriety still, it was like being with a date, she thought, in her parents' house; neither of them at ease because the parents might come home.

"Well, yes, a little. Here, you see, I feel as if I am French. But I'm not, I'm Moroccan. My parents left Casa when I was little. I've lived in France ever since, until I came back to work here."

"What was it like growing up in France?" She wanted to know him, past and present. It was his story she wanted, as well as his present self. Who was he? How had he come to her?

"Difficult sometimes. But it was all I knew. I didn't like school. People said I was stupid, so I acted stupid, never did any work. I thought until recently that I was stupid and now I realize I am not at all, I am even quite intelligent." He laughed and shrugged.

"Don't laugh at yourself, Aziz."

"No, all right. But you know what I mean? Anyway, I decided to be very good at sports instead. So here I am doing sport for a living. My favourite sport is windsurfing. Now I have to do it every day for money. Have to. But I am lucky, too, to be paid for what I like."

He picked up the little drum that lay on one of the chairs and touched its stretched skin with his fingers. The dog pushed at his knees for attention. He looked up from the drum, and frowned his frustration to her. "I can't even play this, not like the people here."

Maybe it was because she, too, didn't fit in. But Americans, he imagined, made themselves at home everywhere. They thought, like the French, they were better than other people. But she, Sarah, did not seem to think that. She looked at him as if he were more interesting than she was. The way she looked at him, he wanted more.

They sat opposite each other at dinner, with Nick there presiding in his usual place, and Yann, drinking, in his; they talked politely, they were far away from each other, a table's width between them and all the dishes, the *tajines*, the couscous, the mounds of food. It was so different from playing in all that sand and water in the blinding light of the beach. For how many evenings that spring did the two of them sit there quite formally among the others and talk? He seemed to have become an expected guest here and nobody questioned it. For Sarah it was both pleasure and torment. She saw him, heard his quiet voice, absorbed his presence, but was far away from him. It was like being at a Victorian dinner table, locked in protocol, a young woman shut in by the social rules of a past time. Across the long table, in candlelight, a sharpish look came to her from Yann from time to time, but that was all. For how many evenings was it that he came for dinner and sat about the house? She couldn't remember. It's when things begin to feel normal, that you begin to forget.

Chapter seven

Horses and Sea

T he horses were purebred Arabs, not tall but fine-boned, with alert dish faces and large eyes. They fidgeted in their stalls and poked their heads out, jingled their bits and stamped. She stood with Aziz under the green canopy of the veranda while the men who looked after the horses moved about with buckets and carried saddles on their arms. She breathed the sweet dung smell and the oiled leather smell of stables and the sweat of men and animals on a hot day. The distant sound of the sea reached her. She put back her head to follow in the blue air above the paddocks, a circling brown hawk. In the paddocks small ponies munched at the new grass—Vietnamese ponies, the stable hand told her when she said, "Are they Shetlands?" "They come from Indo-China looking like Shetlands. They are a very old race of horse."

The three horses that he led out of their stalls were dun, grey and chestnut. They wore brief saddles with high pommels and bridles with dropped nosebands and fierce-looking bits. The dun horse was for Aziz, the grey for her. They came out with their heads low for grazing, reins loose upon their necks. There was the hollow clop of their hoofs upon hard earth. Their guide was a slim, silent man in an American baseball cap, who swung himself up light as a circus rider on to the chestnut and sat perched, shortening his stirrup leathers as his horse pranced close to Sarah's and tried to nip the grey's neck. The stable hand pushed between the horses, gave first Aziz and then Sarah a leg-up, so that suddenly she was up there with him, facing him as they sat their horses and he grinned at her across the yard. The grey moved under her like the waves of the sea, choppy and unknown, its shoulders sliding in front of her, its neck stretched. She felt all the tension in the pit of the stomach that comes from riding a new horse, the fear that was not yet pleasure, that hadn't found its balance in the freedom of movement, the grandeur of horses. She pulled its head up, shortened her reins. It was a while since she'd ridden; the last time must have been in Rock Creek Park in Washington, when she'd stayed with Bill's parents and she and Bill had ridden together, long-stirrup and western-saddled, like cowboys. She saw Aziz snap his stirrup leathers and stand up in the saddle to try their length. He was at ease on a horse, relaxed as when he rode surfboards through waves, he was a man at home with movement. How strange, to compare him with Bill at this moment—her one-time lover, in another life, another country—who'd sat his horse doggedly, heavy-reined, dragging it into submission.

She hadn't time to think about him now. The grey horse threw up his head, ears pricked. The chestnut moved off suddenly, barging ahead through the gate. The guide flicked him with his whip. Aziz's horse pushed at the chestnut, which threw up its hindquarters to kick. They went one behind the other through the narrow gate and the horses pulled and trotted a little and snatched at their bits as they headed down the track towards the ocean. The tide was out and the sand soft and giving under foot. The horses were a body, a herd, connected in their need to move. A hot wind came down the beach from the north in gusts so that fine sand blew up like spray. She felt the sand in her face, stinging. The ruined fort sat there, a broken toy thrown down on the beach; waves of sand moving about it like water. Far up the beach, floated the silhouette of a single camel, moving towards them or away, it was hard to know. The camel prints were single deep holes in sand, beginning to blur. Had the rider gone on up north, away from them, or had he turned to come back? He and the camel were one, a wavering long black blot, shape-changing, far away. Sarah's horse floundered in the prints of the camel, stumbled then put up its head and regained its stride. She rode it at a trot, looked ahead between its pointed ears, saw the ocean blue and green in stripes and the sky mauve with afternoon heat. The horses circled the edge of a shallow lake and came down close to the ocean, leaving deep curved marks all the way behind them. The grass on the sand hills and the tamarisk bushes gave way to the empty hardness of sand. The horses jogged sideways in the slight wind. Under foot there were oyster shells that crunched, and patches of dark weed. At the water's edge the sand was newly bared and wet; the horses sank softly in as they went. The water at their fetlocks splashed up muddied and shallow and they shook their heads and tugged at their bits.

"Can we let them go?" Aziz leaned sideways and shouted to the guide against the sound of the ocean.

"If you want."

Ahead of her, Aziz drummed his heels and let the dun horse have its head. He was away in a minute, churning sand and water. The horse's rocky canter lengthened into a gallop and it headed back out of the water on to the wet sand. It toiled with the softness and the headwind and Aziz leaned forward and urged it on. His black head was before her and his back curved down in the saddle and she let the grey horse go.

The sudden speed of it, bone and muscle all moving together, so that there was nothing for it but to go with the horse, clinging there between sky and earth upon the only solid thing in the world, a hot neck and a coarse flying mane. Out of the corner of her eye she saw the man on the chestnut as she passed him and he fought with his horse in the shallows. Then she was behind Aziz and the gap was closing between them. She came up alongside him, the grey stretched and shuddered, they were close, neck and neck, the horses' feet pounding up sand, and he shot her a glance of pure pleasure. Close, level now as the horses' stride evened out, the gallop steadied into a canter as they tired and no longer pulled to be free. Poised, motionless in all this movement, there's a moment when you are going as fast as you can through the universe and it simply stills and hangs about you; you let go of everything and you are simply there at the centre, not moving; she was there, a yell of elation only just held back inside her. She saw him rein and turn his horse's head, turning inland, and draw a circle in the sand at a canter and come back to her. The grey horse slowed to a trot and came to meet his. The dun's neck was dark and soaked with sweat and seawater. Sarah's grey had whorls of hair in soaked dark patches on its neck. She stroked it through rising steam and her hand came away wet. The two horses whinnied at each other and pretended to bite. Aziz reined his in and stopped a foot away. They stared at each other in the middle of all this space.

"Isn't it great? But—ouf! Exhausting!" He looked as happy and excited as a boy.

"Wonderful." She was grinning at him, vacant with fatigue and pleasure.

The horses lengthened their strides and settled down.

The man on the chestnut came cantering up slowly, his horse like a rocking horse against the sea. He slowed to a trot and sat down in the saddle, loose and easy. He had a joint in one hand and hooked one leg over the pommel and his face was expressionless. They rode back up the beach three abreast, the guide at once sleepy and alert and smoking his joint. Aziz made his horse trot a bit and rode at heaps of driftwood. In the blue-mauve sky above the dunes, three kites rose and dipped, tugged their long tails and moved all together, one blue, one white, and one green. You couldn't see who held them but they rose and then swooped downwards and curved and sank before pulling upwards clear and fast again.

They rode back in to the edge of town: past shacks and heaps of garbage and a procession of old women going home with laden baskets and a man leading a donkey that stopped stock still and wouldn't move out of the way. Children were coming home from school and a policeman directed traffic in his startling white clothes, and trucks were coming in from Agadir, and a slow blue bus. The guide put up an arm to stop the traffic. The sight of the traffic scared Sarah, but the horses glanced sideways and obeyed.

"They're good horses." She spoke to the guide in French, as they crossed the road abreast.

"This one, the one you're riding, was a Fantasia horse. For years he worked only in the Fantasia. You know what that is? It's hard work for a horse, quite violent. Now he is tired, he doesn't want to do it any more."

"He doesn't seem tired."

"Tired of that, I mean. No, some horses go on till they are twenty. Just as some men go on riding the Fantasia until they are eighty. Age doesn't matter so long as you want to do it. *Eh, mon ami?* Then if the will is gone, you have to stop. A man or a horse. He is tired of doing what he has to do, you understand? He prefers to play on the beach!"

"They're all stallions, aren't they?"

"Yes, here we don't cut our horses. It's better. They run better. You cut a horse, he loses something, he is not so interested. But you have to keep them away from each other or they bite. They want to fight, you see."

A long whinny sounded from the stables as they approached. The grey horse put up his head and neighed back. Aziz rode his through some mimosa bushes and came out dusted with yellow pollen. He handed her a twig of mimosa while his horse munched on a mouthful. She rode into the yard with the yellow flowers in her hand and the reins slack on the horse's neck, Aziz's black head with its dusting of yellow pollen before her. In the moment. In the memory.

Light came down through the green filter of the pergola. On the ground he stood close to her when they'd handed their reins to a stable boy.

"Can we come again tomorrow?" Aziz gave money to the guide.

"If you want. Come again when the tide is out, it is better."

"Will you have time again tomorrow?" Sarah asked him.

"Perhaps. I hope so. My boss is coming tomorrow, he may want me, I suppose. He may have plans for me, he usually does. But I could slip off for an hour or two, leave him to Habib. Did I tell you that my boss is coming by plane from France, tonight?"

"No. Who is your boss?"

"My boss is called M. Antoine Dupuy."

Stiff-legged they passed through the gate and out on to the road and along it to the beach again. Barefoot on the warm sand, boots dangling from their hands, walking together towards the base without saying much. Her body aching from the exercise, face stung with the sun, the oily dust of horseflesh on her hands—she was happy just walking beside him in the freedom of nothing that needed to be said. As they neared the base, Habib came towards them, held out a bunch of papers written in Arabic. He smiled from his immense height, shy about recognizing these two together, perhaps, this foreign woman and his friend Aziz.

"Here, Aziz, it's the programme for the *Fête*."

"*Fais voir.* You see, Sarah, I can't read Arabic. It's a nuisance, but I have to get him to translate for me. So he could be telling me anything, *n'est-ce pas*, Habib? Tell me, what am I supposed to be doing?"

Two French windsurfers came out of the base in their wetsuits and made a small urgent queue for his attention.

"There's something every afternoon. And then in the evenings too, the week before the *Fête*." Habib smiled gently at Sarah, as if apologizing for having to interrupt.

"What's the *Fête*?" she asked.

"The *Fête du Trône*. It's to celebrate the King's birthday and Moroccan Independence." Aziz shrugged. "Impossible, no? I'm busy. Can we tell them I'm busy?"

"Listen, Aziz. Friday, a meeting with the mayor. The afternoon, at the sports centre. Then in the evening—" Habib opened his big hands outwards.

"I can't do it. I'm going riding with Sarah."

"The evening?" Habib pleaded.

"Evenings too. All night." Aziz laughed, screwed up his eyes. "And on the Saturday—"

"What are we doing on Saturday, Sarah? I know. Poetry. We're rehearsing Hamlet. That's what we're doing. Rehearsing Hamlet. All day. No, okay, sorry, Habib. *Mon cher ami.* I'll go through it with you later. They could make me do anything, you see, and I would have no idea what it was. I never learned to read and write my own language, *c'est chiant, n'est-ce pas?*"

"I'll leave you to it."

Habib was obviously embarrassed by having to talk business in front of her, and Aziz was frowning with annoyance at having to think about it at all.

"See you later then." He said, and added, "Till this evening. *A ce soir.*"

She walked slowly back to the house, went up to her room and washed off the smell of horses and her own sweat, the fine grains of sticking sand, the black grime from the leather, the salt crust of the ocean. She stood in the shower for a long time, letting hot water rinse her from head to toe, and thought of the evening ahead, and Aziz laughing about rehearsing Hamlet, and pages of written Arabic that couldn't be understood. Then she squeezed water from the darkened tail of her hair, wrapped her head in a towel, noticed in the mirror how tan her face and arms were, how pale the rest of her by comparison, an echo of faint brown only where her swimsuit had not covered her, the parts that it had covered, white. Her thighs ached already where she had gripped the horse's sides; she'd be stiff the next day. She lay wrapped in white towels on the white bedcover, one foot propped on the other, and committed to memory the vision of Aziz on his horse riding through mimosa bushes, pollen spattering his black head. Just in case, she would store this sight deliberately against a future in which he would not be.

When she came down, clean and dressed, there was a man in the armchair by the fire. Aziz's boss Antoine, presumably, come on the Marseille-Marrakesh flight. He sat with a large glass of cloudy pastis in one hand. Nick, Yann and Aziz crowded around him. The room had become the site for a men's meeting, with papers spread all over the table, a bottle of Ricard and cigarette butts in ashtrays.

Aziz said, "Sarah, *viens voir*. Come and look."

They were the plans for a new windsurf base along the beach, new bungalows, a disco, a restaurant, a swimming pool. She shook hands with Antoine: *Bonsoir, bonsoir.* He was a large man with dark hair streaked across with grey. His handshake was firm but damp. He looked at her briefly and then back at the papers. Aziz fetched a chair and gestured to her to sit down. "*Rebonjour*," he whispered to her. Then, "Look!"

The plans showed a spread of new building across the beach and foreshore at Sidi Kaouki, a few miles to the south of the city.

"This looks like you're planning to change things quite a bit."

Antoine Dupuy said, "There is no advance without change, *Madame.*"

"But will you get permission for all this? It's supposed to be a holy place, isn't it?" She was appalled at what she saw drawn there.

Nobody answered. An American, objecting to change? Aziz glanced up but sat close to his boss and said nothing.

Nick said, "It's not Europe, or even America, Sarah, there's a million miles of empty beaches here. Anyway, the tourist trade's good for the country. They need it."

"And you've seen what development's done to the rest of the world? What mass tourism does? The ugliness, the greed?"

"It's jobs, Sarah, it's money. It's what they don't have."

Antoine Dupuy began to roll up the papers. He glanced at his watch and fidgeted in his chair. This obviously was not a discussion he wanted to have. He was exhausted, simply exhausted, he said. The roads, the police blocks, the drive from Marrakesh, the difficulty of leaving work in Toulouse, getting to Marignane on time. He must get some sleep tonight. But how much did Nick think he would have to reckon for one unit of housing, what would the initial outlay on the land be likely to be?

Nick stood up. "Excuse me, Antoine, but I'm going out to dinner tonight. I have to meet someone. Perhaps we could talk about

84

it later? Sarah, I'm taking you out to dinner too. There's no dinner here tonight, apparently, Aisha's gone out somewhere and Omar hasn't had time to do anything."

He stood there in his dark blazer and his clean jeans, waiting for her to join him as if there were no question about it. "We're going to Chez Sam. I'm meeting a friend from Marrakesh. You'll like her, you'll get on. And the lobster's marvellous."

He smiled around at the assembled men. It was diplomacy; he would get her out of here.

She wasn't going so easily. "No, thank you, Nick, I'm not hungry. If you want to invite me to dinner, do it properly, not like that."

Nick shrugged. Aziz didn't look up. Antoine Dupuy got out his pocket calculator and began playing with it. She had the distinct feeling that a woman putting her oar in was not what any of them wanted now. The plans lay half-rolled on the table. She watched the white, plump hand on the calculator, its fingers twitching.

"I'll stay here," she said.

"All right." Nick's face said, don't say I didn't try. He went out quiet-footed as ever, not voicing his reproach. She sat, not looking up. If you didn't fit in with Nick's plans, there was always the hint of a suggestion that you might miss out on the best thing anyone ever planned for you.

Yann was saying, "Sidi Kaouki, one of the most beautiful places in the world."

"You know it well?" Antoine Dupuy spoke in a neutral tone.

"Of course. And Sarah went there on a horse. Didn't you, Sarah?" He winked at her, his old maddening daredevil blue eye.

"Not as far as that, no."

"Ah, not quite as far as that. "Antoine Dupuy said, "No, that would take all day, I imagine. You didn't take quite the whole day off, did you, Aziz?"

Aziz just shook his head, eyes on the plans.

"You like riding horses, then, *Madame*?" Antoine Dupuy said to her.

"Yes, yes, I do." She would not allow him to humiliate her; neither could she stand to hear him drop his hints to Aziz. If you could dislike someone on sight, she disliked this man already.

"And you are a writer, I hear? Tell me, how is it that you speak French? I thought no Americans spoke French."

"Some do. I lived in France for a while when I was young. I studied French literature at the university of Aix." Her voice shook slightly. It was like being cross-questioned. Why was he doing this? There was such an undercurrent here.

"Ah well, maybe we will have a chance to talk about literature too, one day. Now, Yann, what were you saying per hectare?"

Yann said, "Me, I'm not well up in these things."

Aziz said at last, "Maybe we could talk business later, Antoine? It is good to rest after a long journey." His face as he looked up was impassive.

Antoine Dupuy shook his head. "I've only got a week. Okay, I'm tired, but it has to be done. Somebody has got to think about it. We can't all be as laid-back as you people here. Some of us are here for business. Still, I don't want to bore this charming lady with facts and figures. Perhaps we could include some horse riding? That would be good for the clients. For the days when there's no wind. Perhaps you could organize it, Aziz."

Yann said, "I suggest another pastis, *tu veux*, Antoine? Aziz is right, it's late to be talking about all this, you've had a tiring journey. Perhaps we can sort out all this when Nick's here."

Antoine Dupuy said, "Nothing ever gets done in this country, if you ask me. But still—in deference to this charming lady—perhaps we should talk of other things?"

Aziz said suddenly, "What about Hamlet? You know Hamlet, Antoine?"

He grinned across at Sarah and then looked away. She saw a flash of his playfulness, his horse-riding devil-may-care self. Perhaps he and Yann together would be enough to put Dupuy off, at least for tonight.

"Hamlet? Ah, Hamlet. Shakespeare. *Pourquoi pas?* To be or not to be. That is all I know of Hamlet. But what does it mean?" Dupuy looked melodramatically at Sarah, as if she being Anglo-Saxon held the answer.

They all drank more pastis and she went to the dark and empty kitchen for a glass of wine. It looked as if Aisha was on strike. Sarah missed her suddenly—her ironic glance, her way of standing with one hand on her hip making everyone pay attention, the sudden vehemence of what she said. Where was she tonight? With her invisible family? With her child? Aisha wouldn't have let this men's meeting go uninterrupted. Thinking of her, Sarah said, "I'm going out for some *harira*. Any of you want to come?"

"Heavens, yes, we have not eaten. Of course, I ate on the plane. I don't eat a lot but I have to eat often. My digestion is not good." Antoine Dupuy glanced down at the slope of his stomach.

Yann said, "I'll come with you." He stood up, snapped a light to the cigarette hanging in the corner of his mouth, signalled, "Let's go" to Sarah.

Aziz said, "I'm hungry, too. Let's go round the corner to Tariq's. Leave your calculator behind, won't you, Antoine?"

"No, no, I'll bring it just in case we think of anything extra during the meal that we have to discuss."

"I was joking, *patron*. I know you won't be parted from it for a minute, not even when you go to bed."

Antoine Dupuy got up slowly and rolled the plans, fastening them with a rubber band. "You people seem to think you can leave everything to tomorrow and it'll still get done. Why I do business here, I can't imagine."

Aziz said, "Because here are the best beaches and the best wind and because you can't do without us. *N'est-ce pas*, Antoine?"

"Yes, Aziz, that's true. Now, let's escort this charming lady to find some dinner or we'll be accused of machismo. *Harira*, you said? What sort of a dinner is that? A peasant soup, is that all you want? Really?"

Antoine opened the door for Sarah, urging her with exaggerated politeness to go first. The three men followed her out, and Yann walked beside her as they went up the Rue Yassin towards the little square and Tariq's restaurant.

At Tariq's, Aziz ordered the food for them all in Arabic, and she thought she saw him share something else, a joke, a rumour, with Tariq, who slapped him on the back and laughed. Yann stretched out in his burnous on one of the low couches, Antoine Dupuy sat upright next to him. Aziz and Sarah sat next to each other on the small couch. A boy brought the thick, hot soup and the loaf of good bread sliced in a basket. Aziz offered her tastes of his *tajine* and she dipped her fingers in and licked them afterwards. On the wall above them, Aziz showed her, was a large coloured photograph of Sidi Kaouki, with the saint's white house on the empty beach. It was where Antoine Dupuy wanted to build his tourist paradise: one of the most beautiful places on earth. Sarah grimaced and bent to her soup.

"Excuse me, but have you been there, Sarah? Have you seen it?"

"Not yet. I've been wanting to go."

Antoine Dupuy said, "Come with us. I am going there tomorrow. I will take you. Aziz will drive us. I'll show you what we're planning to do."

Yann said, "I can't believe it, you've been here all this time and you haven't been to Sidi Kaouki? You should certainly see it before Antoine wrecks it." He lounged on one elbow, tearing off pieces of bread to eat, and smoking.

Antoine said, "Next time you come, it will be quite different. Much improved."

"Well, as you said, it's a day's ride on a horse and I don't have a car."

She saw Antoine was trying to be friendly now. Anyway, she didn't want to behave badly and make things hard for Aziz, whose brief warning glance at her she had seen.

"Tomorrow," said Antoine Dupuy. "How about that? Tomorrow I will call for you at ten o'clock."

She closed the heavy blue door to the street behind her and went up the first flight of stairs. Nick was back, sitting with his friend from Marrakesh at the low table in front of the fire. The friend was a woman of about thirty, beautifully dressed in soft leather pants and a cream top and she had black hair pulled back in a knot at the back of her neck. Her lips and nails were red, her whole self glossy with care, and she laughed charmingly at something he had just said.

"This is Sacha. She's staying here for the weekend. Sacha, this is Sarah. She's from America. She's writing about Moroccan women, so you can tell her a thing or two. You know Yann. So where is Antoine?"

"Gone home to bed," Yann said, "With his calculator, *bien sûr*. He wants to see you in the morning. Business deals. How to get round the Mayor, I imagine. But first he wants to take Sarah to Sidi Kaouki."

"Okay. Business deals, eh? Looks to me as if he's carved up that foreshore pretty thoroughly. Well, I'd better not drink too much. D'you want something to drink? Tea? Whisky? We're having whisky."

Sacha said, "I never drink whisky. Today is the first time." She stared at Sarah with brilliant dark eyes and held out her hand, plump and ringed and cool to touch. Sarah let go of it, said, "Excuse me, I'm going to bed, I've had a long day."

"And you're going to Sidi Kaouki in the morning?"

Sacha said, "Sidi Kaouki, what is that?" Nick said, "It's a few kilometres south of here. It's very beautiful. There's a marabout on the beach. I'll show you. Or you could go with Yann, he knows it well, he wants to go and live there and be a hermit and write his book. Miles away from everybody. Don't you, Yann?"

"Goodnight then, Sarah," Sacha said. *"A demain*. Sleep well. I think I have the room next to yours, don't I?" She smiled, white teeth, red lips, a soft insistent stare of dark eyes.

*   *   *

He knocked on her door about twenty minutes later. She heard his step on the stairs and his quiet knock, got up from where she'd been lying, fully dressed, across the bed and went to let him in.

89

"Excuse me coming like this? I am not disturbing you?"

"No, it's fine. Come in."

"Last night I asked Omar which was your room. He showed me, we were down in the hall, I saw your light on, and then just as I was about to come up and knock on your door, the light went out. Just at that moment. So I didn't dare."

"You could have. Sit down, Aziz. I'm glad you're here."

"Are you reading? I thought you might be writing, working. I don't know. And then you said you were tired, so I thought perhaps I should not come."

"Tired was just an excuse. Angry was more like it."

"Ah."

She'd been lying across the bed on top of the white counterpane, reading Yann's latest copy of "*Libération*." He saw the dent of the body-shape, the opened pages. He sat down beside her on the bed. "Can we talk?"

"That Antoine, isn't he incredible? I don't like him. Does he ever stop thinking about money? And what the hell are they up to at Sidi Kaouki? I thought it was a holy place."

"I know. I agree. But he's a good man really, just a little annoying at times."

"You think everyone's good," she said.

"But so they are. You just have to know what handle to take them by, like everything in life. There's no point in focusing on the bits you don't like, you only get frustrated. Everybody has two sides to them, everybody, and every situation, don't you think? Can I sit here?" He perched beside her on the bed, at a distance.

"Sure. *Fais comme chez toi*, as you said to me. Yes, but it's hard to live by. Especially when you're with people like your boss. How do you do it?"

"I have to. I can't do it any other way. Otherwise I'd get too annoyed. By my boss, by all these clients who just seem to be out to annoy me sometimes. I have to remember, they are like me, struggling with things often, not getting them right."

"Those plans, to build at Sidi Kaouki. Are those really going to happen? That's worse than just annoying. That's wrong."

"Don't talk about them now, Sarah. Leave them till tomorrow. *Ouacha?*"

His hand played with the edge of the newspaper, folded it and smoothed it again, and she watched it. Then it reached across to hold hers and for a moment she saw and felt their two hands palm to palm, asking and answering. His, warm and brown and calloused with holding ropes and no bigger than hers. Fingers interlaced strongly for a moment. A heartbeat. Then he got up and moved away. He walked about the room looking at things as if to memorize them. She sat, her heart pounding, throat dry. He picked up a whole conch shell that still spilled sand from the beach, looked at the laptop and papers on the rickety thuya table.

"This is where you work?"

"When I'm not at your writers' refuge on the beach."

"You are reading the Qur'an?"

"Yes."

"I've never read it. I have not been in a mosque for years. You'll know more than I do."

He smiled and came back to her. "Sarah. I would like to stay with you. *Tu veux que je reste?*"

"*Oui*, Aziz."

They lay across the bed, whispering together. She heard Sacha go into the room next door that had been empty till today. There was a thin partition wall between the two rooms, with a mirror and a door that closed over it. On this side there was a mirror and a door. She'd taken care to close that door, but could still hear Sacha moving about, clearing her throat, hanging up her clothes, almost as if she were in the same room.

"Ssh. Ssh. In this house you can hear everything." He snapped off the light and came down to her.

"Aziz."

"*Oui?*" His voice just a breath in her ear.

"There are so many things I want to know. Yann told me the story of Aisha Gandisha."

"Oh, that. Old wives' tales." They whispered, close.

"And about the man who feeds seagulls."

"Who?"

"The old man who goes out with the black plastic bags full of scraps and feeds seagulls? Yann said he had slept with Aisha Gandisha and lost his wits. Well, I know that's just a story. But who is he, do you know?"

He was stroking her hair now, her face. But she still needed to ask.

"They say he was beaten by the French, before Independence. For bringing food down to the town from Casa. The people here were starving, there was a blockade. He smuggled food in, they caught him, they put him in jail, they beat him up till he was crazy."

"D'you know his name?" Whisper, question, answer; while their hands moved elsewhere, grasped each other.

"In Casa they called him El Saouri. The man from Essaouira. Essaouira has always been the Arabic name for this town. The French and the Portuguese called it Mogador."

"Mogador."

"You know, Sarah, there are many stories in this town, not all of them true."

"But this one is true, Aziz?"

"As far as I know."

"Then he's the same person."

"The same person?"

"The one my mother knew. The young student she knew in 1936. The one who was friends with El Fassi."

"Allal el Fassi, you know about him?" He withdrew from her, was still. "He was arrested in I think 1937. He was deported somewhere, but others who were with him, they were imprisoned. Now, he is a national hero. Streets called after him, everything. Your mother knew these men? How?"

"At her uncle's house in Rabat, where he was consul."

"*Tiens?* And your mother—is she dead now?"

"Yes. How old do you think the seagull man is?"

"No idea. He could be very old. People here often don't know how old they are. How old was your mother? If that was 1936 and this man was, say, twenty, well now he must be in his eighties. Yes, that would be about right."

"I think," she said, "That he brought her here, to Essaouira. She remembered coming here, said it was called Mogador."

"Yes, before Independence. When this country was divided, a Spanish and a French protectorate, so-called. Then they went back to the Arab name. So, Sarah, your mother had a Moroccan man in her life. Is that why you are here? Then history repeats itself. Only, I am not revolutionary and nobody will put me in jail. *Insh'allah.*"

They lay in the darkness, side-by-side, breathing, hands joined. Heard the crackle of the fire downstairs and the chirp of the caged birds disturbed in their sleep. She turned to him, wanting him close. He was no taller than she, they fitted easily from head to toe; hands and feet measured against each other, the same size. They lay close, simply holding each other. Then he pulled off his shirt and came back to her and her hands moved on him, his skin grainy to her touch, the muscles in his back, hard. She'd made no decision, she was simply there. His hands went in under her clothes and began parting them, helping her off with them till both were naked. His hair crisp and curly under her hand, she held his head. His penis against her stomach. She, wet and open to his searching hand. She wanted to talk, to tell him things. Perhaps this was too soon. Perhaps she had no words that meant anything. He said only, "Sssh, sssh, don't talk, *mon amie,* come, like this, like this"—and swept aside the talking, the explanations, with the movements of his hands. Their mouths, lips closed together to contain sound. He slid inside her, and began to harden and move strongly. The image in her mind was of the great Atlantic wave rolling in from somewhere else; a wall of water.

She hung on to him and he whispered into her neck. "Sarah." Then, "Excuse me. The first time. I should have waited."

"No, no." It was all right. She wanted just to be here, to have this, not to be able to escape. His weight, his exhaustion. To be pinned down by it. This simplicity. Just this: motionless, wet, alive.

"It's nice, no? Like this. *C'est bien?*"

"Yes."

"But I can't stay. Don't make me stay, Sarah. I don't want to go. But it isn't what I want that counts, it's what is sensible. Antoine expects me, he'll have left the door open, he will hear me come in. Let me tuck you in before I go."

It was about two in the morning, perhaps. He pulled away from her, got up to go. Once again sound was sharp in the silence—the shuffle of stiff cloth as he pulled on his jeans, the scrape of a boot on the floor. He drew the sheet to her chin and kissed her.

"Can't you stay? Really? Does it matter?"

"This is Morocco. I work for him. It has to be so, excuse me."

For weeks, the outside handle had been loose and tended to fall off every time she opened the door from the inside, but this time there was no crash. The lights were still on downstairs, the fire still smouldering. She saw the glow from the well.

He gave her a little wave of his hand against the light, closing the door behind him. She lay there, thinking of him going along the empty Rue Yassin, through the town gate and out along the path towards the Atlantic and its stripe of moonlight, to wherever it was he slept.

Chapter eight
Sidi Kaouki

Sacha was already up, eating her breakfast at the end of the long table under the pitted mirrors and the portrait of Mohammed v. She dipped a croissant into her coffee and smiled at Sarah. Blobs of croissant came away in her coffee and she tipped her head sideways to pack it all into her wide, painted mouth. Then she dabbed her lips with a napkin.

"Bonjour, Sarah. I hope you slept well?"

"Very well, thank you."

"Oh, I did too. It's so quiet here. I heard nothing in the night, nothing at all."

Sarah saw the smile, went to the kitchen to get coffee. Yann had put on his tape of "La Bohème" so that once again the huge emotions of opera washed around them. Aisha came in to take the trays away and pulled a face, mock heroic, her eyebrows arched, imitating opera. It was the first time anyone had seen her for several days. She raised her hands and shrugged her shoulders at the barbaric noise, and looked down at Sacha, who ignored her.

"*Bonjour*, Sarah, *comment ça va?*"

Maybe, Sarah thought, her expression of scorn was habit rather than actual derision.

"*Ça va bien, merci.*"

"Me, I have been away. I have been to visit my family in Sidi Kaouki. I left Souad there, with my mother. The air is better. The air here is terrible."

She looked across at Sacha reading her copy of *Le Figaro* and sniffed.

"I didn't know your family lived in Sidi Kaouki," Sarah said.

"Ah, there is much that people do not know, Sarah. There is more that they do not know than that they do know. That is my observation. And some people, they know nothing. Nothing at all."

When she walked past Sacha, she made a wide circle around her, as if to avoid contamination. Sacha raised her head from the paper, to say, "Bring me some more coffee, will you?"

To Sarah she added, "I know you fetch yours from the kitchen, but really, I don't see why we should, it only makes the servants lazy." She said it before Aisha was out of earshot, making sure that she heard.

At ten o'clock, Antoine Dupuy came up the stairs and held out his hand, which she felt obliged to shake. "*Bonjour, mademoiselle.* Or is it *Madame*? So, are you ready? I have a car waiting downstairs."

"Yes, I'm coming."

He looked at his watch. Coughed and folded his arms. "Forgive me, I forgot to ask you. Did you sleep well?"

"Very well, thank you. And you?" Yes, she'd play the game too, the endless politeness, the handshakes, the formal addresses, the pretence. She thought of Aisha, who was in the kitchen brewing coffee for Sacha with hatred fizzing in her every movement; of Sacha's artful: "I heard nothing, nothing at all."

This careful walking through the minefield of every day.

* * *

In the street just outside the city gate, the red Renault was parked, with Aziz at the wheel. He was wearing dark glasses and he took her hand. Sarah put on dark glasses too and got in the back. Antoine Dupuy heaved in beside Aziz and leaned forward as the car moved down the street, and out along the Avenue Mohammed v, beside the sea. He looked from right to left, as if he were searching for something. Aziz, the driver, turned on the radio, lit a cigarette with the car lighter, and accelerated down the Agadir road between the masses of yellow mimosa. From his back view she could tell nothing about him this morning, so she looked out of the window over Antoine Dupuy's loud-checked shoulder.

Out there, people with donkeys and camels were going slowly home after working from dawn. The first time she'd seen a donkey and a camel yoked together, she'd been on the bus from Marrakesh; how strange that coupling had looked, until she realized that they ploughed in circles, the little donkey going round on the inside, the camel with its long stride on the outside. It made sense, as so many seemingly strange arrangements here did. It was the sign, she thought, of a country whose subtle thought-processes technology could hardly touch.

Children stood back on the roadside and stared at the car as it went by. They passed a cart with an old woman in it, waving. One day she too would be an old woman watching others pass; not sitting in a cart, but like that anyway, all skin and bones and eyes. She looked at Aziz, the back of his neck, his shoulders in his yellow T-shirt, the way his hair grew, the muscle bunched under the shirt. What happens to you, the day after making love with a man you hardly know, or don't know enough? It was frightening, the possibility of making a mistake. Only hours ago, this man and she had been that close and now there was no way of knowing what he felt. Perhaps in the way that men are supposed to, he had simply taken some pleasure where it was offered, and then moved on. Perhaps he thought she just wanted a Moroccan experience, a kind of sexual tourism. Perhaps he regretted the whole thing. The gaps were so wide—gaps of culture and upbringing as well as sex—the ones that are easy to ignore in the dark. Did it mean anything? Nothing? Just that softness inside her now, which was entirely hers and made her feel weak? She looked at him from the back and felt it invade her, the weakness. Then she saw his glance in the mirror, unreadable because of his dark glasses.

Aziz turned the car down a rough track towards Sidi Kaouki and the sea. Young palm trees grew against the horizon and the baby dromedaries that grazed beneath them were springy and leggy like the trees. The sea was a pure blue strip and the country all around was green with spring. Beyond the low stone walls and houses set in soft green turf, he pointed out to her the saint's house, the marabout, a white washed pebble. All along the roadsides there were black goats grazing, with kids scrambling off after their mothers between the olive trees. Donkeys ran and bucked with their furry tottering foals fumbling after them, and dromedaries strolled and stretched their necks and glanced downwards through their eyelashes, reminding Sarah of Nick.

Aziz slowed the car right down, not to surprise them. Sarah rolled the car window down to smell salt and fresh dung and new grass on the air. Antoine Dupuy looked at his watch.

"I only have till lunch time, Aziz. I have an appointment at one."

"Never mind, Antoine. It will do you good to slow down. You can look around, relax a little. It is not good always to rush. You must be tired after your journey." Aziz spoke quietly but firmly, she heard his voice, not about to give in and go at Antoine's speed.

"I? No, I am not tired today, not at all. But you, Aziz, perhaps you are a little tired? Perhaps you are talking of yourself?"

"No, not at all."

It was the first time he'd spoken as himself, this morning. He was simply here as Antoine Dupuy's driver, to do as he was told, a Moroccan in the pay of a Frenchman. But he wouldn't drive fast through Sidi Kaouki, no matter what. He was still angry at what Dupuy had said to him that morning. "Don't forget, you're at work here, Aziz. I don't want to hear any more stories about going off horse riding for the whole day. And foreign tourists are strictly off-limits, you understand?"

Aziz had said nothing. The words themselves were spoken

casually but with that authority that doesn't even consider being wrong, or being disobeyed. Worse was the deep sense of shame. That was old, from way back, from being an immigrant child in a white school, from having curly black hair and brown skin, from eyes in the street, eyes in stores and employment centres slogans upon walls, headlines in newspapers, voices yelling a casual insult, wherever he went.

Aziz said nothing, but the long slow-burning fuse of his anger went creeping through him that morning so that any ease and pleasure he'd felt the night before were scorched away and he was left feeling wordless, stupid and alone. She probably hadn't wanted him for himself, anyway. He had no idea what she wanted, who she really was, why they had done what they had done. There was a pain in him today that he found hard to understand. It felt like shame.

Antoine said, "The trouble is, the work is never done. This may be a holiday for you, Madame Sarah, but for me it is work. For Aziz it is work too. You only see that we are in a beautiful place, but what I see is work. We have to get the building programme started by April in order to make the most of the season. And I only have a week to get things organized, to get all the permissions through, before I go back to France. It would be nice to have all the time in the world, yes, but unfortunately that is not the case. Yes, Aziz and I will be very busy, this week."

Sarah said, "It's very beautiful."

He'd arched above her in the darkness and then come down close, she remembered the texture of his skin, wanted to touch him again, feel the crisp dryness of his hair, the unfamiliar graininess and muscle of his back, and hear him laugh in her ear, and to be open again, not scared and tight. She wanted him to speak to her. Damn Antoine Dupuy, damn him to hell.

The Berber women shoo'd goats before them on the track ahead. They wore headscarves and dresses of scarlet, green and blue, like Aisha's. The children jumped up and down and waved. There was a brittle, spring-like freshness about everything this morning, with the women's dresses vivid splits in the green. She wanted to be out there walking with Aziz towards the ocean and along that beach to where the saint's house was, with the vast Atlantic curling back from it in long drawn waves on the wet sand.

Aziz said, "Shall I park by the sea? So we can be tourists, just for a few minutes?"

"No, park up by the house, it'll save time."

Aziz glanced back, his dark glasses pushed up on to his head. His eyes still told nothing, he was masked, a servant. He shrugged and raised his eyebrows. Then he turned the car up a narrow grassy track with boulders in its way, and bumped and jolted it up to the locked iron gates of a house. Suddenly the sea was way down behind them, quite remote, and the marabout was out of sight. He got out to unlock the gates, leaving the car door hanging open to the smell of bruised grass and dung.

"This is the property I've bought," said Antoine Dupuy. "And the land."

It was a tall, squared-off modern house, Sarah saw, with steep steps up to the front door and symmetrically placed shuttered windows. The door and shutters were painted the traditional blue, but otherwise there was nothing that fitted with the rest of the village of Sidi Kaouki, its low crumbling stone walls, its one-storey houses with no windows, its wells and stables for animals, its calm and almost invisible presence. Antoine unlocked the front door and motioned to them to follow him inside. Beyond the iron gates, women and children gathered and leaned on the stonewalls to stare, and dogs barked until a little boy with a stick shoo'd them back. The wind was soft in from the west and the sun hot but she followed Aziz indoors obediently and stood in rooms while Antoine told them what would go where and strode through his house. They looked at the plumbing, stared at the places where showers would go, examined patches of damp. Sarah thought of Ramon the plumber and his complaint that Moroccans, the people who had transformed southern Europe with their watercourses hundreds of years ago, couldn't do plumbing.

"They just don't know, they can do nothing right, everything leaks and they don't care."

Antoine muttered and kicked at rotten plaster. He opened shutters and let light in through the dusty glass of the windows. He pointed to show the extent of the land he was buying, all of it already inhabited by people and animals and dotted with simple houses. He closed them again and they followed him blindly in the sudden dark. He drew in the dust on the floor with his clean shoe and showed the walls that would be demolished with a wave of one hand. He led them up on to the roof where the three of them stood in the dazzling light and looked down.

"This will be the place for barbecues," he said.

She stood with her back to him and to the house, looking towards the sea. The far-down beach was white as salt, and from up here, the marabout was entirely visible and shone like a tooth. On the beach the sea drew dark whorls upon the sand and withdrew. The tide was going out. There was nobody there; just the Atlantic Ocean at play.

Aziz stood beside her on the parapet. He laid his arms on the low wall and his forearm brushed hers as they leaned and looked. He said, "Look, the saint's house."

"Who was the saint, Aziz?"

"Sidi Kaouki. Sidi means lord, or sir. He lived here on the beach and other people came to be here, where he had been, they built the place bit by bit, to live in. They just wanted to be where he had been. That is why it is holy. It was not planned; it just grew. That is how marabouts come about. The saint and the place have the same name, you see, the man and the place are the same, he didn't need to build it."

"So the saint didn't live in the building?"

"No, he lived on the beach."

Silence for a moment, as they looked down towards the pearl on the beach. Behind it was the deep blue of the sky, with a few long trails of high cloud.

"Can we go down there?" She wanted it more than anything today, to be down there, alone with him—free. But it wasn't in the plan.

"You and I? Not today, I think. There is Antoine."
"One day?"
"One day," he said to her, "Yes."

*   *   *

Antoine came up behind them then.
"Aziz, *viens voir*. I need your advice. How many people do you think we could fit on the second floor? I need to be able to estimate the number of units we can put in before we start on the other buildings. I want this part to be up and running for the season. Excuse me, Sarah, I know that for you it's just a nice view, but that is not all that matters."

Aziz went back downstairs with him, with a quick look backward for her. For a moment longer she stayed alone on the roof, looking out. Sidi Kaouki, one of the most beautiful places in the world.

Outside, they stood at a slight distance from each other and looked down on the wide beach while Antoine pointed out where the new windsurf base would be, and the restaurant, and the disco, and the other units of housing for tourists, and the stores. To Sarah the beach and foreshore had a peculiar innocence about them. The beach was deep and shelving where the currents were strong. The water changed colour where it changed depth, suddenly. The white waves fanned out on the white shore, each time drawing the same patterns and then erasing them again on the clean wet sand. It was a place of purity, untouched by man, left free by the light breath of the saint, his not-wanting anything that was not already there.

"I'll have to think about transportation," Antoine Dupuy said, frowning. "We could run a bus out from town, say twice a day. Otherwise, taxis. I'll have to get a licence for a bar."

Neither Aziz nor Sarah answered him. Aziz had his dark glasses on again and turned away from the breeze, cupping his hands to light a cigarette. Antoine looked at his watch and said "Right, we should go. I have an appointment in town."

She followed him back to the car, Aziz walking beside her,

smoking. There was no other choice today; he was in charge. Of the place, of the day, of Aziz, and by extension, of her. As Antoine walked on, Aziz threw his cigarette away, reached and touched her hand, and her heaviness lightened, she curled her fingers around his. It was like talking in code: a promise, its meaning withheld only for now.

Antoine made a sign that she should get in the front, so she sat next to Aziz as he drove. They passed the low stone walls of the village and the people, Aisha's relatives probably, who lived among them, their houses built so close to the earth that it was hard to tell which was house and which containing wall. She thought of the people she had seen get off the bus from Marrakesh and apparently walk off into nowhere. Places where nothing appeared but crumbling stone were home to some people; people who simply climbed down off a bus, took up their bundles, and walked away into the landscape.

Aziz's right hand moved on the gear stick but the rest of him was immobile and his eyes were on the road. Antoine crouched in the back, leaning forward and peering out, probably assessing everything out there in terms of real estate. A group of young camels wandered free on the track and Aziz slowed down behind them. They swayed off to the verge with their languorous, long-legged gait, their faces held horizontal. Without loads or hobbles, naked of tackle, they looked like mythical creatures among the small argan trees, a black donkey rushed after them, kicking. A cluster of brown chickens hurried off the track way.

"All these animals!" said Antoine Dupuy.

"You can't rush them," Aziz said, "they are not used to cars."

He reached the main road and turned left down the broad asphalt expanse of it, with mimosa bushes growing on both sides.

"*Ça va, Aziz?*" she asked him, breaking the silence.

"*Ça va.* I've got toothache, though."

"You don't have to drive this slowly on the main road," said Antoine.

"I thought Sarah might like to see the mimosas. *C'est beau, non, le mimosa?*"

"Oui, c'est beau."

Sarah said, "You have a house in a very beautiful place, Antoine, you are very lucky. But what about the village, what about the people who live there?"

Would he say, like Nick, that they would all be much better off living somewhere else?

"Yes, but it will be even better in the summer, and then you will see. At present there is nothing. Only a view. But it has such possibilities, you will see. I think the people will not be a problem. *N'est-ce pas, Aziz?*"

Aziz looked sideways at Sarah and smiled. Antoine jumped about in the back like an impatient boy, wanting all his plans fulfilled at once, hating being driven home at the wrong speed.

In town, Aziz stopped the car to go into the pharmacy, and while he was in there, Antoine Dupuy clambered out. "I have to go to lunch," he explained. "Come with me and I will introduce you to Jiska. He makes fine leather clothes. There will be many things you want to buy and he will give you a good price. We will have a drink together."

"What about Aziz?"

"Aziz has work to do."

He began walking away from the red Renault, leaving its doors open again, the keys hanging in the ignition. She went too. Hating him, wanting to wait for Aziz, she followed him as if she had no choice. Why? Because of the assumptions made by men like Antoine Dupuy and the weight of them laid upon others: and the way it was so easy to collude with them. As if life and its outcomes were not made up of small chances to say yes, or no.

Chapter nine

Le Cavalier et le Vent

*W*hat happened to him?

I never knew. It was the time before Independence. Long after I knew him.

What do you remember?

A room in a stone house. The fire, lit in the morning.

The smell—can it be a smell?—of cold stone.

In Rabat, was this in Rabat?

No, the house in Rabat was not a stone house. This was in Mogador. Where he took me. Abdel Jadid. Is there anything else?

"Do you remember anything else? Anything at all?"

There was something. He loved birds. He told me about the migration of birds.

What happened to him? To you?

He told me about the Eleanora falcon. I remember that. It came and nested there, on an island, this bird that came from far away.

What did it matter, the smell of cold stone, a fire lit in the morning,

105

the migration of birds? A man's life had been ruined. While she, the white woman, had simply left. Scolded, yes. Shamed, perhaps. But free.

* * *

Back in her room, Sarah kicked off dusty shoes and took her clothes off, to shower and then lie across the bed. She walked wrapped in a white towel, her head dripping. She reached for the old photograph, held it away from her so that it didn't get wet, and lay there studying it. In a photograph, light was light and shade was shade and you could get no more from the expression on a face than this, you could not turn anything by one degree nor change that moment in which it had been taken. In life, you could change things, if you knew what to do. Nothing had to be repeated, if only you could remain conscious. The shame was in letting things happen, unawares.

Shade from the palm tree sliced across the photograph so that Marion's face was mostly light, and Abdel Jadid's face mostly in the shadow. It was a strange accident. Uncle Hajji, a little apart from Marion, had his face also turned towards her. Marion herself, in her pale linen summer dress, was at the centre. She had let it happen, Sarah thought. What had happened to her was nothing compared to what happened to him. His life was over, from the moment this picture was taken. She went home. Disgraced, maybe; but you get over social disgrace, time passes, people forget, it no longer matters what indiscretions you committed when you were young. But he'd never recovered from it. One thing had happened, and then another, and the long, linked line of events led inevitably to that place where the French had him in jail and blotted out his mind.

* * *

Nick was sitting at the long table, jotting figures on an envelope. He looked up and said, "I thought you were going to Sidi Kaouki today."

"I've been. Been and come back."

"That was quick. Oh, you went with Antoine, that explains it.

You should have gone there with Yann, he knows lots of people in the village, Aisha's relations all live there, they would have invited you in."

"I haven't felt like going anywhere with Yann, since what you told me about the poison."

"Oh, that. You're probably right. Anyway, he's gone to the beach with Sacha today, so that'll put another cat among the pigeons, won't it. Or budgies, if you prefer."

"Didn't you warn her?"

"Sacha's lived in Morocco all her life, she's a real Marrakshi. She knows the score. It'll amuse her. She can look after herself."

"And you don't think I can?"

"Sarah, what's the matter? You look all put out today."

"Nothing. Oh, everything. I can't stand what Antoine Dupuy is up to, if you want to know."

"Him? Oh, he's fairly harmless. There are bigger sharks around than Antoine Dupuy. Worse people, let me tell you, who could be taking an interest in real estate round here. But no, I don't think you can look after yourself, not in the way I mean. We Anglo-Saxons have too much heart."

He gave her his sudden quick look from beneath thick lashes. Today his eyes were greenish. He breathed in smoke and flicked ash towards the ashtray and looked away.

"Anyway, I told her that I was busy today and that Yann would love to accompany her to the beach. But you know what Yann is, he's probably telling her he's a bachelor in the sand dunes at this moment."

"Nick!" Really, he was incorrigible.

"Well, what's wrong with that?"

"You know what's wrong with it".

"I suppose Aisha may get all steamed up again. But I think Sacha's a match for her. Don't you?" He slipped on his jacket, grinning, and went off to a meeting with the mayor.

* * *

Sarah walked up to La Skala to look at the ocean. There were these two alternatives, always. Some people went up to the ramparts to watch the Atlantic breakers roll in, others went out along the beach towards the ruined fort. There were always rows of people looking out to sea, not in the way westerners do on beaches, more as if there were something here that they had to pay homage to daily. The fact of it, the Atlantic Ocean, was what demanded this attention. Alone, or in twos and threes, people came to pay attention to the ocean. At sunset there were crowds up here on the fortifications and also by the railings close to the port. The sun going down was an event, like the tolling of a bell. Before, there was daylight, and afterwards, dark. It was that sudden. When the sun rolled down into the sea it was soft as an egg, misshapen, glowing. Above it, there were shreds of cloud.

*   *   *

That evening she counted the fishing boats going out in their procession, passing between the land and the island. Thirteen of them moved in the haze of golden light that would in a minute turn grey, ghost ships caught in the changing light and in the spray from the sea that rose like mist. When it was too rough, they didn't go out. Sometimes the waves that rolled in at sunset were as shocking as moving walls. Then it seemed that anything that went out into that ocean would be wrecked and you wondered how anybody dared.

Nick, Yann, Aisha, Sacha—the machinations of humans in a house, so small beside the vastness of this water. Aziz. What did he think of her now? She had the brief touch of his hand, his sideways grin to go on. Did he regret it? Was he ashamed, angry, or like herself, simply vulnerable and scared?

Coming back, she passed the line of workshops that were hollowed out like caves beneath the ramparts of La Skala, where men were closing up the big wooden doors for the night. Some still glowed with yellow light from deep inside, where a solitary craftsman still worked, carving a candlestick or a spoon, smoothing the surface of a box inlaid with mother-of-pearl. The street smelled of oil and thuya wood and salt. The sound of the ocean was still there booming on the other side of the walls. She walked along the narrow street towards the gleam of light at the end that was the Place Moulay Hassan. There was always this sound, day and night, wherever you were, in bed, on the street, in a *café*—the roar of the ocean.

One day, people said, the town would be washed away. In the January storms the sea had come right up inside the ramparts and made holes in the street that were now loosely filled in with rubble. Walking here in the dark, it would be easy to trip and fall. You had to almost feel your way through the darkness where underground alleyways came out on to the street.

He was there, standing at the sea wall, throwing the scraps like a man throwing seed into the wind. A mass of gulls hung above his head and flapped about him; then swooped down and fell on the pile of scraps and bones. Tall, in his brown *d'jellaba*, a skeleton of a man, hooded in darkness, his face glimpsed for a moment scowling and serious with the effort of feeding the seagulls.

She caught his glance at her, said quickly, "*Labess, beher.*" She hesitated in front of him and he held his bag of scraps high and paused as if surprised.

"*Labess.* All's well."

Was that the gaze and voice of madness? Sarah caught a quick dark stare before she turned away and went back down the Place towards the lights of the *café* and the Rue Yassin. She must speak to him, but not yet. She had to be sure, and un-afraid of the outcome before she did.

Nick was there when she got back, standing in front of the fire, holding a glass of red wine. The black puppy, Ibrahim's dog, lay curled asleep in one of the armchairs, its pink tongue furling out like a conch shell, little yaps coming from its open mouth as it dreamed. Ibrahim himself sat in another. In the kitchen somebody was banging pots and pans. Upstairs a door slammed. Perhaps the door to the roof had been left open? A wind was blowing through the hall.

Nick said, "Ah, hello, Sarah. Have a glass of wine. Sarah? Have you just seen a ghost, darling? Hey, I must tell you, you've just missed the most enormous scene."

He sounded so pleased with himself. "Aisha's furious. That's her yelling in the kitchen. I dread to think what we'll get for dinner. Yann went to the beach for the entire day with Sacha. When they got back Aisha went for Sacha and screamed at her in Arabic that she was a whore and so on. I only understood about half of it but it was pretty graphic, with lots of insults about mothers. She said Yann was her man and that Sacha'd better keep her hands off him or it'd be the worse for her. Omar's trying to calm her down and Yann's run away to hide. He's probably getting drunk or stoned or both. I expect Sacha's packing her bags to get back to Marrakesh, but she may be made of sterner stuff."

"Nick, you set that up."

"I? I didn't. You can't make people do what they don't want to do, can you. All I did was say I was busy today, which was true. Then Yann said he'd take her to the beach. I didn't say, spend the day with her lying in the dunes in full view of Aisha's relatives, did I? I didn't tell him to tell her the story of his life. He's an idiot. He could have pretended. He didn't have to come back all covered with sand saying what a lovely time they'd had. Apparently the baby's not well, either, so that probably made matters worse."

"Oh God. What did Sacha do?"

"Stood her ground. Yelled back, said she wasn't interested in stealing Aisha's man, he was beneath her interest, and what did Aisha take her for—did she think she was that desperate? At least, that was what I understood."

*   *   *

Sacha came down the stairs wearing her tight leather trousers and high-heeled sandals and an openwork silk sweater that showed the tops of her breasts where they bulged over her bra. Her hair was combed back into its dark chignon, she wore chunky gold jewellery and was beautifully made up. Sarah smelled what she thought was Femme de Rochas. Every time she saw Sacha, her own clothes, jeans and a shirt today, seemed to her like rags. But she held the wine glass Nick had given her and smiled at Sacha anyway, waiting to hear her version of the drama. She greeted them in English, "Hello, hello, did you have a good day? How are you, Sarah?"

"Very good, thank you. How are you?"

"I? Oh, it was all right, only that fool Yann never told me that he was practically married and that his wife would be having hysterics by the time we got back. What a scene. I would never have gone near him if I had known. Anyway, he is so stupid. And why would I be attracted to a foreigner? I told him he wasn't my type at all, I am only interested in Moroccans. I am not interested in white men, especially stupid ones like Yann."

She smiled provocatively at Nick, who was still leaning against the fireplace, his legs crossed in his white pants, his wine glass in his hand. He inclined his head towards her, smiling back. *Touché.*

"Do I get a glass of wine? What are you drinking? Don't you get any French wine here? I find this local stuff pretty rough, to be honest."

She lit a cigarette and perched on the arm of the chair. The tops of her breasts moved under her sweater. Ibrahim got up to offer her his chair, but she saw the sleeping puppy first and sprang up again.

"My God, what is that dog doing here? Nick, you don't mean to say you let animals wander all over the house? *Ça, alors...* Get it out of here, I don't want fleas. Ugh. Now, Sarah. Tell me about your day. You like it here? I must say, the beaches are beautiful. I hear you went to Sidi Kaouki? I will go there tomorrow. I hear that fool Yann has a wife whose family live there. Perhaps I should meet her? That will kill more than one bird. That is what you say, *non?*"

"Two birds with one stone," Nick said.

"*Voilà*, that is what I meant."

Nick held an opened bottle of Côtes du Rhône and poured it for her almost humbly, bending before her in a bow. She took it like a queen.

After dinner that night, Yann came and squatted beside Sarah with his arms around his knees. They both looked into the sparking fire.

"Sarah, I am ruining myself. Too much wine, too many ciga-rettes. It is not good. I am getting old."

"How old are you?"

"Only forty-seven. But tonight I feel I am old."

"I hear you went to the beach with Sacha."

"Such a fuss about nothing. If I can't tell a woman that she is beautiful, what is left in life?"

"Do you think she's beautiful?"

"Yes, but not intelligent. Or, intelligent in the wrong way."

"What's the wrong way? Standing up to people?"

"Sarah, you know me. I like things to be subtle. Life is subtle, love is subtle."

Sarah raised her eyebrows, as Yann continued, "This wine, for instance, it is a miracle, a transformation. And we take it as ordinary, we drink too much, we forget to taste it. It is a miracle. We should taste it like the blood of Christ. And love too. Especially love. We make everything ordinary, and that is dangerous."

"And Sacha? What about her? Is she a miracle too?"

"Dangerous too. But I will not be here any more. I am going with Ramon to Spain, it is decided. I am leaving tomorrow."

"Tomorrow!"

"The plumbing for the new bathrooms is finished, Ramon has been longing to leave. And Nick says it will be better for me. Anyway, I have to leave to get my papers in order, to be able to return."

"Nick's sending you, then?"

"Not sending exactly. But he thinks it would be better for my health."

"You mean, there might be chameleons in the yoghurt again. Or dead budgies."

"It is possible."

"I see."

He stretched out his arms and yawned widely.

"And you, Sarah, do you know the story of the *cavalier* and the wind?"

"No?"

"It's an old French legend. The knight who comes when the wind is up. Eh bien, there was wind last night, *n'est-ce pas?* Did you hear it during the night?"

"Yes."

"There was wind and I think there was also a *cavalier*, wasn't there, Sarah?"

His hand closed on hers for a moment and grasped it. He glanced sideways with his sudden flash of blue, and the ring he wore hurt her fingers.

"Never mind, *ma chère*, it will remain a secret between you and me and the person concerned."

He raised her hand and kissed the back of it like a farewell. There was a complicity that he insisted on. She removed her hand. "Promise, Yann?"

"But of course. My word of honour." And he put his hand on his heart.

*   *   *

When Sarah finally went to bed that night, she lay awake listening for footsteps on the stairs, for a quiet knock, a voice whispering her name. She heard Sacha come up to her room and move around just on the other side of the partition. Then there was quiet.

There was the hiss of the dying fire downstairs; the wind, in this city of wind, as it came in from the north; the muezzin's late cry. But there was no cavalier.

*   *   *

During these days, Sarah struggled with a feeling that grew in her, that she had not felt since childhood: a helplessness in the face of what happened around her that made it hard to act or even speak. Antoine Dupuy's arrival seemed to accentuate it, that sense of being an accessory, a person made meaningless because powerless: a woman in a society governed by men, in which a woman had no voice unless, like Aisha, she resorted to retaliation by poison, or like Sacha, to wiles and power games. Where she had felt at ease in the house, she now felt at a loss. Even with Aziz, there was no way of being someone who could initiate things. He came, or did not come; spoke to her or was silent; slid out of the way. The house had become a place of men's plots, their machinations.

She stayed in her room, trying to read and write, as the spring days lengthened and the midday sun grew fiercer. She sat at her table, looking out over the Riad, the palm trees newly planted there, the line of the ocean beyond. It was a strange sensation, almost like being sick. There was no name for it; but there was a kind of aimless floating through the days, a baffled hope kept alive, a nameless fear kept only just at bay. Since she had been with Aziz that night, it seemed that people avoided her. Or was she imagining it? There was no one to talk to about this. And if there had been, how would she have named it?

Later, she would look back on this time and discover, perhaps, what had been working on her, in her, and what was its name. At the moment, it felt like not completely existing. Like being marginalized, kept out of reach of the real, tangible world. It was a sickness, but not one she recognized. The closest she came to understanding it, was by remembering what it had been like to be a child, to have her life planned by others, her deepest wishes kept out of sight. A little girl, a female, a minor; someone not yet realized, someone who had to be both protected and ignored. At the root of the sickness, the helplessness, lay a fear: that her understanding of the world was flawed, that it had been from the outset, and might never be made right.

Chapter ten

The Knight's Move

When Aziz thought about her, *l'Américaine*, he relaxed. Her eyes on him, her touch, encouraged him to be himself. Words came from him. He was bigger, more capable. When he saw her coming, her light hair flying about her face, her hands moving, her skirt about her knees, he became alert, more of a man. To him she was all light and flying. Her quick way of talking, the way she had of using her hands enchanted him. Her accent, tripping over words. Her husky voice as she sang. Her challenge: pointed chin up, hair back, the cool thoughtfulness of those eyes, the pale arc of her eyebrows. He'd been studying her. And when she came out of the sea to him, hair plastered to her skull and dripping rats' tails on her shoulders, he wanted to wrap her in safety like a big rough towel. He was surprised by her—that she was here at all, with him.

Why had they met? He wanted to ask her this; wanted to hear if she might know. Perhaps she had come to him from another life. As the winter sun burned her, he saw her changing. Like a chameleon, changing colour. She laid her forearm against his—"Look, still lighter, but not much."

She measured herself against him—hands, feet, length of leg. His love for her, he thought, like love for a sister. That was why he had no qualms; he was not afraid, even when Antoine said things to him. And when she lay above or below him, all along him, her light body with its shallow curves and slight hills, and he moved inside her (like the sea, he said to her, *je suis comme la mer*) it was innocent and he knew his innocence, his lack of guile, received.

He'd never known this innocence before, with a woman. He was enchanted in it, by it. She was his absolution. She blanked out the scrawled insults on the walls for him, she silenced the voices. He couldn't, wouldn't give her up. Not yet.

Antoine Dupuy said to him, "Think of Anne."

When he thought of Anne, he no longer knew who he was. Perhaps that life was really over. He'd been blown here on a long gust, down the Mediterranean, across to the Atlantic, back to where he first came from, he was all wind now, hollowed out, blown clean by the wind, shaped by it. It had sculpted his back and hands, formed his feet to clench on the narrow board. He was the wind now, the north wind that blew in Essaouira three hundred and forty days a year. *Le vent alizé,* they called it here.

When Antoine told him he must stop seeing Sarah or lose his job, Aziz was neither impressed nor scared. He knew it made no sense, as either-or never made sense. It was like when Omar sat opposite him and made a chess move that seemed to be about to check him, but he knew better, knew that one intelligent move of his own would counter-act the check. His were the knight's moves of the imagination. He remembered the time in her room, the typewriter, the papers, the clothes on the back of the chair, the way she sprawled reading on the bed. Sand trickling out of the conch shell on the knotted, sea-damp wood. The way she had told him, "Yes, I'm writing some articles about Moroccan women."

And how he'd laughed. "What about American women?"

"Oh, nobody wants to know about them. They aren't sufficiently oppressed."

The self-deprecating laugh, that seemed not to value what she should value. Yet, at other times, how she would take herself and her points of view so seriously that he was shocked. In his world, people did not assert themselves like that. He was challenged and alarmed, as if she ran some excessive risk without realizing it.

Who was she?

Married, she told him, divorced, oh, a long time ago, with a husband, who had married again. A life, reduced to one sentence. She'd been travelling with somebody, a work colleague. He didn't matter. How could a woman, he wondered, live like that?

"What about you?"

He said, "I was married."

He didn't talk about Anne because in his world you didn't discuss one woman with another. Also, because he didn't know what to say. She didn't ask again. Probably, it didn't matter.

He said, "You are my teacher."

"No, you are my teacher."

"I will be your windsurf teacher, I will teach you to dance with the wind. Maybe you should write about that, not about women."

"Maybe."

"Will you write about me, Sarah?"

"No. Not about you, Aziz."

She took out a wallet, showed him a small old photograph, black and white. Two men, one older, one young. And a young woman, with a palm tree.

"My mother. Her uncle the British consul. Abdel Jadid."

"Are you sure?"

"She remembered his name, in the end. And it was you who said that was the man beaten up by the French for smuggling food."

"It's only hearsay," he said. "When was this photo taken?"

"1936. In Rabat." She showed him the back, where it was pencilled in, between the little marks where the paper had been stuck to something else.

"And she loved this man?"

"She wouldn't say. Perhaps, perhaps not. But look at the way they're looking at each other. Look at the way he's looking at her."

He said, "Sarah, a man looks at a woman a thousand times in a life."

"Like this?"

"Like this. You cannot see the eyes here; only the angle of the face, and half the face is black from shadow. What can you see there?"

"Something. Maybe. A story. But, he isn't crazy, Aziz."

"He feeds birds. He stays alone. He doesn't speak. So what is crazy? If I do as he does, throw food to birds all day, you don't think I am crazy?"

"She came down to Essaouira with him. To Mogador. She stayed in his house. She remembers the fire, and the smell of cold stone."

"Cold stone?"

"Yes."

"Does that have a smell?"

"Like the inside of a well."

He was silent, thinking about what she was telling him: that there were so many hidden reasons behind the present, the appearance of what is. The knight's move—the move that could take you around a corner.

"Aziz, how can I find out about him? Are there records?"

"People don't keep records. Many people here don't know how old they are, or where they were born, if their mothers don't tell them."

"And people lie about history. They say a man who was beaten up in jail by an occupying power was seduced by a witch. The Aisha Gandisha story, very convenient."

Sometimes he dreaded her fierceness when she was on the trail of truth, he saw her going beyond his, or anyone's, control.

"*Cherie*, it can be dangerous. People believe what they believe. It's the way this country is."

"But why wouldn't they want to know, if he's a hero?"

"Because they are ashamed. They are weak and they are ashamed of weakness. That is why they make their God so strong. Then there is no shame."

It was easy for him to love her. She gave him back so much of himself, his courage for a start. Anne couldn't do that. She saw him as a coward. This woman assumed that he was strong.

He didn't say to her, I love you. *Je t'aime*, it was too French. He had never in all his life said it in Arabic. It was as if a part of him, a vital part, was missing—the words to say it, so that it would mean, himself. He waited, to see if these words would come.

Chapter eleven
Habibti

Sarah woke to hear Yann's voice in the street below her window. She slid out of bed and went to lean on the blue railing to look down into the narrow crevasse of the street. Looked down on the top of his grey-blond head and the battered leather jacket slung across his shoulders. He had a cardboard suitcase in one hand and was talking to Ramon.

"Yann! Are you going?" Obscurely, in his drunken, sexist, poetic way, he'd been her ally. She didn't want him to leave.

He looked up against the light and the white wall. There was that long-distance look, that opaque blue, his eyes screwed up to see. He waved up to her.

"Sarah! *Au revoir!* I got the scaffolding specially put up for you, to reach your window! Make the most of it. You and the *cavalier*! See you in Key West, *insh'allah*!"

He followed Nick and Ramon down the street, moving between heaps of rubble and parked carts. *Au revoir. Insh'allah.* This easily, people came and went. They turned the corner of the narrow street and disappeared, perhaps forever.

She went back to bed and sat there in her big T-shirt, the sheet pulled up around her. She heard Nick come back into the house and pull the door shut behind him. It was still early morning; the sky was milky at the window, the thin white curtains shifted slightly in the breeze. A place for transformations, Yann had said. The transformation she wanted for herself now was not to be afraid. Not to pay attention to the hints, the veiled threats, the innuendoes, the plans that would leave her out. She couldn't bear to be this nervous creature, waiting in her room. She would go down to see Aziz, as she had done so easily in those days before they had become lovers.

He came out of the base and the blue door behind him swung in the wind. He wore his black wet suit, the back partly unzipped, showing the smooth curve of his spine.

"Where were you? Sarah, I looked for you everywhere. I thought you would come back."

"When? I thought you would come to the house last night."

"When we came back from Sidi Kaouki, yesterday. I went into the pharmacy and when I came out you were gone. I thought you would be back in a minute so I waited. I saw the car with the keys in it in the street and nobody there. I felt like a servant. Just the chauffeur, you don't have to tell him what is going on. You know? I waited, I walked round the square, you still didn't come back, and there was no Antoine. So I drove back here. Then last night Antoine wanted me. We went out for dinner. I couldn't eat much because of my tooth. Then I went to sleep."

"I'm sorry, Aziz."

He said, "It doesn't matter."

"It does matter. We both let him push us around."

"For me it is different. I work for him, I have no choice."

He didn't say: you are white, you are American, but she felt it. She felt like a tourist in his eyes now. The shame was still there, that he might believe she had used him. What had happened to her ability to be clear, to explain things? It was not the language they spoke in; although sometimes she longed to speak plain American English and be understood. It was something that had slipped out of joint between them, not of their own making, yet collusion, a failure of faith. He'd waited for her, feeling like a servant. She, feeling like a helpless Victorian woman, had waited for him.

"Well, it happens. Today is another day. But I did go to the house to look for you and you weren't there. There was a scene going on, some woman was yelling at Aisha and Aisha was yelling too. Nobody knew where you were. Then I had to go and have dinner with Antoine and he kept me the whole evening, you know how he is."

"I missed you. How is your tooth?"

"A bit better."

"Why don't you go to the dentist?"

"Because to go to the dentist here you have to wait all day. Then you pay. It's okay. Don't worry about me. Look, the wind is up, everybody's going to be happy today. My clients will be happy, Antoine will be happy because he is making money."

"What about you?"

"Oh, me, I'm always happy. I was born happy. Lucky me. But I will not have time to go riding, not with this wind. And Antoine says he needs me later."

"Tonight?"

"Tonight I will come to the house. Even if it is late. If I am invited."

"You're invited. Aziz, don't let Antoine take you over." Don't let him take me over, either. Don't let him have an effect.

He smiled at her as if she didn't understand. "Antoine is my boss, as I said. It is only for a few days. After that we will have time, *chérie*. I have to take him back to Marrakesh on Thursday. Then there is the *fête*. But we will have time, *insh'allah*."

"*Insh'allah*." It was so often all one could say, and so one said it, meaning: the outcome is out of our hands. People opened their hands as if life would trickle through them.

"Now, let's forget about Antoine for a bit. Why not take a surfboard? I'll come with you. The sea is good today."

"Aziz. I was thoughtless yesterday, I'm sorry. I need to know now. Was it a mistake for you? Is it something you regret?" If it was, don't tell me. Or at least, not now. "Are you angry?"

"A mistake? Sarah, no. If I was angry, it was because of many things, but not you. Never you. You are a gift. Understand? "He held her by her upper arms. "If anything happens, Sarah, it is not you. Now, let's enjoy the Atlantic Ocean, *tu veux?*"

The waves were quick and choppy and rose up like sudden hills. He dived into them and came up on the other side to laugh. Sarah turned the light board and flipped on to it to lie flat and be carried by the coming wave all the way back. Again and again, out to meet the wave, to be hit chest-high, winded, slapped about. Then to rise together to be lifted on choppy water all the way back to the shallows. Laughing and gasping at each other, water running off everywhere. Aziz stood up on his board and balanced on an impossible curve of green water, and then was suddenly wrecked, upended.

She remembered an old friend of Yann's, an old sailor they called Le Capitaine, saying once, *"On ne joue pas avec l'Atlantique."* But they did, they played with it, that stern and unpredictable and sometimes terrifying ocean. That day it seemed easier than being on dry land.

Outside the base, Omar's new bike was propped against the wall and he lay flat in the sun with his arms over his eyes and his legs apart as if he were six years old. Sarah hadn't seen him since Sacha had installed him behind a desk in 'Reception,' as she now called the downstairs hall. He waved a thin hand as they came together up from the sea. Habib was there too, in shorts and singlet, hosing down the floor. The first clients had arrived and were in the changing rooms.

Aziz said, "Shall we have a coffee to warm up?"

So, there would be time for everything, for coffee, for warming numbed bodies in the sun.

"The water's good," Aziz said to Omar. "Cold but good."

At the *café* on the beach, Aziz tipped his chair back and smiled at her and they both watched Omar weave down towards the *café* on his bike. He wore a bright green T-shirt and sunglasses and his legs stuck out like skinny outriders.

Under the blue and white umbrella, at the white table, there was coffee—strong and foaming up the side of the glass with milk. The morning swung on towards midday. Aziz drained the last of his coffee and got up to ride Omar's bike, standing up on the pedals and making it bounce on the concrete. He swooped past the table and carried off Omar's glass of coffee with a swift polo-playing movement and lifted it unspilt through the air. Omar raised his hands to protest and the coffee came back to him. Aziz hooked his leg over the crossbar and slid off.

"He's crazy," said Omar.

Aziz called, "Did you miss your coffee, Omar? Oh, I see you've got it back."

"Crazy but nice," said Omar.

Leaving the *café*, their arms slid around each other for a moment and they walked embraced, as neither of them ever would with a woman in public. Back at the base, Aziz started wrestling with Habib. They pranced and grabbed each other, slipping about on the wet floor. Omar went to change into his wet suit. Close and panting, the other two pushed at each other, Habib much taller and heavier than Aziz, his shoulders bunched with muscle. Aziz put up his hands and backed off in mock surrender. One was always on the outside, here, when two men were together. It was how it was.

"I have to be serious now," he said, "I have to call in at the Hôtel des Iles now. Will you wait for me, Sarah? Don't disappear. I hate people disappearing."

"I'll wait."

She went down to the beach with Omar and watched him drag a pink sail out on to the water and set off looking like a stick insect against the glitter on the waves. The sand was fine and hot underfoot.

Don't disappear. I hate people disappearing. But what safeguard was there against it? This was a place where people arrived suddenly and disappeared again as suddenly as they had come. And what puzzled her was what made this happen: Yann, sent away for his own good, people moved out of houses where their families had lived for centuries, Sacha brought here from Marrakesh, Aisha disappearing for days at a time. What was it that made this happen? Who was in control?

*   *   *

She walked with Aziz towards the port, where Topniveau would slip grilled sardines on to their plates and pour tea for them in a long hot stream, and everybody would see them together. They wore dark glasses as others wore veils, to hide what was going on. In the western way, hiding their eyes, whereas the veil-wearers had only their eyes showing. Aziz was still playful, walking like a man with a prize. That he was like this with her, jaunty, off his guard, made her proud yet scared.

Later she thought, when you feel yourself falling in love, you feel invulnerable to the outside world. Your vulnerability is entirely given to the other person. Together you walk inside your fragile, beautiful cocoon, and you can't imagine that the world might wish you harm, or that accidents happen, or that this state of affairs might not go on. With Bill she had been unsafe, because invulnerable. The paradox. With this man she was safe. With him, but not necessarily among others, in whose world they moved.

His dry warm hand even found hers for a second under the table, as if he forgot too that in this town everybody knew what would happen before it happened, and that nothing was on their side. She squeezed his hand, then took her own away.

Topniveau came and poured from his tin teapot from a height, refilling glasses with sweet, thin tea. Suddenly Sarah saw Aisha cross the square, a small upright figure dressed in black. She came and spoke to the fish men for a moment, ignoring Aziz and Sarah, and then stood, her head down and her hand clenched on the basket she held. Topniveau waved a hand to invite her to his table, but she shook her head and walked away. She walked back across the Place Moulay

Hassan again with her empty shopping basket, without stopping to greet anyone. She had lived here all her life, she knew everybody, and yet she was alone. Being alone here was abnormal, Sarah knew this by now: if you were alone, you had been excluded.

Topniveau said, "It is not good that her man is gone. Not good for her honour. Not good at all."

He spoke sadly. He and Aziz spoke to each other in Arabic.

Then Aziz got up and said abruptly, "Come, let's go. I have to work. You should go back to the house."

He lit a cigarette, bending away from the wind. They left without finishing the tea. He paid for the lunch with a bundle of ragged dirham notes pulled from his pocket. Topniveau watched them go.

"What's up?" Sarah said.

"Aisha, well, she has taken some risks. You and I, Sarah, we are all right. It is other things that are not. But, trust me."

He threw his cigarette into the gutter and smiled at her, his eyes serious. "*A bientôt*. I will come soon."

At the corner by the *Café* Rouge Sarah went back along the Rue Yassin, while he headed out through the town gate, back towards the windsurf base and the sea. It hurt, to have to be this careful, to be aware of who might be watching. Her face hurt with the strain of not letting anything show. She was sick of it; it literally made her feel ill. On the Rue Yassin, she saw Aisha coming towards her with her black cloak and her basket, so that both women reached the blue door at the same time. She opened it and stood aside to let Sarah in. Her face was haggard, she had dark circles under her eyes and her lips were pursed.

"Sarah, today is not a good day," she said. "Not good at all." Then she vanished into the darkness of the house.

In just one day the old door to the kitchen had been blocked up and a large sheet of polythene flapped over the hole where the wall had been broken open. Sarah peered into the unexplored dinginess of the house next door that Nick had bought, its cracked ceilings and scarred columns and the airless rooms in which scores of people had lived until yesterday. It was Nick's kingdom now. He was walking about in it with the architect, Mustafa, stepping over piles of rubble and broken timbers where the roof was open to the sky. He came in with dust on his hair, grinning.

She called to him, "Nick, you've made the exact scene I dream about, do you know that? Ruined houses, knocked down walls."

He said, "Funny things, dreams. But I always think reality's even stranger. Don't you? A dream is just the product of one mind, so it's limited to what one mind can produce. But what really happens, well, that's wide open, that can be anything. Don't you agree?"

When Nick said: Don't you agree?—it felt as if there was nothing anybody could do but agree. He dragged you with him, protesting maybe, but captive. Unless, as she had on the night of the men's meeting, you could tell him quite definitely that you didn't want lobster, or even palm trees.

"You mean, the dream as sketch? Reality as the big picture?"

"Yes. Most people don't even admit it. But in reality, you can have anything happening, all the things you've never thought of. Especially here. I suppose you know Yann's not coming back? The trouble with him is that he just can't admit reality. He's still operating on some narrow little French Catholic notions about good and evil. He thinks that because he's a good Catholic boy, he's safe. He's conveniently forgotten about being converted to Islam."

"He converted? Really?"

"Aisha made him. She dragged him off to see the Imam. He's really called Abdelkader now or something."

"Nick, what'll happen to Aisha, now he's gone?"

"Oh, nothing. People will huff and puff, but they'll get over it. Did you know I had tea with the mayor again today? I told him the palm trees were coming, big mature ones. You know those miserable little patches of earth down by the Riad with dying plants in them? They'll go there. He was thrilled. I even offered him a landscape gardener from Spain. So it meant I could get on with the alterations here."

"What happened to all the people who used to live next door?"

"I've found them houses. Much better houses. They're all thrilled, too. Well, most of them are. Some of them wanted even better houses than the ones I've found. One of them even wanted a car. But I said I had to draw the line somewhere. Have you seen what those rooms are like, where whole families lived? They're so damp you'd think they would all have died within a week. I'm going to have to pull down all those internal walls, open the whole thing up, it's like a sponge. They hung all their washing in there, so it hadn't a hope of ever drying. Then they had to sleep among the washing. They cooked their dinners in those dark little holes. It was terrible, you should have seen it. It's a miracle that people's health is as good as it is."

Sarah said nothing, but thought of Aisha's relatives, who lived where Antoine Dupuy wanted to build his tourist empire. She recognized her feeling of weakness again; it was what happened inside when somebody else was ordering the world about her and it felt shaky, like having drunk too much caffeine.

Nick pulled the cork from a bottle of wine, poured three glasses and handed her one.

"Drink up, Sarah, you're looking peaky. A little peelie-wally, as the Scots say."

Omar brought in a dish of couscous with vegetables all around it and pieces of mutton hidden in the central mound. She sat with Nick and Mustafa the architect at the low table in front of the fire and began to pick at the food, although she wasn't really hungry. The wind roared in the chimney. The candle flames waved and guttered in the draught from the hole behind the flapping plastic.

He came to the house after dinner, wearing pressed pants and a clean white shirt after his meeting with Antoine.

"You see how bourgeois I am getting, Sarah? All these meetings. *C'est chiant.* But at least it is over for tonight."

"What do you have to keep meeting about?"

"Oh, permissions, contracts, all sorts of things. It's this building project. It all has to be rushed through before Antoine leaves."

"How many palm trees does it take?"

"What? Palm trees?"

"That's how Nick does it. He gives the mayor palm trees when he wants something to happen. You should tell Antoine. Is he really going to build at Sidi Kaouki?"

Two people on a white beach, silenced and estranged from each other by the power of the third. She wouldn't forget. That was where the powerlessness had begun, with Antoine Dupuy telling them what they could and couldn't do.

"The first stage is not at Sidi Kaouki. It's nearer to the town. Where we came through the dunes when we were riding, remember?"

"I remember."

"It won't spoil everything, Sarah, it won't change the place so much. We just need more places to put our clients."

"And discos and bars and canned music and fast food restaurants too. And, you said, we?"

He was dressed in Antoine's uniform tonight. "I think that's enough of this subject for tonight. *N'est-ce pas?*"

Omar brought tea without asking. Nick had gone out with Mustafa. There was nobody else around. They sipped it scalding and breathed in the hot aroma of crushed mint. Aziz picked up the guitar that lay on the chair beside him and moved his fingers over the strings.

"Aziz, is there an Arabic word, *Istiqlal*?"

"It means, independence. It was the name of a movement. Why?"

"It was one of the words my mother remembered. *Istiqlal.*"

"It was the Moroccan Independence party. You know, I wish I could play this."

The chords he played were exact but tentative as his hand stretched to find them.

"You will, if you want to."

"You think we can do anything we want to?"

"Yes, if we really want to do something, we can do it." It was still what she wanted to believe, what her American feminist upbringing had meant.

"I'm not so sure. If you are Nick, yes." Or American, he thought. He gestured towards the missing kitchen wall. "Then, you can do exactly what you want. But this, I don't know if I have a good enough ear. You have a good ear, I hear it when you sing."

Omar, with his perfect tact, had left them alone with the tea. But the next step on the stair was Antoine's, and he came in without hesitation, stood looking impatient and glanced at his watch. He refused Omar's offer of tea and stared down at Aziz.

He said, "I can see why you find it difficult to leave Sarah."

"I'm not even trying to leave, Antoine. I'm here till the middle of next month, at least." She felt tired by the very sight of him. How good it would have been to have simply said, "Go away, Antoine, we're having a private conversation."

"Ah, I have forgotten that you are not simply on vacation here, that you have an occupation."

"Yes, I have an occupation." God, this was exhausting.

"And if you have found somewhere where you can occupy yourself, then why not make the most of it?"

"Exactly."

"And what is it, if I may ask, that you are writing about?"

"About inheritance laws under Islam. The way women only get half of what their brothers do. Among other things."

"Ah, well, it sounds a little deep for me. Well, Aziz. *Tu viens?* We must go. Sarah, *bonsoir.* I promise that we will not disappear. You will see us again."

Aziz looked up and raised his eyebrows. He said, "*Oui, je viens, Antoine.*"

* * *

When they were gone, she took Nick's position in front of the fire. The candles were lit in the candelabra and the fire noisily swallowed dry pieces of timber from the roof of the house next door. It was burning the heaps of wood left among the rubble, and whatever Nick said about dampness, these were dry enough to crackle and flame up at once. She stood still, smoking one of Nick's cigarettes. If only she could suddenly become Nick: English, upper class, male, imperturbable. In charge.

Omar came to take the tray away and move the big candlesticks. His black glance glittered up in the firelight.

"He is good, Aziz. A good friend."

"Yes, I know."

She walked about the empty hall in firelight and candlelight. The battered gilt mirrors swaying on the walls reflected it all back, the room, the house—this world. She walked up and down, trying out what Nick did, leaned on the iron rail around the deep well at the centre of the house. How did someone get to be Nick? You probably had to be born that way. The candelabra hung there on its pulley, hauled up by Omar every evening from the floor below. The ropes went right up to the roof to hook under the glass pergola, and the iron frame swung just slightly in the void, like a clapper in a bell. The candle flames flickered and changed shape in the draught. For those few minutes, when nobody else came and the whole house was quiet and empty—perhaps you could borrow it, this power, slip it on like someone else's coat. She stood at the centre for a minute, seeing her own reflection in the mirrors, solitary, real. But female. That was the problem.

* * *

When Aziz knocked softly late that night, all the other voices sounded down there in the hall. Nick, Sacha, Omar, Antoine Dupuy. How they all came and went. Somebody was strumming on the guitar. The fire cracked. The birds chirped occasionally in their cage. Somebody opened the front door and closed it again and Omar's surprisingly deep voice sounded up the stair well. Sacha laughed. The bedroom door opened and Aziz came in quietly and closed it behind him. The white of his shirt in the dark.

"I think Antoine noticed me leaving. I pretended I was going downstairs, then I came quietly up again."

He sat on the edge of the bed and pulled his boots off then leaned back with a sigh, propped on his hands. "Put the light on for a minute?"

"Is it safe?"

"People will think you are reading, working, if they come."

She switched the little light on and he lay back on the bed, his hands beneath his head, his face marked with pallor and lines of fatigue.

"Does it matter if Antoine knows?"

"I would prefer him not to. *Mon Dieu.* I am exhausted. I have a backache, perhaps from the position you have to take when you are windsurfing."

"Turn over, I'll give you a massage."

He rolled to lie face down like someone who has been hit over the head. She found the bottle of argan oil from the market and spread her hands across his back where the shirt was pushed up and the pants loosened.

"*C'est bien.* I am making myself at home, *non?*"

"You may."

His back felt muscular and tense. She spread her hands, dug fingers down into the tight places, felt the knots begin to loosen, moved down to the hard curve of his buttocks. He turned his head sideways on to the pillow and grinned with the old bike riding, horse riding, daredevil grin.

"You know, this makes me think about something else? You know, I think I'm not so tired after all…"

He stood up and began pulling his clothes off with the quick abandon of the men she had watched on the beach, whose natural state seemed to be naked. He twitched the white cover aside and stood to pull her long T-shirt over her head. Then he rolled her onto the bed and began. This movement of his from total stillness to action was beginning to be familiar. He glanced, with a question that did not get put into words, then reached one hand out to switch off the lamp. He smelled of the nutty oil, his body was firm and slippery, compact and small. She held him. In the darkness, gaining privacy not from each other but from an outside world beyond themselves, they found their way back together, at first with more determination than ease. He was on her in the darkness, when he whispered in her ear—*habibti.*

"What is *habibti?*"

"In Arabic, darling. Treasure. Beloved."

Immediately, she was open to him. His hand was there, and then his mouth. In her hand his penis grew and straightened like a flower in water. She put all the questions to the back of her mind. No why, no how. No past, no future. Just now. *Habibti,* the Arabic word, to caress her. She arched towards him.

"No, wait. Like this, first."

His mouth on her, sucking, nibbling. She wanted to scream out. He knew it, clamped one hand across her mouth. His penis in her right hand leapt, she whispered to him in French and English to come in. It was like the ocean again, beating up against the ramparts at high tide, and she bit into his hand to keep silent and came at once, only seconds before his own orgasm made him gasp. He arched and fell.

"*Ma foi.*" He looked at her, and laughed. She was crying, tears running down her face in the dark.

"Sssh, sssh, I have to go."

"I know."

She lay across the bed and thought, this is only sex, he could be anyone, in a sense he is anyone, I was bound to get to feel like this at some point in my life, I must be grateful that someone has brought me to it, and that is all.

It was clear to her that it was his unlikeness to any man she had ever met that gave her the safety to feel such pleasure. It was as if she'd forgotten who he was.

* * *

At breakfast, Aisha came and gave Sarah a brilliant smile and asked

if she would like an egg. She said she had heard that English and
American people liked eggs for breakfast. That was why they had such
strength. Nick often ate an egg.

"*Non, merci*, Aisha. Coffee and bread will do fine."

"You are sure? An egg gives strength, you know, to these
parts."

She gestured frankly to her own pelvis.

"No, I'm sure."

Aisha sat down on one of the wicker chairs. Her foot swung in
an embroidered slipper, one leg was hooked over the other and her
frilled pants showed beneath a black dress covered with gold embroi-
dery. Her headscarf was scarlet this morning and her jewellery gold.

"May I have some coffee with you, Sarah?"

Aisha's gaunt look of yesterday was gone, but her face still
seemed sharpened, its fine bones giving it strength.

"Of course, help yourself."

"It is a fine morning. Are you well?"

"Very well, thank you. And you?"

"Very, very well. And your wind man?"

"He is well, too."

"My fiancé has left. You know, Sarah?"

"Yes, I know."

"It is because of this bad woman, this woman from Marrakesh."

"I thought it was because he had to get his papers renewed."

"*Ah, non. Non.*" She sipped coffee from the bowl and looked
up over the rim.

"Not just that, Sarah. More than that. Much more."

"Are you sure?"

"Sure. She made him go. She sent him away from me. She used
strong magic. She is bad. But she will see. I promise you that. More
coffee? I will make some more, if you want."

"No, thank you, that was fine. Aisha, can I ask you something?"

"Of course, Madame Sarah."

Sarah wanted to ask her if she had really poisoned Yann, the last time. Yet she changed her mind. It mattered more to be friends with Aisha than to know the answer to that particular question. Aisha looked at her and for a moment Sarah thought, we know each other, we know what each other is thinking. Then Aisha got up to go, smoothed her dress down over her breasts with both hands and patted her kerchief to make sure it was in place.

"No, it doesn't matter."

"Have a good day, Sarah," Aisha said. "Have a very, very good day. Do not let these men spoil it. *Ouacha?*"

* * *

And afterwards?

Afterwards I was sent home. The wife of the French consul complained to my uncle. There was a scandal. A young Englishwoman and a Moroccan, alone together.

Nobody believed me. But it was Uncle Hajji they wanted to get at, really. It was a way to do that. The wife of the French consul, she told about us.

So you do remember.

Memory, I told you, lies at the bottom of a deep well. But it does not disappear. You only lose the rope.

Part III
Accident

Chapter twelve

Eating Hyena

Jan Potocki, who travelled from Poland to Morocco in 1791, claimed in his "Voyage dans l'Empire du Maroc" to be "the first foreigner who came to this country simply as a traveller"—instead of as ambassador, merchant or conqueror. On the 11th April in the preceding year, the sultan Sidi Mohammed ben Abdallah, successor to the chaotic reign of Moulay Ismail, had died. At a time when Voltaire and Diderot were writing about "enlightened despots", Sidi Mohammed had been one, it seemed. After his death, Morocco fell back into a more traditional oriental despotism. At the time of Potocki's journey, three pretenders to the throne were fighting it out. The Jewish quarter in Tetouan was ravaged at this time. How much of this did Potocki see, in his brief visit, from early July to early September 1791?

He had read Lempriere, the English surgeon called from Gibraltar to take care of the dying Sidi Mohammed ben Abdallah. "A Tour From Gibraltar, to Tangiers, Salle, Mogodore, Santa Cruz, Taroudant and thence over the Mount Atlas to Morocco (Marrakesh): including a Particular Account of the Royal Harem," London 1791. He knew of Samuel Romanelli, the Jew from Mantua, who lived in

Morocco from 1786 to 1790 and had fled from Mogador (Mongador on the map of the time) in a Portuguese boat. But every traveller has only his own eyes, his own impressions.

Potocki's are of a welcoming, generous, expansive people; a government that appears to keep the peace. It was in 1911, Sarah read, that the nations of Europe divided up the Maghreb among themselves: Morocco for France, Libya for Italy, and Egypt for Britain. The colonial assumption being that the Arab nations could not govern themselves. The *Entente Cordiale* appeared to have nothing cordial about it. Sarah put down her book and thought: from what loss, what injury, now came the acceptance of the new colonialism in the late twentieth century that was so euphemistically called "tourism"—that took land, imposed customs, changed the face of a people into servants again? One world was being made where there should be many. It was all to be a playground for the rich.

She read for hours in her high room, lying across the bed or sitting at her window, elbows on the table Omar had found for her, her fingers tracing the shapes of the mother-of-pearl inlay. She liked the smell of it, which was like the smell of the workshops under the ramparts, and of the nutty oil she had rubbed on Aziz. It was like sniffing the inside of a cedar chest.

Suddenly, it wasn't just a research project she'd set herself. It was what she had to know. The first Moroccans were "Morisquos" and had come from Hornachos in Estramadura, in 1609, and settled in Rabat. They were rich, and financed pirates and corsairs along the Barbary coast for decades. In spite of a treaty signed in 1681 with Louis xiv, they made no differentiation between French and other ships. Even then, the French had expected special treatment.

She skipped on. It was detective work, hunting for clues. The origins of it all, of the attitude that could make servants of a people, take their power from the inside, make them, as she was, weak. Lyautey, now that was a known name. Marshal Lyautey, Resident General of French Morocco. The Treaty of Fez, making Morocco a French Protectorate, in 1912. The thousands of Moroccan soldiers sent to the front in the First World War. Out in front of the armies, taking the worst of it, the North Africans—Zouaves, legionnaires, colonial infantry. Marching towards the German war machine, mown down in their hundreds and thousands as soon as they appeared. But, also, in a paradox of colonialism, Lyautey's determination to give the country he loved so passionately a legal code that would make it a modern state.

Then—curiosity driving her on, and the dark of early evening purple at the window—she went on to the 1930's, when Great-Uncle Hajji had been Consul in Rabat. Uncle Hajji had been, according to legend, a lover of the Arab people he found himself among; like Lawrence, like so many Englishmen. Probably, he had been accused of "going native".

She found the nationalist leader Abdel Krim el Khattabi, leading the tribes of the Rif in the 1920s. In 1921, Krim had the audacity to fight the Spanish, and actually established an independent republic in the Rif with most of the apparatus of a modern state and backed by huge mineral reserves. The French, naturally, couldn't allow this to go on and joined with Spain to defeat him. Riffian warriors were recruited in Spain's armies, which is why Franco was able to get such a hold and to attack from North Africa. After Lyautey's death, Petain, the same Petain who was to be the head of the Vichy government, was left in charge of settling "the Rif question." Abdel Krim: "the devil with horns according to some, crouched in the dark corners of Berlin, Ankara, Moscow and elsewhere; according to others, he had come from heaven with a fiery sword." This man was exiled to Reunion in 1926 and escaped to Egypt twenty years later. He died in Cairo in 1963. Nothing weak about him, except the appearance of failure, at least in the history books.

In 1931, in Paris, the Colonial Exhibition opened. In France, Arab artifacts were all the rage. Mohammed V, who came to the throne of Morocco as a young man in 1927, held out not for independence—a faint dream at that time—but for national unity in the face of the colonial fantasy: divide, diminish and rule. In 1932, the Franco-Moroccan newspaper *Maghreb* appeared, denouncing the colonialist attitudes of the Protectorate. In Fez in 1933, Mohammed Hassan Ouazzani founded the journal—in French, as it was forbidden to publish any nationalist journalism in Arabic. The nationalists tried to promote traditional dress and to boycott French goods. In 1934, they created the *Fête du Trône* to honour their young monarch and all he represented.

In 1934 *L'Action du Peuple* was seized and the paper was suppressed. Allal el Fassi, the son of a well-to-do Fez family, founded the first Moroccan political party: the Moroccan Action Committee. In 1936 Marion Henderson, a young Englishwoman, went to stay with her uncle, the British diplomat in Rabat. El Fassi, probably Ouazzani, certainly Abdel Jadid, came to the house where the carpets were rolled back for dancing, whisky was drunk with water, and conversations took place. A young woman was there, visiting. The wife of the French consul saw what she saw, and no doubt acted accordingly.

In 1937 there were demonstrations in Fez. El Fassi, their organizer, was arrested. The national party was broken up. Ouazzani, who refused to distance himself from El Fassi, was arrested and interned in the south, while El Fassi was deported to Gabon. Abdel Jadid, forbidden to continue to study the law that Lyautey had so wanted for Morocco, went from Casablanca to his hometown, Essaouira, to distribute food to the starving in the city. What happened to him after that, nobody knew.

In January of 1943, at Anfa in the suburbs of Casablanca, Roosevelt met with Churchill and the allies decided that the final objectives of the War were to be the complete capitulation of Germany and Japan.

President Roosevelt had long conversations with Mohammed v. and concluded that the independence of Morocco was an absolute necessity, once the war was over. He promised it; he gave him his word.

* * *

The point of travel may be to get as much of the world inside you as possible. You swallow it whole, digest and secrete it and its essence becomes an indelible part of you, carried in your cells and memory.

* * *

She would still, in years to come, be able to take a walk in her head around this town, that used to be called Mogador, as easily as she could go physically across the city she lived in. There are places in the world, as Yann had said, that are centres, points of focus. You know them when you are in them. You know that something's going on, that you're there for a reason, even if you don't know what it is. Something has drawn you to this place, and until you have let it change you, it won't let you go.

During those months in Essaouira the place began to inhabit her. She walked around it, following all the tracks and pathways that people had been following since the beginnings of life on that coast, and it came inside her, filled her dreams, pushed up like the ocean into all her empty crevices. She'd see this later. It wasn't just Aziz. Each intimacy remains inside you. It's not infidelity to the place which is now or the person who is now: it's you growing bigger and more porous, with fewer boundaries. More on the inside, the more you live. Intimacy means letting people in; intimacy with a place means letting it change you, inhabit you, and become your landscape too. Either way, it means being vulnerable. Because you come to share the vulnerability of the place and of the person. Everything that hurts them will hurt you too. You want it—you say you do. But what can ever prepare you for what will happen?

These days, she read the past history of the country as if it were also hers. Looking for the source of the weakness, that was acceptance, that was also death.

It was hard to go on mailing articles to New York, or to believe that they even got there. The fax machine in the hall worked one day in three, though Sacha assured her she would get it fixed. The telephone, on the main desk by the front door, was hardly any better. When she called her editors, they sounded like people on a distant planet. What she was sending out of here, her articles for the American public, seemed to her as shallow and ineffectual as telegrams sent long after the event.

The days moved towards the King's birthday and the *Fête du*

Trône, the day when Moroccans celebrate their independence from France. All over town she saw buildings were being whitewashed by men perched on rickety scaffolding, and wielding long brushes while donkeys stood dozing with carts holding the big cans of whitewash. Everything in town was being cleaned, painted, begun again. The blue doors and balconies were painted bluer than the sky at midday. As she sat at her table, she heard the shouts sounding everywhere from men crawling over the surfaces of buildings, while the streets were spattered white as if huge birds had dropped their shit from the sky.

Soon King Hassan II smiled down from every wall and window, as if to reassure everyone that all would be well. And would it be? Was that smile all one needed? Was *"Insh'allah"* enough? You hoped so, you had to, because there wasn't anything else. There wasn't a constitution, a first amendment, the right to pursue happiness. Or the right to pursue anything, depending on who you were.

The house around her was emptier, quieter. Where, for instance, was Nick? He was away more and more often. When he came in, he looked distracted, walked about and didn't settle. Sacha was the one who seemed to be organizing the place. She put vases of flowers all over the house where none had been before. She'd reorganized the kitchen, installed a desk downstairs, removed the clutter of old magazines and cassette tapes left out of their boxes that Yann had left around. She made Aisha wash the floor every day, she threw out the ragged carpets and put new ones in their place. One morning she caught Sarah on the stairs.

"Sarah, there you are. I have missed you. Why don't we have lunch together? You are not busy? You have no rendezvous today with the wind?"

"No, I have no rendezvous."

Aziz was busy with tourists, making money for Antoine.

* * *

It had been a relief to spend the morning in eighteenth-century Morocco, even if there was hardly anything written about women there. The strange thing was, you knew that at every single time in history, there had been women. Silent, invisible; but present. It wasn't like researching the activities of Arabs in Spain, for instance, or Africans in America. They weren't brought from anywhere as slaves, they didn't come and go: they were simply there, witnesses to everything that went on. She looked at Sacha, who was wearing white today, her smooth brown skin glowing against it. Sacha was visible, very visible, and certainly not silent.

"Fine. Then what about the Chalet? I can't eat fish every day, and besides, they take so long to serve it down on the quay. It is all so inefficient, it annoys me. Very picturesque, yes, but not every day. Tell me, what do you think of this? I could not bear how the chairs were, all stuck in one corner, and as for that dreadful heap of books. Look, I thought a pot plant there, and a little table in the window with some flowers? It was all so depressing before. I asked Nick and he said, do what you think best. Men haven't a clue. Not a clue. I said to him: My dear, I know that this house used to be a brothel, but there are limits. We don't want it to get like that again, do we? Oh, and another thing. I hope you do not mind, I took those pictures from your room."

"The blue flowers?" She'd particularly liked her gouaches of blue iris above the bed.

"Yes. You see, I had a perfectly terrible picture in my room. I could not sleep. I had terrible dreams. I had to keep the light on all night and even then, there it was in front of me. Ugh. I was sleepless, totally sleepless. Don't worry, I didn't hear a thing. But this picture—a serpent! Imagine putting a picture of a serpent in somebody's bedroom. Two people, a man and a woman, both quite naked, under a tree, and a serpent. Horrible. I simply had to get rid of it. I said to Nick, with this serpent there I shall never sleep again."

"That must have been Adam and Eve."

"I don't care who it was. To you Christians it may be normal, but to me it is an abomination. A-bom-in-ation. So you see, to be able to sleep, to have peace of mind, I took your blue flowers. Maybe like that I will borrow your sweet dreams too. Who knows?"

"Okay, have them for now." She'd never thought before what

effect the images of the Garden of Eden might have on somebody raised as a Muslim.

*   *   *

Against the sea wall, the tide splashed up. The tipped umbrellas swayed in the wind, strained at their bases, and the tablecloths were pinned to the tables like old-fashioned men's shirt cuffs. The glasses on the table shivered, and every now and then a diner shrieked as the wind took a napkin or a hat. Sarah sat in the sun, facing down the beach. There was the white square of the windsurf base at the edge of the long expanse of sand; far out to sea she saw two sails bucking before the wind, one green, one pink.

"Not too much sun, Sarah? Not too much wind?"

"No, I like it."

"Well, if it gets too strong we can always move indoors. At least we will get some proper service here, not like on the quay."

Sacha waved the menu card and when the waiter came, ordered for them both. Salad and a big omelette, would that do, and what would they drink? Water? No, not a Moroccan salad, a green salad. Were the lettuces fresh? With plenty of dressing. A mushroom omelette, why not? And a cold beer for Madame.

The waiters had all appeared as soon as she looked up. She tipped her dark glasses up on her forehead and looked about her. She laid her wrists on the table, laden with gold. Sarah sat back and looked past her to the choppy green sea, her arms chilled from the wind, in spite of the heat of the sun.

"Well, Sarah, I have much to tell you. I think you will be interested. You know I have a friend coming tomorrow?"

"No?"

"A friend from France. He is coming from Nice. A great man, *un grand savant*, I tell you. He is very interested in coming here. He is *un grand psychologue*. A medium. He knows about these things."

"What things, Sacha?"

"You must have noticed. You must feel the atmosphere in the house. I didn't sleep at all last night, I was so worried. And that serpent… As soon as I arrived, I knew it, there is something very bad going on. You do not feel it? The presence of evil?"

"What? What are you talking about?" Sarah put both hands on the blowing tablecloth to hold it down, so that it felt as if she and Sacha were playing some game involving invisible cards. Hands on the table, look, nothing hidden.

"You know, I was born in this country, I have lived most of my life here and I am very sensitive. I feel things. When Nick asked me to come, I could feel that he needed my help."

"Nick asked you to come?"

"Of course, he came to Marrakesh, to ask me to come. You know I was working at the Mamounia? You know he has asked me to run the house in his absence? He is going to London, then to Los Angeles. He has urgent business. He needed someone of course who would be able to manage things. But I said to him, *Tu ne me fais pas de cadeau, mon cher*, no, this is not a gift you are giving me. *Au contraire.* What a situation. I am surprised that you, Sarah, are not more sensitive to what is going on. Me, I feel it each time I breathe. Of course, you have other interests at the moment, other occupations…"

A big bowl of salad was set down between them. The white napkins scattered in the wind. Sarah leaned forward, her hands holding them down. A glass of water tipped and spilled to the floor.

"Sacha, what exactly do you think is going on?"

Sacha helped herself to a large plateful of salad and then peered at it closely, turning over the leaves as if it might have caterpillars in it.

"Aisha, of course. She is practising witchcraft. Beneath our noses. I know all the signs."

"What? You can't be serious. Where I come from, witchcraft has been out of date for over a hundred years."

Sacha shook her bangles in the sun. "Very many women in Morocco use witchcraft. You know, you can do anything with a drop of a man's semen?"

"No, I didn't. Like what?"

The sea slapped up against the wall and splashed people and

147

several of them laughed and exclaimed and jumped up from their chairs. The striped blinds tugged like sails in the wind.

Sarah imagined a new title for the article she would send back to the magazine, which was trying to rival Harper's in its circulation. It was called "Discourse"; so of course to be challenging was what was wanted. Witchcraft Today. Perhaps it would be okay if you had it happening in North Africa. Otherwise the religious right would be on their backs in a flash.

"Make him faithful to you, make him impotent, make him hate a person he thought he loved," Sacha said. "Make him suffer in many ways. I know, Sarah. I could tell you things that would astonish you. Things that have happened to friends of mine. I will lend you books. You will be fascinated. And it's not just used against men. Women can also get rid of rivals. A drop of poison in the food, or you can take somebody's underclothes—you can make her frigid, barren, make her hate the man she thought she loved, make her never want to touch him again. That, *ma chère*, has happened to me. That is why I am very, very careful. *Tiens*, here is our omelette. They are good here, these waiters. *Merci*."

She made a place for it on the table and began eating at once. "I tell you this because you are a writer. Also because you are living in this terrible house. You have to know. Otherwise it is too dangerous. Nick is so vague, he just lets everything go. Yann was a disaster, it is better that he is gone. But we have to do something. Sometimes a whole household can suffer. So I tell my friend to come. He will be able to advise us."

Sarah dipped fingers and bread into the omelette, copying Sacha. "How to get rid of your rivals". How would that go down back in the States? Probably wonderfully, considering the mess most women seemed to be in with their relationships. "Make him impotent?" No, most women in America were trying to do the reverse. She looked at Sacha's vivid painted face and then beyond her to where the two little sails were, taut and brilliant and scudding before the tide. Aziz and Omar, out there playing with the wind. The triangles of the sails against the dark glitter of the ocean.

Sacha pushed her face closer across the table and tapped her on the hand. "You are dreaming, Sarah. You have beautiful dreams."

Sarah said, "You know, I don't believe any of this. You must have imagined it. I think Aisha's just upset because Yann's gone." Anyway, it would be racist to suggest that only Arab women used witchcraft, as well as untrue. It was, she'd heard, beginning to take off in the strangest places, from L.A. to rural Georgia.

"Yes, because she wants to kill him! Now he has escaped! Now she will kill somebody else, perhaps. It is like—what is the word you say when you cannot stop? Like drinking alcohol, for example?"

"Addiction?"

"It is like addiction. Yann is gone, she will find another victim. Have some more omelette. Go on, this at least will not poison you. I tell you, I have not imagined this, Sarah. Tomorrow you will see. Tomorrow, Sarah, you will understand. Now, coffee or a dessert? The *crème caramel* here is good, almost as good as a French one."

"Coffee would be fine." Sarah smoothed her napkin on her knees.

"You will not tell anyone?"

"You mean Aisha? Of course not." She accepted one of Sacha's Egyptian cigarettes from an old-fashioned cigarette case embossed with blue stones. All this intrigue, this not telling X what Y was doing—was it simply the way people amused themselves here, or was it an essential part of staying alive?

Chapter thirteen
In Haik

Later that same day, she found herself standing like a statue in the downstairs room, as Aisha stood back, assessing her work. ("Come, Sarah, come, I want to show you something.") Now they were down in the little anteroom off the front hall, alone together, and she had dressed Sarah in haik, wound her in white material from head to toe. A handkerchief tied across the lower part of her face made breathing hard.

"*Bien*, Sarah, *bien*. Like this, then, like that. *Comme ça*."

Sarah stood before her with one end of the white material held in one hand and turned around like a cake on a stand, obedient to her touch. Some of the white cloth was tucked into the top of her jeans to hold it in place. Aisha put up a hand to smooth her hair back out of sight and examined her. It was like being fitted by a professional dressmaker for her wedding dress, years ago; passive, eager to please, scared.

"It is good, the haik. No one will know you."

Sarah looked in the mirror. She hadn't felt so strange since that day of her marriage, when, in another life, she had stood dressed from head to toe in white, with a veil. In Boston, that had been, when she and Dave, still students, had married to please their parents rather than each other. Here was the tactile memory: she and that false bride, connected through another woman's touch. Aisha tucked and fitted and looked at her with a critical eye.

"My eyes are the wrong colour."

"Nobody will see, in the dark. I give you some kohl. And you look down. Like so. You do not look straight ahead. Now you will be like a Moroccan woman, Arab, of course, not Berber."

She demonstrated. Sarah had never seen her look demure before. But then Aisha, being Berber, did not wear the full haik that covered you from head to toe, just a black cloak when she went out. It was only Arab women who went draped from head to toe in white. Ibrahim and Malik, Jake's friends, stood and watched and the black puppy slept on its folded *kelim* in the corner.

"*C'est bien,*" said Ibrahim.

"*Zuina,*" said Malik. That meant, "pretty" in Arabic. She didn't think she looked pretty, only entirely strange. The forbidden potency of disguise: it was like being masked, but in reverse. Only the eyes showed. The rest of the body was entirely hidden.

Aisha leaned close with a little pot of kohl and a tiny wooden stick, which she used to smear black around her eyes. "There. Now you go out into the street."

"Not alone, Aisha! Come with me."

"No, you must go alone."

When Aisha had suggested this, Sarah had simply obeyed. It was the first time Aisha had ever sought her out, had a plan for her, and there was something that she wanted to discover: not what it would feel like to be dressed in haik, but what it was like being Aisha, what she was about. There was a way of not being weak, and Aisha seemed to have it just as Sacha had her own *savoir-faire*. It was possible that she was going to need them both.

* * *

Out, then, into the thickening spring dusk. The walls still glowed pink but it was hard to see underfoot and she stumbled on rubble. Her steps in the thick folds had to be small, her hips moved differently. She walked close to the red wall as veiled women did, as if it were suddenly impossible to go down the middle of the street. She walked like a nun, towards the little square at the end of the street where in the daytime carpets hung on pitted walls and people sat outside on chairs. Through the crowds who strolled past Tariq's restaurant. Past the clothes boutiques where men still sat sewing, past the carpet shop and towards the *Café* de la Place where Mohammed was pouring creamy coffee into glasses. The known way. But tonight she walked it as a veiled woman: a concealed body and a pair of eyes. Tonight nobody looked at her or greeted her. She was the one doing the looking, from the inside, out.

She'd never imagined that in haik you could have this power. It was the power of being invisible, the power of looking. She'd imagined that being veiled made you feel powerless, was oppressive in itself. She'd even written about it. The veil, instrument of oppression. But now, in spite of the discomfort, the freedom was of not being looked at, not examined in passing, however briefly, by men assessing legs, breasts, face. Her clothes now were simply protection from that assessing gaze. Fashion, body shape, walk, age, weight, all had become irrelevant. She walked free of what western women live with every day of their lives. The only trouble was, the heat. Her own breath made the handkerchief across her face soggy. Sweat poured down her back.

Every evening the women in haik sat upon the benches of this town and on the edges of fountains and the sea wall. They moved slowly through the streets and then just sat. Sometimes they were in twos and threes, sometimes alone. Arab women wore mostly white; Berbers wore black and sometimes wore scarves on their heads rather than the complete veil. There were different ways of wearing the veil, too. You could have it across your mouth only, or across your nose so that only your eyes showed, or across one eye so that only the other looked out. Sometimes all you saw of women was a glowing eye like a hot coal. Sometimes, in the street, a pair of dark eyes above a veil glanced sideways and she wondered if she was passing a woman she knew, without recognizing her. Now she too was reduced to a pair of eyes and a certain way of moving. Would Aziz know her?

Sarah passed the *café*, glanced quickly sideways to see if there was anyone there she knew. The men lounging at the tables were a different species tonight. Hafid from the carpet shop came down the street, passing the *café* on his left. She walked close to him deliberately. *"Labess."*

He recoiled from the shock of a greeting from the unknown woman.

"Hafid, *bonsoir*. It's me." He'd been there the night of the dancing, when she first saw Aziz.

"Sarah! I didn't recognize you. What are you doing?"

But he was of another species. The sexual jolt was like random electricity. He was a man, and there was nothing to say. And she was as unmistakably a woman to him as if she were naked. Neither said any more. Sarah went on down the Place Moulay Hassan, damp under the long robes, her legs weak. She walked past the groups that gathered by the unused fountains under the Lego trees. God, she hoped that she would not meet Aziz.

How could she walk through all that unprotected space with no walls to contain her and no other women to walk at her side? The glances of men seemed predatory, almost angry. But it was not for her, as an individual. There was no individuality left. She, too, was one of a species. She turned the corner and walked back towards the Rue Ben Yassin, leaving the *café* on her right, with its crowds of alien men who might in another life have been friends. Then there were only yards to go before the blue door of the house.

But the house key was in her pocket and she couldn't reach under the haik. She stretched up to ring the bell; even that movement seemed a strain. The door swung open. Aisha welcomed her in.

"Aisha! I went right round and back through the Place Moulay Hassan!"

"Bien, Sarah, *c'est bien."* She had passed some test, she felt, but what it was, she had no idea.

Aisha began unwrapping the bandaged whiteness, as if from a mummy. The intimacy of it, with Aisha's fingers plucking the heavy material from her—she had to think again of the Boston dressmaker and how she had hated standing there being dressed and undressed in swathes of stuff, pinned and unpinned, made helpless until she could escape, leaving her mother to deal with it all. But with Aisha it was different. The handkerchief still tied gangster-fashion at Sarah's mouth was soaked now from her breathing. Aisha untied it. Then she stepped back and looked straight at Sarah with her challenging black stare. She reached to touch briefly her breasts and hips, a sketch of a gesture, showing her to herself.

"You see, Sarah?" she said then. "You see? That is how it is, to be a woman here. Not me, I am Berber." Then she gave her shoulders a little shake and let her go.

Chapter fourteen

The Carpets of Paradise

In her room, Sarah undressed completely and looked in the long mirror. She saw the body that she had more or less ignored all her life as she'd escaped into the life of the mind with only occasional forays into sex. Long, slim, pale and patched with tan. Not young, not old. Now, it was the body that played in the sea and walked on the beach and made love with Aziz here on this bed. What had changed? What had Aisha done? Her hair was light and lank, bleached by the sun on the surface, darker underneath; her eyes pale, the brows faint above the lids marked with kohl. An unremarkable face, she'd always thought. She could have been one of any number of white American women of her own age. She was forty-four, which was past most things now. Yet her body looked different, alive. Was this Aisha's gift? Was it the haik? Aziz? Her own imagination? She took a long shower, dressed carefully for dinner in black, adding some blue-stoned jewellery from the shop on the corner, and went downstairs.

* * *

Nick spread the thumbed drawings out on the table again and he and Antoine Dupuy were leaning over them as she came in, their arms braced on the table, heads jerking as they talked. He'd had the meeting with the mayor, he was saying. Now it was time to talk money. Sarah sat down a little way away from them in an armchair. She crossed her legs and sat back, trying not to let the men's voices in to her head. It was easier to do this with French than with English. A few words infiltrated, *"hectares," "million," "la plage de Sidi Kaouki."*

Sacha came in and fussed about, plumping up cushions like a housewife, moving a pot, rearranging big bunches of mimosa that had suddenly appeared. She sighed frequently and glanced around with a mocking expression as if men's discussions had to be put up with, but not taken seriously. Omar came in to see if anyone wanted tea, olives, a drink.

"Omar," said Sacha, "these candles are a disgrace. Could you not have bought new ones?"

Her finger picked at solidified dripped wax and she held it up to him, looking disgusted.

Omar said, "I buy new every day. Three dirhams each, for all these candles, you realize the cost?"

"But this system you have for lighting them, when you fool about on a chair like a stupid acrobat! Surely you don't have to do that? Why isn't there a pulley, like the one downstairs? Nick, excuse me, why don't you get a pulley? Then we wouldn't have to put up with Omar wobbling about up there on a chair every night."

Nick said without looking up, "Good idea, I'll see to it."

Antoine Dupuy said, "Now we really do have to be sure of the price of one unit. And what does he mean by the city limit? Where exactly would that be? You do realize, I'm leaving in a couple of days. Aziz, I'm going to have to leave some of this to you. I hope you're paying attention."

Sarah had to hear it now, because Aziz was suddenly there with them, his black head bent over the plans too, as if he had materialized from nowhere. He must have come very quietly up the stairs. He sat there staring at the plans as if he was seeing something else. He might have looked like that, she thought, when he was a schoolboy, with life going on beyond the high windows of some classroom while he waited for release.

Sarah said to Sacha, "I went out dressed in haik this evening. I could have walked past any of you, and none of you would have known."

Sacha said," Whatever did you do that for? It's absurd the way they still wear it here, in my opinion. It's mediaeval. It gives me the creeps. You can never tell who is who."

"That was what was interesting. I've never felt so invisible."

"Who wants to be invisible?" She turned away from the table by the fire, looking disdainfully at the little group of men.

Nick looked up. "Sacha, we will go for dinner later. I'll take you for a lobster *chez Sam*."

"Oh, I am honoured, *Monsieur* Nick. Come, Sarah, they do not want us; you and I will go and drink something delicious in the kitchen. That is the place for women, so they say."

Sarah followed her into the kitchen, the jut and wobble of her in tight white pants and a gold top. She helped them both to Nick's gin. They leaned against the worktops and ate olives. Sacha spat the stones into the sink. Then she lit a cigarette.

"That Nick, he thinks he can have what he wants for the price of a lobster. He will see. 'Sacha... I will take you for dinner'... What does he think I am, a teenage girl? An idiot?"

"A lobster or a palm tree," Sarah said. "Depending on who you are."

"What is this about palm trees?"

"He gives them to the mayor. In exchange for building permits."

"Ah! And that Omar, he is no good. He is so slovenly, he has to go. Aisha, well, we will see. We will see when Jean comes tomorrow. My friend, you know, from France. This house, it needs so many changes. You have seen what I have done with the mimosa? So easy, just to go out and pick some flowers. Men do not think of such things. It was like a morgue before, so gloomy. And they are too busy with their stupid buildings, their plans, all that."

"Where did you get the mimosa?"

"Oh, I went with Aisha to get them, this afternoon."

"You went with Aisha? After our lunch?"

"To Sidi Kaouki. Her family is there. You know, they will not build there, all this is nonsense. Yes, after we had our lunch, you and I, our little *tête-à-tête*, I went with her. I want her to be a friend."

"I thought you were trying to get rid of her."

"Get rid, no. I want to know her, to understand. We are women together, no? We have to understand each other."

"So you actually got her to take you to Sidi Kaouki?"

"*Bien sûr*. I met her family. They were very pleasant. Of course, they would suffer from this idea of building all these things there, they would be homeless, that is clear to them."

"You told them?" Jesus, things moved fast around here.

"They knew already. They are not stupid. I told them a little more, that is all."

"And did you tell Aisha that you suspect her of witchcraft?"

"Of course not. What would be the good of that? What you do not understand, Sarah, is that everybody does it. It is not so unusual. I do not think she is strange to do it, I understand only too well. There is a time for each of us when we have to do what we can. Do you not agree, Sarah?"

"Uh-huh."

"I just try to stop her, this time. I understand her, with that shit Yann she has to deal with. But she is doing it in this house—this house is to be a hotel, it is not good, you see? What you do not understand, Sarah, is that you only tell somebody something if it is useful to do so. Otherwise, you stay quiet."

She mimed it, with a finger at her full red lips. Sarah drank the gin and stared at her.

"I want Aisha to like me," Sacha said. "That way everything will work better."

She stubbed out her half-smoked cigarette and put her glass beside the sink.

"What are you thinking, Sarah? You are thinking hard, *n'est-ce pas?*"

"Nothing."

If Aisha's family knew that they would be turned out when Antoine built at Sidi Kaouki, then Aisha would try to stop him. Aisha had one reliable way of stopping people. And if Sacha had told Aisha's relations about the details, it meant that Sacha didn't want the building plan to go ahead either. So she might join forces with Aisha, if 'everybody has to use witchcraft sometime'. So why was she importing Jean Whatshisname from France? Also, now Yann was gone, Aisha had no real motive for poisoning anybody except Antoine Dupuy. So perhaps he would be the next victim.

Oh, what a tangled web, thought Sarah. How interesting.

"You are American," said Sacha, "you say always it is nothing when it is something. You pretend to be direct but you are not. Americans are liars."

"I'll tell you later." Now she was doing it, trying to keep Sacha on her side. And what was her side, after all?

"Perhaps you will, perhaps you will not. You can trust me, Sarah. Now, shall we go and disturb those men? They cannot talk business all evening; it is most rude; I will not put up with it. You are with me, Sarah?"

"*Bien sûr.*" She finished the drink, its sour juniper-tasting smokiness.

Sacha went and stood over Nick with her hands on her hips and said, "It is ungentlemanly to keep ladies waiting beyond a certain time, do you not agree, Nick?"

Nick stood up. He raised his hands as if he had a gun pointed at him. "Antoine, it looks as if you will have to excuse me."

Antoine said, "We will have to continue later, then. Aziz and I will continue over dinner. Aziz will see to this when I am gone, it is important that he understands everything. We will eat a quick dinner at my place and then start early in the morning. I have the impression that sometimes you do not get enough sleep, Aziz. For a sportsman, enough sleep is essential, wouldn't you agree, Sarah?"

When Antoine went to the toilet, Aziz said quietly, "Be patient, he will go soon."

The day before, Aziz had taken her to the Bordj el Berod, the old palace of the Sultans of Morocco, half buried in sand. The summer palace, where the Sultans had come to make love in the fresher breezes from the ocean. But there was so little time; he had always to be back for another meeting.

"About time."

"Sarah. We will have time to—"

"Rehearse Hamlet?"

"Yes. Everything we want."

"You aren't angry with me, are you?" Sarah asked.

"No. *Au contraire.* But remember, even the Sultans of Morocco had to find the place and time for love."

"But you don't stand up to him, Aziz. You know what he's trying to do, don't you?"

"It's my job." He turned away, shrugging his shoulders. "If I stand up to him, as you say, I am out of a job. How many Moroccans do you think there are in France without a job? You have to understand this. Anyway, he is not so bad."

"I think he is. I think he's appalling. Not just the way he treats you, but this whole project."

"Oh, you American, you are such a democrat. Sssh, he is coming back. *Cherie*, I will try to come later. I cannot promise. You heard what he said."

"Yes, he wants you to have an early night. You're not a child!"

"You think I don't know that?" A flash of anger, rare.

Antoine called him sharply from the stairs, and he went. How easy it would be to drop a little something in Antoine's coffee and watch him turn yellow, shrivel up and at last, disappear.

She opened her eyes and looked at the patch of bare wall in the moonlight where the blue flowers had been. She glanced at her watch.

It was nearly two. The moon had moved right round so that now it flooded the room from across the rooftops. She heard the quiet wuff-sound of the front door opening and she heard Aziz's footsteps on the stairs.

He came in. "Are you awake? I am not disturbing you?"

"No, no, I'm awake. I had a dream, it woke me."

He was taking his clothes off fast. Naked in the moonlight. Then his hands were rough and warm, the pressure of his body was real and his breath smelled of tobacco. He pulled the sheet back and came down close. He undid the front of her shirt and pulled her breasts and shoulders free into the moonlight, then slid the rest off her. The same gesture as Aisha's, undressing. People were unveiling her, pulling off the wraps. His hand moved all the way down the front of her body, feeling its way. Wherever his hand paused, she felt herself grow more distinct, more solid. The gesture with which he had made her naked was like a sculptor's removing the cloth from clay. He was drawing her with his hands. He tipped her backwards to come in as deep as he could. Sarah shuddered. It might mean that she didn't know who she was any more, she might be the woman wrapped in white who went with only her eyes showing through the world of men, her body secret and vulnerable and only to be guessed at, her steps and gestures small. She stopped him.

"What is it? I am sorry."

"No, I'm sorry. I've been totally thoughtless about you and Antoine. I'm sorry about that."

"Antoine? You are thinking about Antoine? Sarah, at a time like this?"

"I just wanted to apologize. Before—"

"I forgive you. Now, forget Antoine! Please!" A few moments later: "You are not with me?"

"It's okay." She mumbled into his shoulder. This time, it was he who had forgotten her.

"No, no. In Islam, did you know, a man is taught that a woman's pleasure is sacred, it has to come before his own?"

"No, I didn't know that."

163

"Sexual pleasure is supposed to be a foretaste of paradise. So nobody should live without it. There is no virtue in celibacy, but you should not have too much sex or you will forget about paradise, you will not desire it. And to be sure that the woman does not go without it, in sex the man makes her go first, as in the street he makes her go after him. You see? What is inside is the opposite of what is outside. This, Sarah, is our foretaste of heavenly pleasure, so we have to make it good, eh?"

*   *   *

She heard her voice mixed with the long chant of the call to prayer that sang out from the mosque.

"Sssh, sssh, they will hear you all over town and then they will not want paradise!"

Then he was in her, the salt of his sweat in her mouth, a groan stifled on her shoulder. Two bodies shivered together in the dark.

Chapter fifteen

Strange Medicine

Jean Simon, newly arrived from Nice, settled himself into his chair and stretched out his legs in beige pants with knife-edge creases and feet in polished brown shoes. He was pale, with light, reddish hair smoothed sideways to cover a bald spot. His eyes flickered behind half-glasses as he looked from Sacha to Nick. Sacha hovered about him, brought a glass of water, a little table to place it on. Sarah thought the man looked more like a lawyer than an exorcist.

"Madame," he bowed to her as they shook hands. To Nick he said, "You have a fine house, very fine. I want this afternoon simply to absorb a little of the atmosphere."

Sarah sat in the window, her nose in a book about buried treasure that Yann had left behind, and settled in to eavesdrop.

"Yes, well," Nick said, "It used to be a rather superior brothel. Did Sacha tell you? We're making it into a hotel. It's not finished, as you see. Have you seen the house next door yet? It's through the hole in the wall, just over there."

"Ah, *Monsieur*, the atmosphere is not about whether it is fin-ished. It is what goes on in it, what still goes on. A brothel, you say.

Well, well. And yes, I have looked, I have glimpsed the house next door." He shuddered as he spoke.

"Are you cold?" Nick asked.

"No, no. I am simply very sensitive to these things, you know. It is my business".

Sacha said, "You will tell us about it later, *n'est-ce pas?* We do not want to tire you."

"All in good time, yes. But you must feel it too? Madame, you must be sensitive to the ambience?"

"Yes," Sarah said out of her corner, "I love it. It's a great place, isn't it?"

"Well, *chère Madame*, great is perhaps not the word. Perhaps there is another word. Perhaps indeed. Well, I must retire for a few minutes, if you will excuse me." He got up like an old man, and went to the stairs to his room.

"He's an exorcist!" Nick stood beside her, bouncing on his toes with excitement.

"Didn't you know? I thought Sacha had been telling everyone."

"She didn't tell me."

"I thought you asked her to get him. That's what she said."

"She just said she had this friend, a great parapsycho-whatsit, very well-known in France, blah blah blah, and she wanted to invite him to stay. Well, you know me, I like meeting weird people. I thought, why not? And now she's told Aisha to come to dinner, she wants them to have a good chat, she says. Can you imagine? This is Aisha, she's a witch; this is Jean Whatnot, he's an exorcist. I know you'll have a lot in common."

"You could stop it."

"What's the point? Let's see what happens. It could be rather fascinating. D'you know, he had the nerve to tell me that in three months he could exorcise this house completely? I said, why three months, can't you do it in an evening? He said three months was what it would take. I said, if you get a pest-control firm in they do it quicker than that. I think he was a bit pissed off. But three months!

I thought that if I gave him one free dinner, bed and breakfast, that should do it."

"Nick, what's he going to do?"

"Search me. But it's all rubbish, isn't it? I mean, you don't believe in this stuff, do you? Have you noticed this famous ambience? There's only Yann, and he got what was coming to him. She hasn't got a reason to poison anyone else, has she? You feel quite well? Anyway, you've got an alibi now."

"An alibi?"

"The wind bloweth where it listeth, Sarah, and some of it's been heard coming from your bedroom."

* * *

The exorcist started the next day by placing bowls of water all over the house in strategic places. When Sarah nearly tripped over one at the top of the stairs, he apologized.

"You will be patient with me, Madame? My work is for the elimination of evil."

"How do bowls of water help?"

"It is just a beginning. First the water, then the fire." He showed her the little bundles of leaves and sticks that he had placed on the window sills.

"How d'you know where to put them?"

"Evil has a smell, Madame. You become able to recognize it straight away."

"Do you think evil exists on its own, then, as a force in the world? Or are there evil people?" She asked him quite politely, like a good student.

"Both, Madame. Both."

"But everybody has good in them, surely. People are born good, it's just what happens to them that makes them behave badly. What about babies? You can't go into a room full of newborn babies and say that some are evil, can you?"

"Yes, I have seen this. Even babies." He bent to move a second bowl a couple of inches nearer the centre of the room. Dust danced in the air in the sun from the open windows. Outside in the street, the Javel man passed, yelling out his cry, "Gabi! Gabi!"

"I think that's nonsense. If you look into a new-born baby's eyes, all you can see is goodness."

"Then how do you account for the presence of evil?"

Aisha came upstairs in her black cloak, carrying Souad. The baby blinked and looked about her with a serious stare. She was wearing a little red hood and her cheeks were rosy from the cold air of the morning.

"*Bonjour*, Sarah," Aisha said, ignoring the man.

"*Bonjour*, Aisha, *bonjour*, Souad." She took Souad's tiny cold hand and the baby stared at her thoughtfully. Aisha put her down on a folded rug and laid down her own cloak. She wore scarlet this morning. She began tucking up her long dress and knotting it over her white leggings, to begin on the housework.

"What is this? What is this water?"

"It is for cleansing," said the exorcist.

"What is this, cleansing? Every morning, I wash the floor. Or Kiltoun or Myriam does it. I do it again today. What need is there for this cleansing?"

She poked the basin with her foot so that the water slopped.

"It's just an experiment he's doing," Sarah said.

Aisha sniffed and went into the kitchen. The baby started crawling off her rug and let out a little crow of excitement. Then she began making straight for the nearest bowl of water.

"I think you'll have to do this another time, *Monsieur*." Sarah scooped Souad up and removed her to the kitchen while she wriggled and squeaked.

"Sarah. There is something I must tell you. Listen." Aisha pulled her close. The plastic sheeting still flapped and sucked air, as there was no door to shut.

"Sarah. They will send your wind man away. If you do not do something. But I will help you. Together we will stop them, these men."

"Send him away? What do you mean?"

"The man who is going to France, the smelly one, he will make him go back to France. So you will have no more wind in your bedroom. My poor Sarah, *ma pauvre*. They did this to me, they sent my man away. He is gone, my Yann. But this time it is not too late. I will tell you what to do, I will help you. Yes? This man here is a bad man too, we must make him go. There are many, many bad men. They make bad things happen. You have heard, they wish to destroy my home at Sidi Kaouki? We must stop them, Sarah. Here, give her to me now."

"But how?" Antoine and Aziz? Aziz leaving for France?

"Medicine," Aisha whispered.

"Poison?"

"Not poison. Not so strong. Just medicine. I will tell you."

"One minute, Aisha, how do you know Antoine's going to send Aziz back to France?"

"I hear it. I am outside the room, I bring coffee and I hear it. They do not want your pleasure, Madame Sarah, just as they do not want mine. So they get rid of him, like they get rid of my man, my fiancé, my Yann—the father of my child. So. I make some coffee, yes. I let my baby sleep. Then we talk. We leave this stupid man with his water. I tell you what I know. There are things we can do. You will be happy, Sarah, I tell you."

* * *

I learned on this occasion that there were many hyenas in the neighbour-hood, and many stories told about them: one of which was that their brains have the power to make those who eat them crazy. People even describe a mentally deranged person as 'having eaten hyena.'

Jan Potocki, "Voyage dans l'Empire du Maroc," 1791.

She'd read the passage only this morning. Eating hyena: a good description of a certain state of mind.

Sarah walked back towards the town barefoot, her swimsuit dangling from one hand. Down the long beach, along the sea wall, all the way back to the Chalet. The windsurf base was behind her, where Habib was sweeping, his wet suit partly stripped off, his hair drying like slate in the sun. Where she had heard him tell her, "Yes, he is going with M. Antoine. At five o'clock, he said. But he will come back here, his things are here. He will not go without seeing you, I know that, *j'en suis sûr.*"

"*Merci*, Habib." What else could she say? He was going to France at five; Antoine was sending him away.

She was nearly at the Chalet de la Plage, when she saw the tall figure in the brown burnous, burdened with the black plastic sack. He turned towards her as she approached. She was still barefoot and carrying her shoes. He paused in mid-movement, about to throw crusts at the waiting gulls. The gulls came down to wait on the sea wall. She saw strong yellow feet and mean little eyes. His face moved as if he wanted to speak, but no sound came out. He bowed to her. The trajectories of two lives, entirely separate, touched just for a moment. It wasn't the right moment, not yet. Again, she went on her way.

* * *

Aziz stepped into the driving seat of the Renault and adjusted the driving mirror. His skin felt to him oddly chilled, as Antoine settled in beside him, laid his hands on his knees and waited for him to start the car. There was something wrong going on, he was doing what he should not be doing. It hurt him that he had not found Sarah, when he went to the house. Even if he was only going to Marrakesh, he wanted to say goodbye. His safety seemed linked to her now, in some way he had not yet understood. But if they arrived in good time for Antoine's plane, he could drop him off and be back here before midnight, at the latest, and then perhaps he could get Omar to let him in, so that he could find her in her room. Habib had told him that she'd come by the base. If Antoine had not been in such a hurry to leave, he could have gone back there just to see if she herself had been back to see him. But Antoine wanted to leave at five, so at five they were already turning out of town and taking a left on to the Safi and Marrakesh road.

The ocean lay behind them in a strip of shining metallic

blue. The country, with its hillocks and argan trees in clumps and its scrambling black goats, surrounded them; he glanced at Antoine, who was checking his tickets. Still, Aziz felt a physical discomfort that he couldn't account for. He shifted in his seat, moving his head from side to side to ease an ache in his shoulders and neck, felt the chill on his skin. Antoine shuffled tickets on his knee, in a Royal Air Maroc folder. Aziz glanced down at them as he settled into the right lane. There were two distinct folders on Antoine's knee.

Antoine said to him, "I have your ticket here, Aziz. You will be coming with me. I am sure you understand."

Then, he felt all the rage that had curdled in his stomach since first he'd walked into the school yard and they'd taunted him, the boy from Casablanca, calling him names he'd never heard before. The wish to kill, you could feel it all your life and never act on it; you made yourself calm, humble, accepting, you looked on the good side, you took what life gave. But now—was it from knowing Sarah?—it was harder to take. This man believed that he had the right to arrange his life for him. To send him away, to send him home. To buy plane tickets in his name and trick him into accepting them. He slowed the car and drove on to a grass verge, turned off the engine. The two of them sat there without moving, the tickets to France open on Antoine's knee. Aziz felt blood thud in his wrists, at his temples. His hands wanted to come up on their own and hit Antoine Dupuy, even to leave him dead. He searched for a calm place inside himself, that place he had found as a child, where life was possible. It was there, he found it. When he spoke, his own voice sounded harsh and old to him.

"You had no right to do that, Antoine."

"Have you forgotten that you work for me?" I was going to leave it to you, the work at Sidi Kaouki. But I'll have to send someone else, you are simply not reliable."

"I work for you. I am not your slave. You did wrong, to buy that ticket and not tell me."

"My dear Aziz, it is for your own good. When I saw how you were entangled with that American woman, how you neglect your work, I saw it was time to remove you. Have you forgotten that you have obligations? What is he thinking of, I said to myself. Then I saw that you must come with me. Don't worry, I will find you another windsurfing position, somewhere else, maybe southern Spain."

"I am not yours to dispose of, Antoine. My life, excuse me, is my own affair."

Still the anger burned in him. But it was better than shame, than giving in. He imagined Sarah, her grey-green gaze, the way she looked at him, as a man, simply a man, not an Arab or a Frenchman, no better and no worse than anyone. It meant he could not give in now to Antoine Dupuy, whatever happened, whatever choices he might make in the future. It was not possible.

"I won't do it, Antoine. I'll drive you to the airport and leave you there, *comme tu veux*, and then I'm going back."

"I think you don't realize, you don't have a choice. Please drive on, Aziz. I have no more to say."

He started the car again and drove on. In the silence, he heard his own blood buzz in his ears; an anger like bees swarming, like heavy black clots of them that hung from trees. The tickets stayed open on Antoine's lap, as if they were cards he'd flung down, ace cards, making him the winner. But he, Aziz, was a chess player, not a card player. The moves were different. He began to know what he would do.

Chapter sixteen

The Nature of Men

The two young Berbers, Myriam and Kiltoun, sat perched on the edge of the worktop in the kitchen where the charcoal burned for the *tajines*. Their round faces were streaked, as if they'd been crying for some time. As Sarah came in for her breakfast coffee, Aisha seized her arm, her eyes blacker than ever, and pointed with one finger at the girls.

"Sarah! You know what he is doing, *Monsieur* Nick? He is telling them they cannot work here any more. What have they done? Nothing! They work well. It is her fault, that woman from Marrakesh, that Sacha, that whore. Sarah, you must help them. Tell him they work well, that it is not right to send them away. They have families, they work for their whole family. Nobody pays as well as *Monsieur* Nick. That is why they are crying."

"I don't believe it. He wouldn't just send them away like that."

"He told them this morning. He told me. When will you believe, Sarah? He listens too much to that woman. I know her, I see through her. She wants to go to Sidi Kaouki to see my family, pick flowers together, make nice talk, make it all nice. But I see what she is doing. Oh yes. First they send my man away, now they take my girls. I know why they sent Yann. I know why, it was because he looked at her. But she is a whore, that is why men look at her like that. He is just a man, what can he do? A man has eyes. But he is stupid, my Yann, he does not protect himself. He is greedy like a child. So I have to do it, I, Aisha, I have the power. Will you talk with *Monsieur* Nick, Sarah? He will listen to you. Look, they have no work, no money. They only speak Berber. It is not right."

"Well, I could try. But Aisha, I was looking for you last night. I have to talk to you—about what we were talking about yesterday."

"Yesterday, what is yesterday? Yesterday is gone. But you have no worry, Sarah; I have done what I can. So now you will do this for me?"

"Oh, God. Aisha. Look, I made a mistake. They haven't sent Aziz away, after all."

"No? Where then is Aziz?"

"He had to drive Antoine to Marrakesh, that was all. He's coming back."

Her derisive coal-black stare. "You think that is all? I know more. I tell you, Sarah, that is not all. I have done what I can, I cannot say more. Now, will you speak with *Monsieur* Nick? Look, they are crying, they will cry all day."

"Okay, I'll talk to him. I can't believe he'd just give in to what Sacha said, though."

"Men are fools, Sarah. She speaks to him in a certain way, he cannot resist. He is like soft pastry in her hands. But you, he will listen to you because you are American. *Ouacha?*"

Ouacha.

"I will trust you. As you trust me. Yes?"

Her face up close, the intensity of her gaze. "I made this house, Sarah, and I will bring it down. They will not get rid of me. Now that Yann has gone, they think that they can do it. But I was here with Madame Sadia. I was here first, and I will not go. Sadia gave the house to me." She gestured to the wall with the blue decorated plates hanging on it. "This. All this I make. Now she wants to change it. New kitchen, she says. Now she wants me to go. No, I say, no."

She walked about the kitchen, very erect; she poked Myriam and Kiltoun up from their slouching positions on the worktops and spoke to them sharply in Berber. Then she picked up the coffee pot, peered inside it, and poured two bowls, to which she added milk and sugar.

"Come, we drink coffee together for a minute. Then you see *Monsieur* Nick. I forgot, *ma chère*, that you have not had breakfast. I have not had breakfast either. I was up very early, then I find this mess. I am tired, Sarah. Come, we will rest together for a minute."

They sat in the window, next to the birdcage. The two budgies were still surviving and had even produced an egg.

At last Aisha said, "Sarah, if Yann were here, they would not treat me this way. They say I poisoned him, but he is my man, Yann, he is the father of my child, he should be here, not"—and she spat on the floor—"in Europe. He is Muslim now, he belongs here. Why should I use poison to hurt him, answer me that?"

I made this house and I will bring it down.

"Did you? Did you poison him?"

"Sarah, I tell you, sometimes there are things you have to do. In themselves they may be bad things. But it is better sometimes than not to do anything. Sometimes you have to do these things, for yourself, for your child, for your family? A woman must think of these things. You know? Have you been married, Sarah?"

"I was. I'm divorced."

"Ah, that is not good. Here that would not happen. Who sent him away, your husband?"

"I did, I suppose."

"Ah, Sarah, that is not good. Here you would be able to do something else. You see? Here you make him change. You make him better. Here, men go, we bring them back. Another woman, we make her ill. He has another woman, your man?"

"Yes. But it was a long time ago."

"Here, we make her change. We make her not want him. We

make her hate him, refuse him even. All this can be done. And then he comes home. Yann, you see, I did not want to hurt him, only to bring him back. He is my man, you understand. And at that time he not only looks at other women, he touches them, everything. That is not good. That makes a man weak, useless. So then I do something. Yann is French, he is not Moroccan, and he does not understand these things, that I do it for his good. I have to teach him, to show him. You see, Sarah? It is the nature of men. It has to be corrected, and that is what I do."

"I see."

"That woman, that Sacha, she wants me to be out of the house. She says nice things, asks me to dinner, but I understand. It is all what we call sweet pastry. She is not so intelligent. I can see into her head. She wants to be married with *Monsieur* Nick, to be the mistress of this house. But I am already the mistress. I was here with Madame Sadia, from the beginning. They are fools, all of them. They do not understand that Madame Sadia gave me this house, it is mine."

"Do you really think she wants to marry Nick?" Sarah said, trying to imagine the combination.

"Of course. He is rich. She wants money. So she makes plans." Aisha's fingers rubbed together in the universal sign for money.

"He told me he would never marry."

"Ha! If she wants to marry, he will marry, even *Monsieur* Nick."

Sarah went on up to the roof terrace, and there was Nick himself. He was lounging on the golden carpet that was laid out on the whitewashed floor to air. His shoes were off and his shirt was open to the waist. One slim foot balanced upon the toe of the other.

Sarah said, "Hi. Am I disturbing you?"

"No, sit down. I want someone to talk to." She sat cross-legged at his side. It was like being on a magic carpet that could lift up at any moment and fly over the rooftops.

"Are you really sending Kiltoun and Myriam away? They're very upset."

"Oh, God." He closed his eyes and jiggled his bare feet. "Is there a scene going on? Sacha thinks they don't work well enough, they're always just hanging around giggling or gossiping in Berber. She thinks we should have someone more efficient."

"Why does it matter what Sacha thinks? It's your house."

"Because I've asked her to take over while I'm away."

"Oh." So he was going, it was official.

"She knows about hotel management." He yawned, looking at his feet.

"What about Yann? Has he gone for good?"

"I don't think Yann will come back. He doesn't settle anywhere for long. I spoke to him on the phone the other day, told him I thought he should stay away for the good of his health. We don't want him turning yellow and getting the shits again. Didn't you notice how ghastly he was looking when he left?"

"He drinks too much, that's all." Sarah said, "It's affecting his liver, I guess. And his fingers are yellow from the nicotine."

"That among other things. But he's only about forty-five and he's getting to look like an old man. He looked quite sprightly when he got here. I think he ought to stay away."

"What about Aisha and Souad?"

"Well, Aisha cooked her own goose, in my view. She told him she was too old to have a baby."

"Jesus, Nick, anybody can make that mistake."

Nick opened his eyes and gave her his green stare from between those astonishing lashes. He lay there without speaking. She sat, silenced. Omar had said of him: *il est comme un roi.* He's like a king. A statement, not a matter for surprise.

At last he said, "That man from Nice. What's he up to? He thinks he can come over here and do his stuff, waving incense around, collecting dust, I don't know what, without knowing the first thing about Moroccan magic. It's ridiculous. It's like sending a shrink out of Beverley Hills to deal with Haitian voodoo. Or a dentist to cure schizophrenia."

"So you think there's something to cure?" She crossed her legs, sitting beside him, and took one of his cigarettes.

"In Morocco there's always more going on than meets the eye. So I'd be stupid to think there wasn't. He's no match for it, that's all. This stuff is centuries old and it's practised daily. I meant it, about Yann. I'm saving his life by telling him to stay away, in case you thought I was just being mean to Aisha. You'd tell somebody to stay away from nuclear fall-out if you got the chance, wouldn't you? You wouldn't agree that it wasn't happening just because they couldn't see it? You wouldn't wait till they started getting cancer? Well, then."

"Nick, all Aisha wants is for Yann to come back and not have people trying to get rid of her and her girls." It seemed unwise to mention that she and Aisha had been discussing poisoning Antoine Dupuy. An American upbringing was supposed to make you immune to such thoughts.

"That's all, is it? She wants to run this place, to be a second Sadia. You know she worked for Sadia for years? Doing what exactly, don't ask me. I imagine she was rather a good, high-class whore. But I bought this house from Sadia, it was a legal transaction and I paid a lot for it; by Moroccan standards anyway. Aisha didn't seem to recognize that, she just stayed put. It was like she came with the house. Then that dope Yann started screwing her and that was that. Baby, marriage, the works. She sees herself as married to Yann and running the place. You know she even got him to convert to Islam? Yann, out of one of the most bigoted Catholic families in the whole of France?"

He sat up and then pulled himself up to sit on his haunches.

Sarah said, "Well, she is in an impossible position here unless he marries her, isn't she?"

Nick stood up and walked away, restless again, and leaned on the whitewashed parapet. Some of his words were lost, as he turned his head seaward.

"I think your notions of international sisterhood are getting in the way here, Sarah."

He turned and frowned. The sun showed lines of fatigue on his face this morning. He looked as if he had not slept.

*   *   *

"Let's stop for a moment," Aziz said, as they came up towards the T-junction where the road from the south came in, at Chichaoua. "I need to pee. Antoine, do you need anything?"

"No. Hurry, please, we don't want to be late."

"We won't be late." In the little roadside *café*, there might just be a phone that was working. He went to pee in the stinking little pit at the back, bought a bottle of Orangina and asked if there was a phone.

"No, *Monsieur*, no telephone. We had one, but it is broken. I am sorry. *B'slama.*"

"*Merde!*" Aziz muttered. But there would be a telephone at the airport. The truth was, he was simply relieved to have escaped from Antoine for a few minutes.

"*Bon, merci, b'slama.*" He stumbled out into the growing dark. It was decided: he'd drop Antoine off at the check-in, say he was going to park the car—Antoine was too lazy to want to walk—and then disappear. It felt terrifying, as if his life were at stake: perhaps this was what it felt like when you confronted a fear that had been with you as long as you remembered, the fear of the white man's power, the belief that he could run your life.

"*Putain de merde*," he murmured to himself again. Swearing seemed to strengthen his resolve. Antoine would fire him, could even make his life a misery, but he could not make him get on that plane.

He got back into the driving seat, switched on the lights again, and started the engine. Antoine just sat there, so sure of his power. Aziz thought, I must remember to ask for the ticket before dropping him off, so he'll believe me. And he accelerated up the road towards the junction with the road that came in from the south.

179

Chapter seventeen

The Red Flag

Far down in the house, the phone began to ring again. It rang for a long time and then it stopped.

Nick walked up and down the terrace. "Look, all the flags are going up. You have to, you know, it's mandatory for the king's birthday. And you have to have a picture of him up on your wall. They come round to check that you've got one. And it has to be big. I've got a nice little one of him when he was a kid, but I'm not sure that'll count."

Then he said, "Sarah. I don't want to interfere, but there are always problems, you know, if you get involved."

"Involved with the natives, oh, yeah, that'd never do!" She had to call out to him, from the golden carpet.

"There are ways of getting involved that aren't intelligent. They don't work. For instance, if you start mounting a campaign about labour relations in a country like this, you'll just come unstuck. And affairs of the heart, too."

"But we're all human, Nick. Hey, it's hard to talk to you when you're walking around."

He came back, squatted down. An intelligent man, but also remote and infuriating. "Being human means being intelligent. Not splashing your feelings all over the place. Wouldn't you agree?"

"I guess so. Excuse me. I shouldn't have said that. But what about you? How do you manage? How do you stay so aloof?"

He looked genuinely surprised. He took a cigarette from the old-fashioned case in his shirt pocket. "I? You think I stay aloof?"

"You seem to avoid involvement, yes. I guess that's aloof."

"I don't allow myself the luxury. I fall in love much too easily to allow myself to get involved with anybody. I'm far too susceptible."

"What about Sacha?"

A gull-shadow cast its fleeting cloud as the big bird wheeled overhead against the dark blue sky.

"What about Sacha?"

"Some people think you're going to marry her."

He burst out laughing. "Sarah, what do you take me for? Sacha? Jesus, I'd rather marry a man-eating tiger."

Then, the quick scuff of *babouches* coming up the stairs, slowing towards the top. Omar arrived on the roof terrace, panting.

"Nick, telephone. Nick—come down. The police, in Chichaoua. They are taking them to the hospital in Marrakesh. An accident! Please, come—they have to speak with you!"

"What happened? What accident?"

Nick tucked his shirt into his jeans and buttoned up the front. He ran his hands through his hair. Omar panted and trembled and was close to tears. "The car. The one with Aziz and *Monsieur* Antoine. They crash, on the road to Marrakesh. There is a truck, with oranges, coming from the south. The roads are blocked for the king. This truck comes from a side road. The car is hit. Oh, come quickly, they will die!"

He began to sob loudly. Nick gripped his shoulder with one hand and massaged it with his fingers. "Omar, tell me. How badly are they hurt?"

Nick left and ran downstairs to the phone. Omar stood with his face in his hands.

"Ah, Sarah, Aziz, he is my friend, he is my friend."

"But Aziz was driving. How can he have driven into anything? He is so careful. Omar, what's happened to him, how badly is he hurt?"

"I don't know. Perhaps they will tell Nick, not me. He is alive, *Hamdulillah*. You know, that road is not good for trucks, they come up from the south because they cannot pass on the high road through the mountains, the Tizi n' Test road. Ah, Sarah, my friend, we must pray. You know, I would give my life for that man."

She stood and held on to both his arms, feeling nauseous.

"Sarah? Are you not well?"

She mumbled and pushed past him and went to vomit in the little shower room where Yann used to wash. She held on to the wall, cold and shaking.

"Sarah! Come, sit down inside. I will get you a tisane."

She came out, shivering. "Omar, there is something I have to tell you."

"No, do not tell me. It is better not. I have seen Aisha. It is better we forget these things, you understand? Come Sarah. All of us, we will forget."

She looked down at the carpet Nick had been lying on. There was an uneaten orange that he had just begun to peel. There was a bunch of keys. There was a scrap of paper with a drawing on it like a wishbone, or two roads meeting. There was a metal ring. She stared at these things that lay close together on the golden carpet and felt she couldn't move, until she had understood what they were. There was a game, called Kim's Game, where you had to memorize a selection of random objects. Her stomach heaved and wrenched. Then Omar tugged at her arm, "Sarah, come down with me, we will go together." And she went.

Downstairs she sipped the thyme tea that Omar brewed for her, and breathed in the steam from the pot. Suddenly she'd thought it: I'm either pregnant or I've been poisoned. This could not simply be shock; she'd been feeling ill on and off for days.

Nick came back from the phone.

"They're both alive, anyway. I'm to call back later for the details. Don't worry, Sarah. I'll take you to Marrakesh, if you want. I have to go to the airport, I'll give you a lift, so you can go and see him." His kindness, a hand stroking back her hair even, brought her to tears. She sniffed and thanked him. It was all right to be looked after, to be weak. But, oh, God, pregnancy or poison, which was worse?

*   *   *

The men came up on the roof that day and nailed up the red bunting so that this house, like all the others, wore red for the king. They climbed up a wooden ladder and clambered about shouting to each other. Down in the town, in the Place Moulay Hassan and by the quay, makeshift wooden stages had been hammered up overnight for the singing and entertainments. It was all red and starred with the five-pointed star of Morocco, the sign of the absent king. Sarah lay back on the carpet in the shade with the books that Sacha had lent her on sex, magic and Islam. The men came and went. The wind lifted the red banners and carried them streaming sideways. The hours went past and the day grew hotter, yet she shivered from time to time with sudden cold. Omar brought another tisane. He stroked her forehead and urged her to go indoors.

But she wanted to be up there, high on the roof where the air was fresh, on the golden carpet where Nick had lain: remembering the carpets of paradise and the flick from their fringes that is the allowed taste of pleasure on this earth. She rearranged the objects he had left.

Nick came back and dropped down beside her, joining his own dense shadow on the white floor. "Sarah, how are you feeling?"

"A little better, but I'm definitely sick. Have you heard from the hospital yet?"

"He had some concussion, and a broken leg. Antoine's just cut and bruised."

"Nick, I thought I'd killed them both."

"What are you talking about?" Nick frowned.

"Magic. Or something like it. A connection between an intention and an outcome, if you like."

She told him of her conversation with Aisha about medicine.

"You really think that Aisha messing about with a few herbs in the kitchen could make a truck come out and hit Aziz's car? On the road to Marrakesh, a hundred kilometres from here? You really think that? Sarah. Come on."

He picked up the copy of *Sex, Magic and Islam.* "In that case, I'm going to change your reading diet. Why don't you go back to old Yann's treasure book?"

"Sacha lent it to me. I'm really reading about nationalism in the thirties. Anyway, things happen like that, you said it yourself."

"You really think Aisha did magic for you and made the car crash?"

"I think that's what I'm afraid I think, yeah."

"Sarah, this is nuts." Nick said, "You're a journalist. Look, don't you think your job as a writer is to see the real connections between things and not get taken in by the false ones? You may be sick, but you have to see this in perspective. It was a coincidence. It's a dangerous road. Aziz may have been tired. The truck driver may have been smoking hashish. Anything could have happened. But it wasn't magic."

"Why not?"

"This is a deeply superstitious country and I'm beginning to think you've been here too long. Can you imagine even thinking this in New York? Sarah."

"But I'd been thinking I wanted Antoine stopped. I'd even been thinking of killing him."

"Look, wanting somebody to stop doing what they're doing isn't the same as killing them. You haven't killed anybody or even injured them. It was an accident. Right? You have done nothing. I don't know what Aisha did, but it certainly didn't cause that accident."

"You really think that?"

"Of course I do."

"But you said you'd be a fool not to believe in the poison."

"Sarah, I live here. It's different." He took out his cigarette case and offered her one, but she shook her head.

"D'you mind not smoking, just for now?"

"Sarah, God, you aren't preggers, are you? I hope you don't mind my asking."

"I don't know. I don't know what I am, I just feel nauseous."

"Well, you know, if I can do anything to help—when we go to Marrakesh, you could see a doctor."

"Thanks. But you know, I have friends in Marrakesh. An old college friend. She'd help me."

Nick looked relieved. "Look," he said gently. "You came here to get to know Morocco. You've let it in much more than I have, you've been braver than me, you've got involved in ways I haven't. But you don't belong here. You're going home. Just remember that, Sarah. It's all going to look very weird to you then, whatever happens, you won't even believe you said the things you just said to me. It's not our world. It's not our way of thinking. And you need to look after yourself just now, and keep these ideas out of your head, or you'll get lost. So, will you do this? Come on. Let's get you feeling better, then tomorrow I'll drive you to Marrakesh to see him."

He put out a hand to her.

"Come on, let's go down. Soon there's going to be no shade up here."

"Nick, what are these?"

"Oh, they must've fallen out of my pocket."

She followed him, her head splitting. Perhaps it was cracking in two, one half of her brain in the western world, the other stuck here in the world of this house, this city, the maze of its streets, the complexity and contrariness of its beliefs. Suddenly she thought of Bill. "It's too like Europe, I can't stay here." She remembered walking out of that room in Marrakesh without another thought, because she knew that he was wrong. If he had gone where the danger was for him, she had followed her own route, and it was here, it was inside her. In her room, where the window was open and the white curtain sucked back with the wind from the sea, the book that was open on her thuya table had its pages blowing as if meaningless in the gust.

Chapter eighteen

The Death of an Exorcist

The red flags fluttered against the white wall at the end of the square. A slight breeze lifted them towards midday. The whole town was bandaged and swathed in red. Sarah walked down to the quay, carefully staying in the shadow of the wall.

On the narrow wooden bench at the plastic-topped table, she sat and sipped bottled water while Topniveau cooked his fish. Of course, the everyday smells—charcoal, grilled fish, hot bread, cumin, onions—made her nauseous again. The sun was hard overhead here, she shielded her eyes and wrapped a scarf around her head and shivered. Probably she should have stayed indoors.

Topniveau brought a pale pink snapper, so recently alive that its eyes gleamed and its gills were a vivid red.

"You will not have something, Zahrah? Even have a little sole?"

"Not today. Maybe tomorrow." She looked away from the fish. "Just a little mint tea, perhaps."

"Tomorrow I will cook something special for you, *ouacha?* Today you are sick."

The rank salt smell of sardines. The sky coming down closer until there was only its weight and the hardness of the hot, flat land, and herself jammed in between the two.

"Look," said Topniveau, "here are your friends."

Sacha and the exorcist. The two of them walked across the flat expanse of the Place Moulay Hassan. Sacha, with her hand in the crook of his arm, as if he were blind. He seemed to wobble on his feet. He put up a hand to ward off the sun. Sarah, watching, felt suddenly sorry for him, wanting to push the sun away. Walking like an invalid with a nurse, he tottered beside Sacha to a place in the shade, under a tipped umbrella. He looked terrible.

Sacha waved to Topniveau to come.

"Bring him some water! He feels faint. It is the sun. Quick!"

Topniveau slid sardines from the blackened grill on to a plate for a customer and seized a water bottle to carry it across. Over on the dock, some fishermen dumped their catch and the gulls flew down screaming. The air was full of their noise, the beat of wings. Sacha held the man against her like a mother. His pale face tipped against the brown of her neck. His bulk slid gently sideways till he was against her breast. She looked down on him. For a moment it looked as if they were embracing. But no, she was simply propping him up, holding him braced against her to stop him from falling. She looked up, screamed. "He is not well, help! There, Jean, ah, take some water. It is that house! It is not good! But he should not be in the sun either, this sun is terrible, terrible. Somebody, help me!"

Sarah ran, her head pounding, to where Sacha sat with him, and Topniveau and his brother followed. The man's eyes were half closed, he murmured and groaned. His weight was too much for Sacha, who gestured to Topniveau, to the other men, to support him. A pale, fat man caught in pain and sunlight, his hand moved like a baby's to feel the air, and all the dark-faced men holding him up, holding Sacha up, made a little struggling crowd around him. Then his mouth opened and his eyes opened and one arm shot out suddenly across the table as if he were grasping for something. Topniveau came from behind and caught him as he slipped backwards, he held him under the armpits that were stained with sweat. A spasm shot him forwards again and he fell across the white-topped table among the fish-stains, his head between his outstretched arms.

Sacha screamed, "A doctor, someone get a doctor! An ambulance! Sarah, run! *Nom de Dieu, vite, vite!*"

Topniveau's black head was down close to the man's throat, his hands felt across his chest for the heart. He was tender and expert as if gutting a fish.

He looked up. *"Il est mort."*

The man slid from his hands. The body lay out heavy and relaxed across the table.

Nick came striding across the Place Moulay Hassan, with Omar beside him. They both wore dark glasses. They walked like cowboys through swinging doors, pushing everything aside. Now no one need do anything, none of them need move.

*　*　*

The last Sarah saw of Jean Simon was a weighty body piled into the back of Nick's hired car, slumped right across two seats. His shirt had pulled out at the back and there was an expanse of pale flesh. With the life gone out of him he looked heavier, bigger. Omar, Nick, Topniveau and two fishermen had dragged and heaved him to the car. It was like a scene from a film, when everything takes a long time and nothing fits and you are supposed to laugh on that account. But nobody laughed, not even when a foot with an expensive shoe on it trailed out of the car and had to be shoved back inside. When one human being is dead, it takes five to move him, Sarah saw; and the living men push and heave and pant to deal with death, to bundle it away.

Sacha and she stood and watched. It was not what women had to do, thank God.

Sacha herself was sobbing and catching her breath in little hiccups. The fish sellers on the quay waved their arms just the way that the live lobsters and crabs waved theirs. A few tourists stood in little groups and then were embarrassed by their own curiosity and shuffled on, pretending not to look. Nick, in the driver's seat, waved and called to Sacha to go with him. She walked to the car on her high heels, her hips shaking. Seeing her into the car was like seeing off royalty. There was a silence as they left. Even the gulls stopped screaming as they fell upon a pile of fish bones and offal tipped down for them on the ground.

The car turned slowly in a three-point turn and left the Place to drive away up the Avenue Mohammed v.

Topniveau said, "It is better to die like that than to die slowly. He will feel nothing."

He spoke as if life were a burden. He stood with his hands folded, like someone at a graveside. "There was a man here who died and they buried him without knowing he was still alive. He was only dead for a few minutes. Then he was alive. When he was in the ground he awoke and knocked on the lid of the box he was in and they had to dig and let him out. It often happens. But when the heart has stopped, usually the person is dead. I think that man will not wake up again."

He shook his head at a couple of tourists, telling them he would cook no more that day.

Sarah stood beside him and watched as the car turned the corner and merged with the rest of the traffic out on the road to the hospital, on the far outskirts of town.

* * *

"It's surprising how heavy a dead body is. Why do you put on so much weight when you die? Is it that when you're alive you don't let yourself be your true weight? Or is it that life itself is light and makes you sort of float, like a buoy in water?"

Nick walked up and down, smoking, although when he saw Sarah he stubbed his cigarette out.

Sacha said, "You must get the police, Nick. You must tell them. You must have a thorough investigation. Heart attack! It's rubbish. You know it. You cannot fool me. He was suffering. You cannot be that sensitive and not suffer from what goes on in this house. I myself,

I suffer, I cannot sleep. Sarah too is not well. Who will be next? You must do something, Nick, you must stop this wickedness, or I will do something myself, I tell you."

They all stood in the hall, beside the unlit fire. Omar went to make tea.

Nick said, "I talked to the doctor at the hospital, Sacha, and he confirmed that Jean died of a heart attack. It might have been brought on by too much food or too strong sun, or both—but it was heart failure."

"But these doctors!" Sacha said, "They are useless! They will say anything. Moroccans are all the same. You cannot believe anything."

She clasped her hands before her like a much older woman and her distress was real. Nick stood over her and looked down. He put out a hand and grasped her shoulder in a sudden gesture of tenderness that then tightened and ended in a little shake.

"The police will come anyway, as a matter of formality. You can't have somebody dropping dead practically on your doorstep and not have the police take an interest. But I shall tell them that I am certain it was a heart attack and show them the doctor's certificate. Okay?"

Sacha sat up and sniffed and smoothed back her hair. Omar came in with his tea that smelled of hot crushed mint and poured it from a height with his usual grace. He had not made one comment on the exorcist's death. Except for the quiet twittering of the birds in their cage, there was silence in the house. Sarah sat with Sacha and they sipped their tea as if they were at a tea party. Sacha even had her pinkie crooked as she raised her little glass.

The chief of police and Nick went to sit at the table in the window. Two other policemen sauntered in and smoked cigarettes in the hall. They were young and smooth and well fed in their pale uniforms decorated with red. They leaned on the iron balustrade and looked down into the well of the house and murmured to each other in Arabic. The chief sat with Nick and thumbed through papers. Sarah looked down on them from where she stood leaning with Aisha on the upper floor, arms folded along the iron balustrade, seeing the black, cropped heads of the policemen, Nick's smooth cap of light brown hair.

The chief of police had his hand inside the birdcage and was trying to get the male budgie to sit on his gloved finger. There was the murmur of voices and Nick's laugh. The chief of police closed the door of the cage carefully again. The papers flicked through experienced hands. Another awkward fact had been disposed of, Sarah thought. Nick had become fluent in Arabic in just a few months. It was just a matter of a little friendly chat and some papers shuffled and possibly some money changing hands. It was just a formality. The king's official birthday was about to begin, the *Fête* was under way, and there was little time to spare: the police were busy, the roadblocks had to be maintained, they had to keep an eye on who was coming in and going out of town. The death of Jean Simon was, after all, a straightforward affair. A heart attack, yes, it was unfortunate, but this climate had never been good for Europeans, and you have lived here long enough, *Monsieur*, to be aware of that. That was what they would be saying, down there, in yet another men's meeting; the facts, rearranged, always fell in a particular pattern, the one which would make least trouble for those in charge.

Then the chief collected his bored men and they all clattered down the stairs in their clean boots. Nick leaned where the young policemen had leaned, and was motionless. Sarah saw the top of his head and his shoulders in the white shirt and a tanned, languid hand dangling a cigarette over the parapet. Aisha, once the police had gone, slipped away downstairs, without a word. It was over. Whatever Nick thought privately, order had been maintained.

An hour later, Sacha, clearing papers from the table, putting glasses away, said, "You know what really happened. You know it, Nick knows it. These English, such liars. They cover everything up. They want everything covered over. And Aisha, where is she? Hiding. She will not dare to come out. Ha, of course not. Sarah, you have read the books I gave you? Then you will understand. I have seen this before. One day a man is well and the next day he is dead. The police here are so corrupt, they will never investigate. Of course, he gives them money. Otherwise they would not go away like that. Where is the investigation? Where is the justice? I know what I know, Sarah. You will not convince me otherwise."

"Sacha, you know it was nothing to do with Aisha."

"I know what I know, Sarah. Let me tell you. And you too. You are sick, *n'est-ce pas?*"

Omar came in, a towel over his shoulder, and took the tray of tea things left by Nick and the chief of police. "He looked sick, that man, when he came. He had a bad colour."

*   *   *

Nick said, "Sacha, I am going to London on Monday. I want you to look after things. I'm leaving you in charge. Okay? You understand?"

"I understand. I understand you, Nick. I understand you only too well."

Nick said, "D'you know what the chief of police said to me? He said my picture of the king wasn't big enough. Said I'll have to get a bigger one by tomorrow. What do you think of that?"

Aisha came back to where Sarah was sitting with a spoon lifted high and approached her as if she were a baby.

"What is it?"

"Cumin. Very good for the stomach, you will see. Here, take it. I take this too."

She stood over Sarah in her scarlet gold-trimmed dress, her sleeves rolled, her arms slight and soft-skinned but powerfully veined. She mimed swallowing, the way people do to encourage small children. Sarah swallowed what felt like a spoonful of dust. The smell of cumin was strong but there was no taste to it, only dusty dryness. She choked and Aisha handed her a glass of water.

"There. Now you will be better."

"Thank you, *merci* Aisha."

Aisha stood back. "She will go," she said.

"Who will?"

"That woman from Marrakesh. As soon as the *Fête* is over, she will go."

"I don't think she will. Nick's going to London and he says he's leaving her in charge."

"Nick will never do that. Yann will come back and he will not have her here. You wait, you see."

"Hmm." The last thing she'd heard from Yann had been: See you in Key West.

"How is your sickness, Sarah?"

"Better. The cumin seems to be working."

Aisha put out a hand and touched her shoulder. Her face was softer, reflective.

She said, "Good. *C'est bien* Sarah, I am glad that you are better. We will all be better now that man has gone, I think. Tell me, do you sometimes miss your home?"

"Sometimes." It was hard to remember where her real home was; she thought of her mother's house on Cape Cod, and that was enough to make tears stand in her eyes. Lavender, fuchsia, lilac growing in the gardens; low, mossy stonewalls, the softness of grass.

"Cry, Sarah, it is good to cry. It is sometimes hard to be a long time away from home. I will not leave my home. All my life I have lived in this town. Since I was young, in this house."

Sarah laughed, and then the tears came and Aisha held her to her bony chest with a firm hand, patting her as if she was Souad. "Good, Sarah, good. You let this badness go when you cry."

At last Sarah straightened, rubbed her face, accepted the handkerchief Aisha gave her. "Thanks. Aisha, what exactly did you do when you worked for Madame Sadia?"

"I looked after her friends. They were good days. When this house was a woman's house. Men came here, yes, but only to enjoy and then they went away. *Monsieur* Nick, when he speaks of her, does not understand."

"Did you hear, Madame Sadia's dead?" Nick waved a newspaper.

"Apparently it really is true, this time. She was found dead in her bathroom in Agadir. It's in the paper. She killed her maid and then committed suicide. She drank a lot of course, and probably took drugs too."

"What was she like, Nick?" Sarah asked him, thinking of Aisha. This house was a women's house, men came here but only to enjoy…

"Hey, you're looking better. Are you better, Sarah? Oh, Sadia, a queen. The most beautiful woman in Morocco, I told you. She was a kind of myth. But nobody can keep that sort of thing up for ever. She was probably just a lonely old bat underneath. Omar, could you just ring through to Royal Air Maroc and confirm my flight?"

Chapter nineteen

The Official Version

The *Fête* was on.

Sacha said, "Sarah, you know, it's a disgrace, this *Fête*. You know what happens, every single man in the place takes all the money he's earned in a week and spends it in one night. The wives are all supposed to come out and celebrate too, but what can they do, they have no money, they have to take their children with them, the babies hanging on their backs, no money even for a sweet or a cake. Then their men don't come home for three whole nights, they're all out there with prostitutes at this very minute, they'll drink as much as they can and then come home on Sunday night and sleep. Meanwhile, there's nothing to eat in the house. It should be stopped. It's a disgrace."

Nick said, "Aren't you exaggerating a bit?"

"I? I never exaggerate. You know me, Nick. When I say something it is the truth. Okay, maybe it is the truth you don't like. When I say I never slept all night because of that terrible serpent on the wall, it was the truth. Not a single time did I shut my eyes. You know that was true."

"If you say so." He smiled and slipped once again out of reach.

*   *   *

In the morning the streets were empty. There was silence in the Place and down by the sea wall. In the afternoon it would all begin again, the red flags waved, the music tuned up to a wild crackling shout. Each evening there were the crowds that moved like sleepwalkers through the streets and down through the Place Moulay Hassan. The face of the king smiled down from the hoardings, the bunting jumped in the wind. In the mornings, on the benches and along the base of the red walls, only the girl prostitutes were awake. They sat huddled together waiting for sunrise to warm them and for someone to buy them coffee. Sarah went down early and they smiled as she passed and murmured, Bonjour.

"*Bonjour, bonjour.*"

"*Bonjour, Madame. Labess, beher?*"

"*Labess.*"

Which means, all's well. And it was. She felt completely better, knowing that neither of the things she had feared were real. Blood flowed, stomach enzymes ate up food, acid broke down its lumps, the kidneys and liver processed what they had to process, hormones shifted, herbal remedies washed through the system and it began its cycles again. She had been sick, as people in this country did get sick, on account of bacteria, not because of fate or the malevolence of others or the determination of future generations to be born. It hadn't happened. But it could have. She had probably been sick for the same reason that the exorcist had; but his weak heart had given out, and hers, strong, set for a lifetime, had not.

Down on the quay early there was the man who fed seagulls. He pulled his scraps from a plastic bag and threw them into the wind and the gulls squawked and hung in the air above him, their feet dangling and beaks ajar. He threw the scraps like a man throwing seed into the wind. A mass of gulls hung about his head and flapped about him. Then they were all down on the pile of scraps and bones.

He took his black bag and left, striding back towards the town. As he passed her, she said *"Labess, beher,"* to him. He paused for just a second and looked at her. He looked at her as if he knew her. It was the look of recognition that made him seem familiar. And recognition means intelligence.

Maybe if you could no longer feed people, you fed birds, instead?

What happened to him?

There were riots in the city. People were hungry. But I never heard what happened. Perhaps nobody knew.

Did you ever think of trying to contact him again?

It was two separate worlds, Sarah. That was what I hadn't understood.

But, Uncle Hajji?

They moved him, to Damascus. They called it a promotion.

It was still early. Sarah went down to Driss the patissier's shop and asked for *café* au lait and croissants. She was fiercely hungry, actually salivating at the smell of the warm freshly baked croissants. Driss also brought orange juice with fresh pulp in it that stung the back of her throat. In the back room with the green painted railings and the canary singing in its cage, there was Omar. He bit into a cake and nodded to her to sit down.

"I always have breakfast here, it's better."

Driss' boy brought through a big wooden tray of croissants from the bake house on the other side of the swing doors and the whole place smelled of hot butter and coffee. The canary shouted and the light was filtered green through the little courtyard garden under the open sky. Driss himself came from a family of generations of patissiers. He said to her that every sunset he went down to the shore to look at the sea and the moon 'because a man has to be alone with himself.' Fishing, he said, was a sure way to conquer fear. If you fish, you will not be afraid. Anything can happen to you and you will not be afraid. You have simply become yourself.

Omar said, "Are you better now?"

"Much better. Aisha gave me some cumin."

He nodded and stirred sugar into his coffee.

"It's good. You had too much of the sun. You should go to the *hammam*, that would make you quite well. It is what we do to feel better. It purifies you. Or, you could go to the *baraka*, the man who heals."

Fishing, cumin, the *baraka*, the *hammam*: anything, to regain peace of mind.

The room was filling up with men who came in for breakfast and the canary shouted louder than ever.

"Sarah, you are wrong about many things. And also Aziz. Aziz isn't from here. Aziz is from France. It is different for him, for you."

"Why, Omar?"

"Well, we are a poor country. We need money. We need tourists. Tourists like to stay where it is clean, where it is safe, not where there are people like Aisha. And those girls, who never make anything clean. It is right that they go. We have to learn this. *Monsieur* Nick is right. And Aziz, he has money from France, where people are civilized, where tourists do not have to be afraid. That is all. I learn this. If I want work, I have to think this way, I have no choice. Now I have to go. It's me who is doing the cleaning now."

"You?"

"I have to work—the cleaning then the reception. I know how to clean, not like these girls. So, no windsurfing today." He smiled an apology.

"That's a shame."

"And without Aziz it is not the same, eh, Sarah?"

"No, it sure isn't."

Their silence registered the hurt of his absence.

"Omar, I wanted to ask you something. The man who feeds seagulls, the one they say was seduced by Aisha Gandisha, who is he? Do you know?"

"You want to know that? He has one name, but the name he had that everybody knew was El Saouiri? That just means, the man from Essaouira. He was a great leader once, they say. But now he is an old man and his brains have gone. Why do you want to know?"

"I just wondered. Why, if people know he was a hero, do they say he's crazy?"

"Because, if you are a leader and you fail, there is shame. It is better that people say he is mad. Otherwise, there is weakness, failure."

"So it's better to be crazy than weak?"

"Of course. There is no blame."

"I'll see you later, Omar. I'm going to Marrakesh today."

"Tell Aziz—tell him, I wait for him. Yes?"

In those days, people did not talk about things. I was sent back to England. The official version was that I was indisposed. The climate was too much for me, that was what they said. Indisposed.

That was the word Marion had used, and in those days it could mean sick, having a period, pregnant, anything female and alarming.

* * *

The official verdict—whose?—was that she was indisposed. Had she in fact been pregnant, or had it been the food, the sun, the atmosphere? I know what it was, Sarah thought. It was the system. It was colonialism. It was usurped power. If you make love with somebody from the native population, you lose your privileges. You are no longer immune. You are no longer quite white. That's what happens: it isn't poison, it isn't female problems—it's oppression—and it makes you feel weak, weaker than anything you can imagine. You've slipped on to the other side, and you can't really ever get back. All you can do is leave.

Marion had probably never articulated this to herself. She was only twenty, half Sarah's age, and it was 1936, more than fifty years ago. She probably thought she was sick. The climate, the food; female delicacy, all that. She probably swallowed that diagnosis. These places, she would have heard, not fit for white women; only men can handle them, the heat, the lack of hygiene. But men handled them by staying in control, and women, by remaining under the control of their men. Like the French consul's wife, Sarah thought. Women lost themselves to Arab men, brown men, men from the subservient colonized population—and yes, all these years after Independence, it still went on. They were shipped home, sick, in disgrace. It wasn't something you could talk about because its name was hidden, it was supposed not to exist. The underside of the colonial story. That was her mother's secret, so unmentionable as to have been forgotten. Amnesia, Alzheimer's, who knew what forces of the body surged to eliminate the truth, collapse memory, remove what could not even be thought? That was what Sarah herself had come to find out. And it was in the depths of her own body that she'd found it—the meal undigested, the egg that had taken a few days to burst from her ovary. There was the sudden discovery, freed by her own innately healthy American body, of what was really at fault.

Part IV
Djma'a el Fnaa

Chapter twenty

The Road to Marrakesh

That's where they crashed, apparently."

Nick waved his right hand, indicating the place. Sarah, beside him in the passenger seat, peered out. They'd come through Chichaoua, where she remembered having stopped on her bus ride out. A road came in from the right and there were a couple of policeman lounging by the roadside making tea on a little burner, their car parked up on the verge. It looked strangely domestic, the tea ritual, the men's careful hands, as Nick slowed the car beside them. The day was still and hot and the leaves on the trees were a tight, pale green. All the way up from the sea there'd been roadblocks and police. They seemed bored with the ritual of stopping and searching cars; they'd been at it all through the days leading up to the *Fête* and all through the weekend. But still, one of the lounging men had waved Nick down.

He braked and parked at the roadside beside the police car. Hatless and in shirtsleeves, one of the men, got up and sauntered over. Nick put a hand out of the window with his American driving licence in it.

"Bonjour, Monsieur."

"Bonjour. Lovely day, isn't it? U.S. Drug Squad."

"Passez, Monsieur."

Then, as they picked up speed again, Nick said, "Otherwise I have to keep giving them money. If you don't give them enough, they find something wrong with one of your tyres, it's a hell of a nuisance. And I've got a plane to catch."

Sarah looked back. The two men were hunkered down on the grass again beside their teakettle. A pack of cards slipped white between brown hands.

"Easy way to make a living," said Nick.

"So that was where the truck came out? You'd think you'd see its lights."

"It wasn't even quite dark. Sometimes you see less in daylight, and dusk is even trickier. It was on its way up from Taroudannt."

"But Aziz is such a careful driver."

Nick said, "In this country, you can be doing nothing, nothing at all and something'll come out and hit you. You can be as careful as you like."

Silence. The brown earth of the countryside, with its little springtime shoots of green. The line of the Atlas mountains, blue-white, far off to their right. The way she'd come, those months ago. It was actually wonderful to be out of the city, out of the house. She felt as if she'd been going round in decreasing circles lately, like an animal in a maze.

"Nick, about the exorcist."

"Old Jean? I don't think he was really an exorcist. I don't think he had a clue."

"But when you went to the hospital, what happened?"

"Well, he was dead as a doornail on arrival. No question about that. So they took him in and asked me what it was and I said: heart attack. I gave them some money and the guy signed the paper and that was that. Of course, I left Sacha in the waiting room. I didn't want her jumping up and down and putting her oar in, did I?"

"So you don't know for sure that it was a heart attack."

"Well, his heart had stopped, hadn't it? It wasn't still beating."

He accelerated up the straight road and passed a boy herding either sheep or goats up the narrow verge. It was hard to tell which was which; they were all so skinny and covered with dust.

"Sarah, you know what history is? It's the version given by the person who gets there first."

She watched his small firm hands on the wheel as he looked straight ahead.

"Then if the official version was contradicted by another version, it wouldn't have much of a chance."

"Right."

"And if the other version appeared, it would mean that somebody would get into trouble."

"Exactly."

"And the person in whose house this other somebody lived?"

He laughed. "No, Sarah, they'd have nothing on me, and anyway I'd be in L.A. by then, or London, or somewhere. It would be the other somebody, who can't move away, who'd be in for it."

"Aisha."

"Anyway, you don't believe all that stuff, do you, magic and mayhem? Pure superstition, if you ask me."

"You once said that you'd be a fool not to believe it."

"Well, maybe I have to believe it a little bit when I'm here, but not when I'm somewhere else? Geography can make a difference to belief."

"Is that why you're leaving?" She thought, even this amount of geography, even being in a car as opposed to being in a house, does that make a difference?—Nick must have developed his relativist approach for a reason, living in several places as he did. This way, he made himself at home in all of them: talking to the mayor in a small Moroccan town as easily as to film producers in California. She breathed out, laid her arm along the open window, and watched the mountains in the distance. The High Atlas: another place, thousands of feet above sea level, another layer of Morocco, where people probably wore different clothes and had different beliefs. Aisha had told her that the mountain people were Berber and had been there long before the Arabs had arrived.

"I'm going to check out my London house to make sure the pipes didn't freeze and then I'm going to L.A. to make a movie."

"And if someone didn't believe the official version, they'd be barking up the wrong tree?"

He flicked his greenish glance sideways.

"You're the writer, Sarah. Do what you like with it. My only rule in life is not to hurt people."

"Are you sure you don't hurt people?" The people who'd lived in the house next door, did they really all have better lives once he'd moved them out?

"God, you have a literal mind. I've just got out of a police interrogation; do I have to have another one? No, of course I'm not sure. I just try not to. I try to circumvent pain, for myself and for others. And if you must have it in a nutshell, which is what you seem to like, if a murder investigation got under way it would be very bad for a certain person or people and they might land in jail. And if I was in L.A. or London and not in a position to get them out by what we call over here 'sweet pastry', then they might stay there for a very long time. And Moroccan jails aren't fun."

"So you did it for Aisha."

"And Souad. Don't forget that kid's sort of my niece. Bloody Yann's the closest thing I have to a male relation in this world, apart from Jake. And Jake could well be Yann's son. You didn't realize that, did you, Ms. Sleuth?"

She was silent, taking in some of the implications of what he said.

He lit a cigarette from the dashboard lighter. "I never know exactly what happens. You can't, in this country. Nobody can. That's why they have to have a king, to give them the official version. Then everybody's happy. If you question it, all hell breaks loose. So, you can't know the cause of things, but if you have money, and a little intelligence, you can make sure that the effects aren't too dire. That's all I do. I try to minimize the damage."

"I see."

He gave her one of his quick sweet smiles and they began to approach the suburbs of Marrakesh, the Atlas still a rim of blue-white, dusted still with snow. The edge of the world.

"Nick, I want to ask you one more thing. What do you think will happen with Antoine Dupuy and Aziz, and was it an accident?"

"That's two things. Two for the price of one?"

"Okay, two things. You can trust me. I won't talk." She felt like someone out of a Dashiell Hammett novel; but it was an improvement being a fast dame instead of a Victorian victim.

"Trust a writer? Never! Still, it makes a good story, doesn't it. And sometimes a good story is more entertaining than the truth. That's why I make movies, by the way. It's understood there. Well, look, maybe somebody's got it in for Antoine. I don't know. It wasn't the driver from Taroudannt. But other people are interested in what happens in Sidi Kaouki. It's a holy place as you know, it's people's home, and it's also the best stretch of beach in Morocco. It's three completely different things, depending on who you are. So take your pick. There's an American hotel chain that'd kill to get its hands on it. Well, I kind of like the Moroccan shoreline the way it is and I don't like to think of it turned into Disneyland overnight. So I sort of threw in my lot with poor old Antoine. But you see, when somebody tries to get his car off the road just when he's going back to France to raid the kitty to pay off the mayor, I get the message: Antoine's a loser. He's old French money compared to American megabucks; he hasn't a snowflake's chance in hell. Somebody else's going to get their greedy hands on this coastline in the end, I'm afraid. But Antoine grew up in Tlemcen, he's a *pied noir*, did you know? He hates North Africans. A tourist empire would be something of a revenge—he could reduce them all to servants again. That was what he had in mind."

"Oh. So there wasn't an accident?"

"There was a truck full of oranges. There was a crash. There was a man called Jean Simon, and he died. But who can say what was or wasn't an accident? Are these things random, or connected? I prefer to think they are random. The idea of an accident lets all of us, not only the villains, go free."

"What do you think will happen?"

"I hope it'll all quieten down. Antoine and Aziz will go back to France—sorry, Sarah, but what's a windsurfer with a broken leg got going for him? I'll tell the authorities back home that Antoine's out of the market, he's just looking for a retirement home in Sidi Kaouki. You've seen his rickety house that was supposed to be the seat of his empire, haven't you? He'll get his retirement pretty damn quick from the people in Marseille if he screws up on this deal, but he can save his skin and settle down to be a nice guy in the sun if he plays it right. When Aziz's mended up he can come back and be the windsurf champion of Essaouira again, if his leg works. Then the guys can all go on playing football on the sand and Aisha's relations can go on pottering around Sidi Kaouki in peace, which is what they've been doing for centuries, in between killing each other."

'Minimizing the damage.' She'd never thought of it as a possible philosophy before. She watched him as he spoke; his small firm hands on the wheel, the set profile, the blowing, fine brown hair with its strands of grey. This was probably as close as she would ever get to knowing Nick; it was probably as close as anybody got.

"Sooner or later, somebody will come and do it anyway. Unless the world changes overnight and people start wanting different things. I can't change the world overnight; I can just do a little stalling in the face of the inevitable. Give it time, if you like. Buy time. That's all that money can do, really. Hey, look! We're nearly there."

He swerved to avoid a trotting mule with a man astride.

"Can I chuck you out at the taxi rank and leave you to find the hospital? There only is one. You'll recognize it by the queues outside."

"That's fine. Nick—"

"What?"

"Thanks for the ride, and everything."

"What, everything?"

"Letting me live in your house. And for the stories."

"Well, honour among thieves, do what you like with them, I always think plagiarism is the sincerest form of flattery. Good luck, and give my love to Aziz, who as you've noticed, is an unusually nice human being. And something-or-other to Antoine if you see him. Tell him he's lucky to have come out of it with his skin; no don't, don't tell him anything."

He swerved between donkey carts and mopeds at the big intersection that marks the beginning of the sprawl of outer Marrakesh. Huge buses, taxis, bikes and people on foot begging in among the slowed down cars, the sea of constant movement. Animals and people and pieces of metal, all were jumbled up, swept into what made the city. The pink walls of the old town were up ahead. He slowed and drew in to a taxi rank where all the drivers were yelling out their trade.

"This do?"

"Yes. Nick, just one more thing."

She was out of the car, shouldering her small bag.

"What?"

"Sacha wants to marry you. There's a plot."

He grinned, gunned the engine as she closed the door.

"No chance. Me and Sidi Kaouki both are going to keep our virginity, at least in the short term. Sarah?"

"Yeah?"

"Good luck."

Chapter twenty-one

A Narrow Space

When Aziz woke, everything hurt. It was the third day of waking with everything hurting and having to remember all over again what had happened. He moved an inch at a time. His jaw and the side of his face were covered with dressings, so his fingers found softness, as if he were a wrapped parcel. His ribs hurt with each breath, their cracked cage only just holding in his heart and lungs. He was like a crustacean, the hard shell of his pain holding in something soft, jellylike, entirely vulnerable. His brain; how had his skull held in his brain, under such crushing, the weight of what had hit it? He remembered glass flying. The smell of crushed oranges. Oranges rolling in front of his eyes upon the road. The voices of men standing over him, very far up. The weight holding down his leg. Oranges, headlights, darkness. Splinters. A half moon.

Dead or alive, he was stuck now. He waited for nothing. They brought him bowls of soup, injected him, gave him pills, looked at him, hurt him, and went away. Whatever had been happening before the impact of that sudden huge blow from the right of him, was over. If this was his life, it was new. Bandaged, softened, hidden in white, he was a chrysalis, a being entirely given over to whatever change was inflicted on it. He felt under the hard bolster for his wallet, which was all he had now.

* * *

Sarah rode to the hospital on the back of a scooter; the young driver said it was really a taxi; he had a licence but hadn't been able to afford to run a car for several months.

"Going to see your boyfriend, are you?" The young man yelled back to her in French. She hung on to his narrow back as they twisted and dipped through the traffic. They stopped at traffic lights.

"Yes, he's been in a car accident. Broken leg."

"You should take him something to eat! They don't feed them in there. Want me to stop on the way? Get him some dates or something?"

They stopped at a market stall and she bought dates, almonds, bananas, a loaf of bread, still hot in its slip of brown paper.

"Does he smoke?"

"Oh, yes."

"Take him some cigarettes. He'll want cigarettes. Oh, and a paper too."

"He can't read Arabic."

"Can't read?"

"Only French."

She bought *Libération* and *Le Monde*, aware that she knew nothing about Aziz's reading habits. Then she saw Tahar Ben Jalloun's novel, *La Nuit Sacreé* and took a chance on that. The bike buzzed away up the boulevard towards the new suburbs where the hospital was, in a maze of unmarked roads and bare open lots with just a few palm trees growing where everything else had been uprooted. The hospital was the same pink as the old city walls, but smooth and hard-surfaced. She loosened herself from the scooter and climbed off.

"How much do I owe you?"

"Give me five dirhams."

"Five? That's nothing."

"It'll do. I enjoyed the ride."

"Thank you. *Shok'ran*. I did too."

"Good luck, then. *Bonne chance*. Tell your man good luck. Tell him: Get out of hospital as soon as he can. Tell him from me. My name is Abdel. It means, who is come from God."

"*Au revoir*, Abdel. Have a good day."

"*Hamdulillah*. I will pray for you."

She'd imagined long corridors and rows of men in beds, as in pictures of the Crimean War. Starving, dark faces turning to watch for the nurses' approach. But here was a reception room full of women with screaming babies. She asked for Aziz by name. It was the first time she'd used his surname.

"Ah, Aziz Serhane he came in with a French man, yes. This way. Khamed, you show Madame the way?"

The orderly took her by the hand. He was skinny as a boy but his face was old on a child's body. He wore a flapping white jacket over dirty jeans and his humped chest was frail and bare.

They scuttled along corridors. There were more people waiting, lines of them lounging against the wall. A corner. A curtain. A room with beds in it. Six pairs of men's eyes turned towards the entrance. He was in the corner, hung in a contraption like the scaffolding put up for the king's feast. His leg had grown out of all proportion to the rest of him. He was a small man with black eyes like all the rest and a giant stiff white limb that held him still. The side of his face was blanked out in white, cancelled. A half moon. But half a smile spread over the part she could see and drew her in.

"Sarah. I did not expect you."

She walked towards him on sticky linoleum. "But I came. Nick gave me a ride. I wanted to see you. How are you?"

"As you see. But I am lucky. I could be dead. Antoine too."

"Where is Antoine?"

"In a room alone. His head is hurt, but he will be all right. He pays to be alone. Like a cat, to suffer alone. Sit down, *mon amie*. Here. What did you bring me?"

She gave him the wrapped fruit, cigarettes, papers and book.

"Sarah! It's not my birthday. Ah, I need a smoke."

He ripped open the pack of Camels at once, and lit up. "You know, they don't give us anything here. I am lucky to have a sheet. But I can't stay too long, they do not wash them. You know, they give us *harira* every day? Every day, the same soup. You know what I'm dreaming of now? *Pâté. Pâté de foie.* Camembert. A good steak. With pommes frites and a salad. *Coeurs d'artichauts…* mmm. *Tarte aux pommes.* Coffee, ah, coffee. All we get here is mud."

He tore a piece of the round, warm, loaf and chewed in between inhalations of smoke.

"Still, in Morocco there is good bread. *Tiens*, this is new, did you just buy it?"

She told him about the messenger from God on the moped and he laughed. "You are a crazy woman, Sarah. You believe anything."

"But I'm usually right!"

"I want to kiss you. You don't mind?" He stubbed out the cigarette and put the remains of the loaf on his plaster cast with the newspapers, like a still life.

"Of course I don't mind."

"No, it is just these others, that they see us. Hang this jacket on the frame, there, then we are private."

He struggled out of his buttonless, off-white jacket and she hung it on the bed frame as if to dry. Then she went in and held him close. He smelled unwashed, musky.

"Come on top of me. It won't hurt, if you do not lean too hard. Forget my leg, it is only sculpture now."

Her cheek on his smooth chest. She began to cry.

"What is it, Sarah? What's wrong?"

"So much…"

"Could be worse. I could be dead, no?"

"I know, that's just it."

"You cry because I am not dead?"

"Yes, yes!"

It was relief: it was seeing him, but also being out of the house, alone with him in a different place where she was able to act, move, be. She cried into his chest and into the rough, laundered sheet that smelled strongly of bleach. She thought of the bleach seller going round with his endless bird-cry—"Gabi! Gabi!"—Of the scaffolding outside the window and the narrow street walked every day, the city gate, the way to the windsurf centre, the two coloured sails bucking and dipping on a dark blue sea.

"Oh, I can't do more. It's so nice, so nice. I wish I could do more." He groaned exaggeratedly. She laughed, out of her tears. He hammed it up, frustration; rolled his eyes, to make her laugh more, make it possible.

The jacket that protected them slithered and dropped. Five men out there shifted and pretended not to watch.

"Can I have one of your cigarettes?"

"It's better if you take a taste of mine." He spoke in a low voice.

"Oh, I forgot. You don't want them to think I'm a whore."

"Sarah, of course not. Don't be angry. I tell you, it is so good to see you." He hitched himself up in the bed a couple of inches, patted the place on the sheet for her to sit up, look respectable.

"For the last time, eh? You're going back to France." Suddenly, she knew. "You're married." It was not even a question.

"Yes. I should have told you, *n'est-ce pas?*"

"Of course you should." She sat upright, not even looking at him. That was what had been there that she hadn't seen. That fact, that detail; so close that it had been invisible.

He said, "But what would be different? That is what I ask myself."

She took his cigarette and drew on it. "I know what you think, we're all hookers, whores, we have sex all the time, we have no feelings, it doesn't matter if you lie to us, it's just a game! Do you lie to your wife, too?"

"No. And I don't lie to you. There is one life, there. And another, here."

"How convenient." She thought of Nick' theory of geographical belief, and wondered if men of all races held it, always had. A wife in every port. Relative truth, shifting all over the place, leaving women dumb and helpless in its wake.

He wondered how to make this confusion clear. How to tell her, and be believed. That he and Anne had been apart, but that now he was injured he had nowhere else to go, she was his home. He'd been thinking about it while lying here, pinned in place by his broken bones, the failures of his body. He could no longer bear being alone out here without his home, his wife and daughter. He wanted only to go home. And now Sarah—*l'Américaine*—was hurting him with her tongue, with her logic, where he was raw, where he couldn't bear to be hurt any more.

He wondered how to tell her that he was weak, not strong like American men. For the moment, he just wanted her to stop hurting him.

"So you'll tell her, will you, you had an affair with a stupid American woman in Morocco, she was just out for a bit of fun, what else could you do? I mean, you're a man, after all. And she'll end up forgiving you and being all understanding, so you can live the rest of your life in domestic peace. Is that it? Is that how it goes?"

It was important, he knew, to let her know what the truth was, and that while she was angry there was no hope of finding it. Let her be angry, he deserved it. But then he would have his say. "No, Sarah. No, that is not it. Listen. You did not want to marry me, did you?"

"No! Of course not. But I didn't want all this to be based on a lie."

"So, you think it was based on a lie? Sarah? You think so? There are also things you did not tell me. Many things. Also, I like you. Maybe, I love you. For the time we are together. Why not?"

She stared at him, as if trying to work out a problem. His ribs hurt, his head throbbed. He didn't want this, not this way, not at all. But she would have it, her anger. Patiently he went on. "What is really wrong, Sarah?"

"That you didn't say you were married, of course."

"But you do not want to marry me?"

"No!" She said it so quickly. "I just want truth. Truth matters, surely?"

"Truth matters. But this friendship between us is true. That is what I think. This—my leg—is true. The truck on the road is true. What happens, is true. You are true, I am true. No?"

Silence.

"Sarah. If anyone is a whore, it is me. I did not use you, I did not buy you, but Antoine bought me. He used me and paid me. He knew me: I wanted new windsurf equipment, money, prestige. To be the only Moroccan here earning French money. He gave me that. So I would act for him, turn people off their land. I didn't know that, Sarah, but I learn fast. You understand? To love, is not be a whore. To act for money, that is prostitution. That is what I have done. I think that this, this smashed body, is my punishment. I think it is an act of God."

"I thought you didn't believe in God."

"Me too. So God makes me believe."

"You don't think he drives a truck full of oranges up the road from Taroudannt, do you?" She sounded sarcastic, and he heard the hurt. He didn't want to hurt her.

So he spoke quietly. It was like walking slowly up to a wild horse, he thought, an animal about to bite. "Not exactly. But I know now he has our lives in his hands. He brings you to me, and he takes you away. For a purpose. Can you believe that?"

"I'm not sure."

"Sarah, I have to tell you. He wanted me to go to France, Antoine. Not just to take him to the airport. I decided I couldn't do that, that if I did I'd be a slave. I told him: No. I thought I would leave him and drive back to you. Then the truck came."

In the narrow space between bed and wall, between trapped limbs and bandages, between words, between cultures, she tried, against her feelings, simply to understand. The gaps of upbringing, of gender, of expectation of life. All you could do, in the end, was listen to the other person, the person who, out of the whole varied world, you had chosen to love. If you wanted any truth, that was; if you wanted your life to be based on anything other than projection or imaginings or the myth of yourself. She softened towards him at last, her own version beginning its fading.

"Your wife, is she Moroccan?" Her voice was different. Deeper, as if she spoke from a different place.

He looked so relieved. His hand moved close to hers, it lay beside hers on the rough bleached sheet, she looked at their two hands the way she had when he had first come to her room, and she laid her fingers so that they touched his own, just touched, didn't hold.

He said, "No, she is French. We met in school. We married young, so nobody could send me away, you understand? She was nice to me. *Elle était gentille.* It's not easy now in France, to be married to me, the atmosphere is not good. But I go back there because I can't be a Moroccan, wear the *d'jellaba*, earn six dirhams an hour. I have been in France since I was three. You see?"

"What will you do, Aziz?"

"Study, I think. Become a teacher. Now I have understood I'm not stupid, that it's just racism that makes me think that. Funny, I had to come to Morocco to discover that, with an American woman who now I think hates me. *C'est drôle, n'est-ce pas?*"

"I don't...I don't hate you. Of course I don't. It was a shock, that was all. But I helped you to find that out?"

"You, because you do not think I'm stupid. You listen, you are interested."

"And that made the difference?"

"Yes. It is the first time, I think."

"Surely your wife doesn't think you're stupid?"

"She has known me a long time. In school, she knew me."

He glanced up at her, guileless. She thought, I trusted him completely, he didn't tell me the truth, this truthful man; and now I trust him again.

"Yes," he said, "I think she thinks that. She is French, maybe she can't help it. So, *chérie*, I want to show you something. So you understand."

Under the bolster again for the battered wallet. The photograph, a colour print of a little girl with curly hair and his smile. He held it for her to see, she took it in her hand.

"That is my daughter. Félicité, happiness, le *bonheur*, that is her name."

"She's lovely. How old is she?"

"Five. She is at school now, the *école maternelle*."

She looked, then handed back the photograph. As once he'd handed back the photo she carried of Marion and Abdel Jadid. These captured likenesses, carried with us to determine the course of a life. These hostages. All the time he'd been with her, he'd had this photograph in his wallet.

"I thought to work was enough, for a man. Now I know, I will go home. You say you miss me, *mon amie*, I miss you too. But what I miss most is myself. I miss Aziz. You showed me who he is, this Aziz. Not just a man blown on the wind, you see. Also a father, husband, maybe even teacher. So I have to thank you, from the bottom of my heart."

And he laid his hand on his heart in that archaic gesture she would not forget, the one his ancestors had used for generations, when they spoke of hearts, and love.

"I won't see you again," she said. It was, had to be, the truth. How hard, and yet how real. She thought, you have to prefer reality, however hard, because it is all there is.

"In this life, everything is possible, *insh'allah*. We can't know if we will meet again. Perhaps yes, perhaps no. But what is important is that we have met. Do you know, sometimes I think that life, time, is not in a straight line. Perhaps everything that happens is continuing. Perhaps it just happens somewhere else. We think we have lost it, but no. It is simply in the next room. In the next universe, the one we live close by, but cannot see. Like at Sidi Kaouki, Sarah."

"Sidi Kaouki?"

"In one universe at Sidi Kaouki is the holy man living on the beach. In another is Antoine building his restaurants. In another, you and me, making love in that place. Do you understand?"

"You mean, they are all going on in one place at the same time?"

"Yes, perhaps. I think, while I lie here. More than any time before. I have time at last to think. To know that I can think. So I have this idea. That nothing is lost or destroyed, it just moves a little bit out of reach. These men cannot destroy Sidi Kaouki; they just make up another story about it in which they become rich in making it what they want. And you and I, we go to Sidi Kaouki because we love it as it is, and the saint's house opens to us and we go inside to make love. Did you know, Sarah, that the power of Sidi Kaouki is to make women conceive?"

He added this last with his grin, which she had not seen since the times at the house, when they had relaxed together.

"Aziz."

"Excuse me, but it is true. What we desire," he said, "makes a difference. We have a place at Sidi Kaouki because we desire it, *n'est-ce pas?* That is all the saint did. He built no buildings, made no money. All he did was desire to be in that place. His desire for it formed his life on earth. That is what I think. And all others came afterwards and added their dream of Sidi Kaouki, they built their little pieces of it, they came there with their lovers, they came to eat picnics, to pray. All this could exist at the same time in that place, you see. I, Aziz, look down from the balcony with you and see the saint's house. I cannot go there. But my dream of that place is as strong as anybody's. I don't need to build anything there. But in my life, yes, I build it. These others, Antoine *par exemple*, they don't understand this. They think they have to take it, to build, to own. They do not understand."

"And will you go back there, do you think?"

"Who can tell? In that sense, I am Muslim. I wait for the will of God."

He took her hand and the two hands played together the way they did on that first evening, asking and answering a question. She was calm. It was as if the wind had dropped.

She said, "I won't. I'm leaving. I'm going back to America soon."

All we can do is leave. But not, like Marion, leaving damage behind;

going before that happens, before that unlived future arrives. If Aziz had been damaged by her existence, it was only skin deep.

"Why will you leave?"

"Because it's time. But you left first, Aziz."

"I had to do that."

"Yes."

"We can both leave, live elsewhere. There are people here who cannot."

Yann, Jake, Nick, Ramon, Aziz, herself—all of them able to leave. Who could not? Only Omar and Aisha. "I know."

"Can I take your address in America? Write it on my cast, here." She took the pen and wrote, labouring over the bumps in the plaster. It was like writing on a rough white wall. Her name, her apartment, the numbers in her address. She wrote it on the carapace that held him inside it like a creature in transition. He smiled at her.

"Now everyone can see it. Thank you, Sarah. Thank you for coming here. Thank you for your love."

There, it was named, the frail real thing that existed once the veils were drawn away.

Chapter twenty-two
The Dance of Life

The pink, soft walls of the old town were warm in the late afternoon light; a wash of smoke rose in the air as the charcoal fires were lit. She walked alone. The sun sank low behind the palm trees and the donkey carts and mule carts moved more slowly through the narrow streets. Entering the old town was like entering a quieter, inner room. People swarmed about on foot, but quietly. The hour was one of expectation. It was the last movement of the town before it settled for the night. Sarah walked down to the Djma'a el Fnaa, the great open market place at the centre of Marrakesh. She'd thought of going to see Suzanne, but needed first this time out in the city alone. Around her, the air smelled of smoke and carried the stink of the tanneries from across town. She was in her life without Aziz. It was a new place, the city of after leaving him.

Into the evening crowds of the city, she walked like someone entering water. In among the charcoal braziers and the spread cloths covered with jewellery, leatherwork, pots, pans, sweets, herbs and charms. She moved among the live animals tied by the foot, people squatting. On the braziers they were beginning to cook flat bread, roasted meat, boiled eggs, tea. The spices heated on the fires—cumin, coriander, turmeric, oregano. The meat sizzled and roasted. Men smoked the stubs of cigarettes and stared. She breathed the bay leaf smell of hashish, the catty smell of sweat. All essences blended, the smells shifted and changed and became each other as she went deeper in.

Two children ran beside her, chanting—*"Donne-moi un dirham, Madame, donne-moi un dirham, un stylo, Bonjour, Madame, donne-moi un bonbon!"* A woman seized her by the arm. She was a young woman with wild hair and strong, scratched brown hands. She tied a piece of blue wool on to Sarah's arm.

"C'est pour le bonheur!"

Happiness. Was happiness then just a piece of blue wool the colour of afternoon sky that somebody tied on your arm? She went forward, wearing her scrap of blue wool. She gave all her spare change away, a dirham here, a dirham there, until a small crowd ran after her, Madame, Madame. Somebody gave her a boiled egg and a piece of hot bread. She walked on, eating, one in each hand. The egg-seller shook his head when she offered to pay. "It's for your beautiful eyes, madame, *c'est mon plaisir.*"

She went on, circling round and through the market place, unable to find her way out to the circumference. She was drawn in, fed, wooed, pestered, blessed, tugged at and let go, smiled at and glared at, visible and invisible all at once. She came to a circle of people who were gathered three deep to watch what was going on at the centre. There were three musicians playing on small stringed instruments that wailed and sang. One of them let out a deep groan from time to time. They played for a very small dancer at the centre, a figure in a pink tulle skirt over pants who whirled and grimaced. The crowd all around was intent. The dancer, a man, but wearing a woman's wig and false breasts, with a padded rump under the skirt, was so small and lithe and padded that every movement had a ripe obscenity to it. He danced and whirled and pouted and then another man came into the circle and began to circle around him, hands on hips like a flamenco dancer. They began on a long imitation of heterosexual sex. The crowd shifted and sighed and people called out in Arabic. The musicians played faster. The male partner brought his hips up close to the rose pink skirt, he lifted it and began to grind and thrust. The female partner, whose face was like a monkey's, began to moan. The space between the two pairs of filthy pants was transformed into the space between ecstatic lovers. The beat quickened. The female partner's moans came to a crescendo. He became a woman having an orgasm. The other partner threw himself into the rigid pose and a cry shot out of him that seemed to go up into the night sky and stay there. The crowd, nearly all male, shouted with relief. The musicians slowed, all the participants bowed, and applause began.

She saw that the act was grotesque and yet had power and poetry. The man who had worn the skirt was taking it off now and lighting a cigarette from someone else's. His monkey face was screwed up in the light of the flame.

Sarah thought of Nick and Aisha. The quiet suggestive circling that Nick had done that night and the invitation, in all its haughty formality, that Aisha gave him. They'd stopped short of the orgasmic finale, but the same feeling had been there. They'd paid homage to sexuality, rather than imitating sex. The rapt, quiet, unaroused faces of the Moroccans watching, and the dazed longing on the faces of the others: it came back to her now.

A voice in the crowd behind her said, "It is not what you think."

She turned. A man spoke to her in the rich, rolling accent of Moroccans in the south of France. It was Aziz's voice, but it was not Aziz.

"It's not homosexuality, you know."

"Yes, I see that."

"And it's not like what people do in the cinema."

"Why do they do it, do you know?"

"It is what is sacred and forbidden. In the West you don't understand this. For Christians it is one or the other, *n'est-ce pas?*

I have spent many years among Christians. For us it is both. You understand?"

His intonation when he said—'*tu comprends?*' — was so like Aziz. But he was somebody else. He was not the one among many millions whom she had come to love. He was an echo, a shadow, a faint copy. But he stood close behind her as Aziz might have done and he was the same height, broadset in the shoulders and slightly short in the legs.

"Would you like me to show you the rest of the city? It is a beautiful city, Marrakesh. At night, it is beautiful. Come."

"No thank you. No. I am going home."

She pulled back, shocked. For a second she had responded to him, just as if he had been Aziz. Or was this the way that any man would be, finding a woman alone in a place like this? Later, in Paris, in London, in New York she would see a man in a crowd, dark, probably an Arab, with his hair growing just so, his shoulders so, his walk so, and be mistaken. Her body would shout out, just for that second; but then she would know, and turn away. It would be like the echo of a voice in a canyon, empty, repetitive; she would know how memory builds itself into our cells and takes years to wear away.

The Djma'a el Fnaa, the Place of the People, was the centre. It was here that she had to be. All paradox was here. Here, the universes Aziz had talked about surely overlapped. But like someone in a fairy tale, she couldn't stay there after nightfall. Already the sun was going down in a haze of red behind the minaret and the crowds of wrapped men blurred in the dusk. The charcoal fires and the stars were the only points of light. The evening star first, then Venus, low in the sky.

The known stars in the different sky over Africa. She turned towards where she thought the way out was, out of this teeming knot of humanity. She wriggled and pushed her way through, out of the anonymity and lostness of crowds. Behind the waiting, muzzled horses that took people in little carts across town, there was a rank of big blue taxis, that the Moroccans call "*cerceuils collectifs*" or collective coffins. Down by the minaret, a landmark at last.

She left the Djmaʿa el Fnaa behind her, as we all struggle out of the blood and hot alleyways of birth, and she never went back.

I never went back. Nobody talked about what happened. It was all very innocent, not like what happens now. We were innocent in those days.
    It was a white woman and a Moroccan together. It was the fear of disgrace.
    Memory stays with you for a lifetime, and then it falls away, the pieces of it are gone. But who can say where it goes? Perhaps it lingers in the world, once you are gone.

* * *

"Suzanne. It's Sarah. Listen, can I stay the night? I'm at a taxi rank by the minaret, at Djmaʿa el Fnaa. I'll tell you when I get there. Okay, are you sure? Good. See you soon."

She couldn't remember the name of the street where Suzanne and Cherif lived, only the district, out beyond the old city in a new suburb. A radio antenna was close to their house, and it was the only signpost she had. But as the blue cab took her out along the Boulevard Al Fassi, she remembered the way.

"It's right at the cross-roads, about another hundred metres," she told the driver. "Tell me, why was this road called after Al Fassi?"

"He was a hero, madame. A leader for Independence. A great man." So, whatever happened to you in life—torture, exile—you could have a street called after you, a wide new boulevard with four lanes of traffic, leading to a new, clean suburb where professional people lived. Too bad there was not a Boulevard Abdel Jadid. She leaned over the driver's shoulder and pointed the way, navigating entirely by landmarks: a pink wall here, a leaning palm tree there, a butcher's shop, a laundry, the antenna itself, blinking in the warm darkness, the pinkish darkness of Marrakesh.

"Here. This street. About the third on the left. Yes, here."

The streets had no names yet, as the suburb was too new. The driver said, "One day they will have names. Now, no names. Names have not yet been invented." So it was not surprising that she had not remembered the address; just the way she had come that morning, when she'd walked down these streets to take a cab to the bus station, to catch the bus to Essaouira, that place not yet even imagined.

"Sarah!" Suzanne opened the heavy gate to the inner garden, as Sarah paid the driver, tipping him with more than half the fare. He smiled, bowed, wished her happiness.

"Hi. Thanks for having me at such short notice."

"You know you can come any time." Suzanne had adopted the rules of Moroccan hospitality, in a country where nobody ever grumbled about "company," however long a visitor might stay. "Are you all right? What's happening?"

"I want to tell you. I'm fine. Yes, really. Just, if we can sit down somewhere and have a cold drink, and I'll tell you the whole story, because if I don't tell it, if I don't put words to it now, I'm afraid of forgetting. You know, like my mother? I'm afraid of that."

"Alzheimer's isn't hereditary, is it?" Suzanne led her into the house, across smooth wood floors spread with fringed carpets upon which her husband and children lay, watching TV. Cherif looked up to say hello, then went back to cuddling his children, one in each arm, and watching a soap. It was as if Sarah had never been away.

Suzanne pulled out a chair for her at the kitchen table. She took a jug of orange juice from the refrigerator. "Or would you prefer something stronger? Or tea?"

"No, juice is fine. I'm just thirsty. It's dusty out on the street."

They sipped and looked at each other across the Formica tabletop, and at the opened window the night rustled with palm trees and the wings of nesting birds. A cackle of chickens, that flew up into a tree to roost. A cat yowling in the dark.

"So," said Suzanne, "what happened? I guess it must be more important than unpacking, right? I see you don't have any luggage, anyway. What's up, and why on earth were you down in the Djma'a el Fnaa on your own at night?"

"It was fine. I was completely safe, I just needed to be on my own for a while."

"Well, you're hardly on your own down there, you have all the hucksters and bandits and con men of the country with you."

Suzanne, Sarah remembered, had all the fear of being a woman alone out there that twenty years as a wife had given her. Cherif didn't even like her going to *cafés* alone; he said it wasn't done. It was possible, Sarah thought looking across at her friend, that there were many things to miss about America if you were a Moroccan wife, even the wife of an intellectual like Cherif.

"I mean, I needed to be alone in the world. To operate in the world just as me; to be there. D'you understand?"

Suzanne shrugged. Obviously it was not something she did. "Anyway, tell me what's been going on. Have you been on the west coast all this time? We didn't hear from you for weeks."

"Yes. I fell in love with a man. A Moroccan. He lives in France. He's married. I've just been to see him in the hospital. He was in a car wreck. Oh, God, so much has happened, Suzanne."

But this was probably not a story that Suzanne could hear. It was a story about a break-up, about leaving, about the relativity of truth, about love outside marriage, it was essentially disreputable; this was Morocco, and Suzanne, since her student days, had been a reputable wife. She had loved, married, had children by, and been controlled by, this one man. The man who had bought her this house, whose life was indissolubly joined to hers unless he suddenly decided to divorce her, and who objected to her going alone to *cafés* or to the Djma'a El Fnaa—that meeting place of worlds, dreams, states of mind.

Suzanne was silent for a long moment. Then she said, "It's a good thing, Sarah. That he was married, I mean. You had the love affair. You didn't have to have the rest. And that's all I'm going to say. You know Cherif is a wonderful man, I have a wonderful life, my kids are great, I have everything I want. But for you, Sarah, it's good that he was married. You'll go back to America. Your life will go on."

Her friend, her old friend, with whom she'd sat in a dozen *cafés* in the south of France that summer when Suzanne had met Cherif, when they'd all smoked and drank pastis and talked politics, the war, the draft, the fate of immigrant Arabs in France, the threat of racism creeping across the country. Sarah looked at her with love, Suzanne with her smooth, old-fashioned chignon, her smooth wifely demeanour, her kitchen with its purring refrigerator; her loving, demanding, TV-watching husband, her life. Memory. It had no age. Some things were remembered over decades, vivid as the present, making the present what it was, giving it its depth.

Suzanne said, "What exactly are you afraid of forgetting?"

"The details, I guess. And the meaning of things. I think my mother forgot because she had to, because there were some experiences in her life that she couldn't really have. You know, she was sent home from here, because something happened, with a man. And I've found the man. He's in Essaouira."

"You have? Really? How extraordinary. Are you sure it's him?"

"Yes. Ninety per cent, anyway. He was a resistance hero. The French beat him up. The people in Essaouira think he's nuts, because he got seduced by some fantasy woman called Aisha Gandisha. I don't think he is nuts."

"Well, have you spoken to him yet? Does he know who you are?"

"Not yet. I had a feeling that I had to be sure about what I was up to. I don't know how to explain it to you, Suzanne, but I had this long time of just feeling incredibly weak, as if I couldn't take the initiative in anything. I thought in the end it might be to do with racism, and the position of women, women who're involved with Moroccan men, do you know what I mean? It began happening as soon as I'd had sex with Aziz. I felt kind of passive. I couldn't seem to shake it off."

"I know what you mean. It's why it's good that you're going home." It was all that Suzanne would say on that subject, but she sighed and fetched a bottle of Cognac from a cupboard. "I think we need something stronger, don't you? To your mother. To you, Sarah."

Sarah lifted the little glass, "To you, Suzanne. To friendship. To the one who stayed."

Late that night they sat giggling about Bill Jackson, and the way he'd spent so long in the bathroom and the day he'd stayed on after Sarah had left, when Suzanne had not known what to do with him so had set him to making marmalade.

"Marmalade? Bill?"

"Yes, we had all these oranges, we didn't want them to go bad, so Cherif set up a marmalade factory here in the kitchen, we were all chopping and talking and boiling up sugar, it was fun. We made Bill sterilize the jars. He'd never made jam before, imagine."

"Well, American men don't, do they?"

"Cherif thought he needed to learn, anyway."

"You could have changed his life. You could have put him off hunting up the next war."

It was good, to laugh, to chat in ordinary slangy American English and be understood. To be understood not only as she was now, but as she'd been, a college girl in Boston way before Bill, even before Dave whom she'd married, before all the mistakes and compromises of adult life. And as a student in France, as the girl who'd gone home with a new language, new ideas, as the friend of the one who'd shocked everybody by running off with a young Moroccan, to be married and live, of all places, in Marrakesh. Suzanne had been the wild one then. Marrakesh! Where was that, somewhere in Africa? And how could she marry a Muslim? It would never last.

Now, Suzanne poured brandy into little glasses long after Cherif and the twins, her youngest children, had come in to say goodnight and Cherif had taken them to bed. He liked to sleep with Yassin and Karim sometimes, Suzanne said, and he got up at dawn, before they woke. So she and Sarah had the night to themselves, for talk, reminiscence—do you remember the time when we borrowed that motorcycle and took off into the French countryside, do you remember that *café*, what was its name, and the boy you went out with in Aix for just one night, and the lies I had to tell my mother when I got home, and how yours was so sympathetic? And that dress I wore, with grass stains all over it that wouldn't come out? And when I married Cherif, all the dire things people said? And how you said you were going to come to Morocco, all those years ago, and how you never did? And Sarah, tell me about Bill, how on earth did you get together with him, and what was wrong between you and Dave, I heard you'd had a divorce but I never knew why, and what was Aziz like, and how do you feel now, and what was your mother's story, tell me, and what did it mean for her life?

When Sarah left, the following day, she felt all the relief of having talked to someone who knew her so well. Suzanne, whom she hadn't seen for all these years, whose house she had stayed in with Bill as if it were a hotel, whose friendship and concern she'd forgotten, because she was on the track of something else: a man, a story, a plan. What had looked like real life.

"Now, let me know what happens with the mystery man in Essaouira. Promise?"

"Promise."

"And come back here on your way home?"

"Of course."

Whatever she became now, Sarah thought, being a reliable friend was a priority. Memory was not exclusive, for love affairs, for men. It was all the details of life, all the pasts one shared. As Aziz had said, all these parallel lives ran, in one, through one, and each of them must be honoured. Cherif drove her to the bus station and said his courteous goodbyes, after Suzanne had kissed her at the gate of the house. He was on his way to work at the university; it wouldn't be out of his way. She thought, he guessed what was going on with me, and he left us alone; and she was glad for Suzanne, with her thoughtful, gracious man.

Part v
The Man Who Fed Seagulls

Chapter twenty-three

A Boy's Return

When she let herself in, that evening, the house was silent; the fire, dying out in the hearth, the birds quiet in their cage. The silence welcomed her and she went upstairs and slept for ten hours. In the morning, she came down to find Sacha fussing, dusting, moving furniture about.

"Ah, Sarah, there you are. Will you help me? Will you give me your advice? Now that Nick has gone there is so much to do. Look, I want to make a proper salon here instead of this heap of furniture with no sense to it. Don't you think that's better? So, at least there will be somewhere to sit. Now at least things will be a little *comme il faut*. What do you think?"

Sarah stood in her way, wanting coffee. Omar came in and looked helpless too, as if waiting to be moved. Downstairs, Jake was back, drinking tiny cups of espresso with Ibrahim, whose little black dog lay at their feet. She called down over the rail to him.

"Hello, Jake! Welcome back."

He was back from the south, from black Africa—dark tan, his

hair curling to his shoulders. He seemed to have grown, and a faint moustache shaded his lip.

Sacha said, "I told Nick I don't want his nephew and his scruffy friends using the place as a doss house. And now look at them. He arrives as if he owns the place and sits on the furniture. I told him I didn't want a dog here, either. Frankly, this is a hotel or it isn't. What are people going to think if they come into reception and find those two louts lolling about?"

Sarah said, "Well he does sort of own the place, doesn't he? I mean, he's Nick's family."

Sacha lifted a large blue and white pot from a shelf, set it down on the low table, blew dust off it and wiped her hands. "Everything is filthy. Those Berber girls never cleaned a thing. It was like a morgue."

"Well, it sure looks different now."

"You think so? You really think so, Sarah, that it looks better?" She appealed, her hands on her large hips, her sleeves rolled, somewhere between a movie star and a housekeeper.

"It looks more—well, clean."

"Under control." Sacha said firmly. "You see, I think Nick trusted me to do this because I have a certain flair. Also, I am used to it. I am used to making something from nothing. I see what needs to be done and I do it."

Jake came upstairs, the young dog at his heels. He leaned to kiss Sarah on both cheeks. She smelled his young fresh sweaty smell and noticed that he had a blue bird tattoo'ed on one shoulder.

"And you, take that dog out, there will be no more animals in this place and no more hairs all over the cushions."

Jake's face was so often set in a scowl as he screwed his eyes against sunlight or the opacity of language, it was hard to tell if he was scowling more than usual. He was blinking and morose, like someone woken from sleep. He mumbled in Spanish and dropped into one of the armchairs. One hand raked through his hair until it stood on end and the other caressed the dog's head.

"Jake, I said I don't want dogs in here."

"I heard you. Ibrahim's coming back for her in a minute. Cool it, for God's sake."

Omar came back with glasses of coffee on a tray.

"Jake, *bonjour*. You want coffee?"

"I've just had some. Got a cigarette? All I want is some peace and quiet and not to be nagged every minute. Man, it's like an army camp round here." His voice cracked and groaned.

Sacha came back and sat down, sighing. Her bosom lifted the jewellery at her neck and her hands smoothed her skirt down over her knees. "*Tiens*, it is so dark this morning, I think there is going to be a storm. Omar, why don't you light the candles? I can't see a thing."

He was on his feet again in a moment. He brought a stool and the matches, hitched up his striped *d'jellaba* and stood beneath the swaying chandelier to light the ring of candles. Outside the windows, the sky was dark with rain clouds. He was up on the stool between the fireplace and the table, his arms reaching to light the candles as the wind from outside began to gust and bang the windows. He swayed a little and dropped a candle.

Sacha screamed at him. "You're so clumsy! For God's sake, can't you do anything properly? This—this standing about on stools to light candles! This dropping things all over the place! I can't stand it! Get down. I will not have candles dropped on me!" Sarah raised her eyebrows and blew out her breath. If the storm was coming on the outside, it was about to hit in here too.

Jake jumped to his feet and the dog ran behind his chair to hide. "How dare you speak to Omar like that! He's worth ten of you, you stupid cow, he deserves respect, not to be yelled at like that, you shouldn't even speak to an animal like that! You come in here telling everybody what to do; you treat us all as if we were scum! Who d'you think you are? Apologize to him! Apologize!"

He stood and shouted at her, all his adolescent timidity and passivity gone. Jake stepped clear out of it, himself at last. To Omar he said, "Take it easy, man." Then he sat down again and dropped back into silence. Sacha said nothing. She sipped her milky coffee as if nothing had happened and lit a cigarette. Omar went away into the kitchen.

Jake said, "Am I right, or what? She shouldn't speak to anyone like that. It's disgusting."

Sarah said, "I agree with you. But she's upset."

Sacha flicked her ash and said, "Now, can we have a little civilized behaviour or have you got more adolescent nonsense to spit out?"

"She thinks she can walk in here and take over. She thinks she has a right. She treats Omar worse than a dog. And no animals; who said no animals? She won't let my friends come in. This afternoon she told Malik to leave, just like that. And no music. No nothing. We were only playing our new cassettes. What was Nick thinking? And she tried to turn me against Yann, who I've known all my life—he's like my father. I won't listen to what she says about him, I told her, you can't talk about Yann like that, not with me here."

His thin dark young face was already marked and lined by travelling in the sun. His wide mouth with two commas, one at each side and frown lines already between his eyes, the premature lines of travellers in deserts. His blue eyes strangely light in the sallowness of his skin, the only feature that was anything like Yann's. He was the son of Nick's sister—and who? Perhaps even he did not know.

"And Aisha, she says all these terrible things about Aisha, that she poisons people and so on. I tell you who poisons people. It is her. Nobody else. She is poison. Well, I'm not going to stay here to listen to her any more, I'm going out."

Jake leapt up then and left the room with his hunched teenager's stride. He walked as if protecting himself from blows. But he had made something happen. He counted, as a voice in this house. The few candles that Omar had lit guttered and swayed overhead in the draught.

*   *   *

Late in the evening, Sarah came downstairs to take a bottle of water from the refrigerator. Aisha sat by the dying fire in one of the armchairs. Jake was on the floor at her feet. He'd turned towards her so that his arms clasped her knees and his head was laid upon them, face down. He was huddled, his face hidden, and Aisha was stroking his head, ruffling his dark hair where his dark tan ended and white skin began.

Across the room, in another armchair, Omar lounged with the guitar across his knees. He played quietly, as if to himself. In front of the fire the little black bitch lay stretched out, warming her belly with its row of pink and black tits. She twitched and whimpered in a deep sleep. It was nearly midnight. Aisha looked at her across Jake's head and then closed her eyes.

Omar smiled, "Come and join us, Sarah. Tell us, how is Aziz?"

They were at home, a family.

"He's okay. He just has a broken leg, and it's mending. He's going back to France."

"*Insh'allah*," said Omar. "It is the will of God."

It was all one could say, Sarah thought, and it avoided questions she didn't want to answer, not tonight. She perched on the arm of one of the chairs and then slid down into its deep seat and relaxed. Jake snuggled in closer to Aisha's thighs; her hand still stroked and played with his hair.

Omar's face was open and easy as it was when he played music, sang or lay on the beach, but he was unshaven and looked tired. He laid the guitar carefully to one side and went to pick up the little drum, leaned to warm its skin at the fire and stroked its surface gently. When he settled back in the chair, the drum was between his knees. He touched it into a quiet rhythm, feeling for the right beat. It was like hearing a heart begin. When he had found it he glanced up, smiling. Jake sighed deeply. Aisha was still, apart from her moving, caressing hand. Jake, the boy whose life was all movement and shifting scenes, who had no language that was really his own, snuggled in like a baby.

Sarah closed her eyes; saw the teeming crowds of the Djma'a

243

El Fnaa, the dancers at the centre, then the kitchen at Suzanne's house. She thought of Aziz, his words to her about Sidi Kaouki, the stillness of him, white-wrapped in that bed, and everything that had happened since yesterday. Omar's music rocked her on its slight waves, its repetitions. The house was quiet around them. Sacha must have been asleep in the room with the gouaches of blue iris on the walls; maybe she had even been able to put the light out and sink into her pillow tonight and rest. The birds were quiet in their cages under the draped blanket.

Chapter twenty-four

The Sign of the Floating Bed

Aisha was already up on the roof and Sarah was surprised to see her smoking a cigarette, with today's piles of laundry still damp in the basket beside her.

"Sarah! You look better. You are no longer ill, no longer sad?"

"Yes, I am better. No longer ill, no longer sad."

"I too am no longer sad. It is not right to be sad for long. So, you went to Marrakesh, you saw the wind man Aziz?"

"Yes, I saw him."

"And he will return?"

"No, Aisha, he's going back to France. He's got a wife there."

"Ach!" She spat a gob of shining spittle on the white floor. "Ach, these men! Wife, no wife, what does it matter? They all have wife when it suits them. You don't take notice of this, Sarah, it is nothing, it does not matter. But it is good, you are not sad. Sadness is sickness, the same thing."

"I'm not sad because I'm going home soon."

She patted Sarah's cheek.

"To America? So, you will go back to your country, to your

parents, your man? Your children? You will not be sad, Sarah. Never sad."

Sarah smiled and shrugged. It was no good telling Aisha there were no children, no man waiting.

Aisha laid her cigarette on the top of the low wall, pulled out the locket she wore between her breasts on a long gold chain and opened it to show a photograph of herself. "It is me, Aisha. I am Berber. That is why I cannot be sad. I know that Yann will return. I am strong. I know what I know. You want a cigarette?"

She lit it for Sarah with a strong movement of her veined hands on the gold lighter she pulled out from under her dress. Doing this, she became someone of the modern western world; any woman, anywhere, giving another a light.

"Yann give me this. You see, he gives me gold. It is not nothing, gold. It means he will return."

They smoked together, leaning on the white roof parapet.

"You know Sacha wants you to stay?" Sarah said.

"Huh. That one, she does not know what she wants. But I tell you, Sarah, I will be here when she is gone. Long after. After all of them—Nick, Sacha, even Jake. He will not stay, my Jake, he has the wind in his heels, he too. He is young. It is right for young men to go. But Yann, I bring him back. He cannot choose otherwise. You see? Sarah. If you want, I tell you some things, some recipes. You try them in your country. You will see. Without this, men remain fools, there is no other way."

"Recipes?" Sarah said ironically.

Aisha flicked her ash downward, into the narrow slot between the houses. Sarah looked out beyond the rooftops to the line of the sea, dark as far as the island, choppy beyond. Recipes, for staying alive, for taking back one's power, for not giving in.

"Not *tajines*, not couscous, *ma chère*. Other things. You know what I mean, I think. Otherwise men will always run. It is their nature. Like a horse needs to be tamed, we have to tame them."

"I don't think it would work too well in my country," Sarah said, "And I think the ingredients would be hard to find."

"You take them with you!"

"No, thank you, Aisha. I'm fine now. You know, American men aren't really the same."

"All men are the same. If you change your mind, you ask me. You write. But don't tell anybody. You promise?"

"Promise."

"You know, I tell you one thing. We must fight, Sarah. Men will not give us what we need, never. They just know to take and take. So we have to fight, to be women. You understand? Now, I tell you, you go to the *hammam*. It's good. I go there, it makes me strong. You see."

She saw that Sacha had hung the new sign outside the house already, the one that announced its existence as a hotel. The new sign only said 'Hotel' in French on one side, and in Arabic on the other. The old one Nick had commissioned had been a painting of a man and a woman lying together on a comfortable, brightly patterned couch. Or rather the man, who was dark-skinned, was leaning back against the pillows and the woman, who was paler and also naked to the waist, seemed to be reaching out of bed to pick up a floating cup of coffee. They were surrounded by brilliant rugs and cushions and the whole scene seemed to be flying through the air, as in a Chagall painting. The mayor, when he had seen it, had refused Nick permission to hang it up. No amounts of palm trees or money could convince him. He said that it would encourage immorality. Nick had offered to put in a baby, to make the couple into a family but the mayor said that would make things worse. Nick said, but it shows that we are a respectable family hotel. The mayor said, it would have been one thing to have painted a family in the first place, but to have a man and a woman in bed and then to add in a baby afterwards, that was not on. Nick had offered to put in two babies and remove the cup of coffee and cover up the woman's breasts, but the conversation was already at an end. The mayor was sure that it would encourage immorality. You could not hang a sign in the street showing a man and woman in bed together, however many babies you painted in, however many cups of coffee you painted out. It was the bed that was the problem. Nick had said that hotels were bound to have beds, weren't they, wasn't that the law? But the mayor was not listening. It would not do, and that was that.

So the sign that Sacha hung had no beds and no babies and no cups of coffee. She stood in the big open doorway and looked up at it, pleased. It was done. The house of ill repute had become, at last, a hotel.

*　*　*

"Hey, you've changed the sign."

"Sarah, it is better, don't you agree? *Tu n'es pas d'accord?*"

You had to be *d'accord* with what Sacha decided to do, just as you were supposed to agree with Nick when he said, "Don't you agree?" It was, Sarah thought, the benevolent dictator mode.

She didn't like the change as much as Sacha did, and found she rather missed the scaffolding, the rubble, the men upon the roof, the time of transformations, Nick and Yann as well as Aziz. The tariffs now hung in the hall. Omar was permanently there in reception, wearing a white shirt. The season was changing and soon tourists would begin to arrive in large crowds. Everything would be ordered and organized, there would be no more dead budgerigars and poisoned coffee and sudden crashes of falling masonry.

Sacha said, "It is all so much better, much better than before."

She pushed up her dark glasses on her forehead and went indoors to see to the accounts, closing the door behind her.

*　*　*

Aisha came down the street with her basket on her arm, wearing her black cloak. She stood and looked up at the new sign that hung above the blue door, inviting paying guests, making public what had been private. She sniffed and said nothing. Her basket was full of vegetables and fresh herbs from the market. Sarah met her at the door as she came back from the *café* on the corner with her *café au lait* in a glass; caught the sharp whiff of coriander from the green soft leaves.

248

Aisha put down the basket and tried the door. It didn't open. Sarah, her coffee in one hand, got out her key and tried the lock. Nothing happened. It would not turn. Sacha must have changed the locks. They both had to stand there waiting in the street for Sacha to hear the bell and come to open the door, Sarah still with the glass of milky coffee she'd brought from the *café*. When the door swung open, Aisha went first in her magnificent silence, carrying the vegetables. Sarah followed. The cool interior of the house opened to them both, they went up the familiar stairs in the familiar gloom, but nothing was as it had been. In the kitchen Aisha put down her basket.

"Sarah. You have seen that sign, what it says?"

"Yes. Hotel."

"It is ridiculous. Sadia's house, a hotel? For tourists? It will not stay. It will not work. I will see to that. And changing the locks! Who does this woman think she is? The keeper of a jail? But you won't see it. You are going. When are you going, Sarah?"

"Soon. In a few days."

"It is good. But I will miss you, Sarah. That is also true."

Aisha embraced her then. She was small and wiry, hot against Sarah as if fevered.

Outside the house the new sign creaked slightly in the breeze. Indoors, where nobody could see it, the old one was still propped against the wall. The gaudy bedroom still floated in mid-air, with the sated man leaning back against cushions and the woman with a smile of satisfaction, reaching beyond him for her coffee. No babies, no compromise. No tariffs. Just pleasure.

The police came for Aisha that afternoon. Sarah came back from the spice market where she'd been buying dried herbs and spices—lumps of myrrh, black resins from the desert, henna—to take home. She found Sacha walking up and down in the hall, crying noisily, a cigarette in one hand. She stubbed it out with a shove in the ashtray and went on pacing.

"The police, yes, two policemen, they come into this house and take her. I say, she works for me, you cannot do this, she is an employee of *Monsieur* Nick. But *Monsieur* Nick is not here. We must call him, we must find him, only he can do something. Oh, this is not possible, this country."

"Sacha. What happened? Do you know why they took her?" Sarah put an arm round her shoulders and Sacha leaned against her, sobbing.

"I ask them. I beg them. I say, she has done nothing—she is innocent!"

"It wasn't anything to do with poisoning, was it?"

"Poison? No, of course not. No, it is because of the baby." Sacha straightened and looked directly at her from six inches away, her eyes welling with tears but her face stern.

"The baby? You mean, Souad? Why?"

"She has a baby, she is not married. It is not legal here."

"Not legal? Jesus."

"I know, it happens. But Aisha has no man here to protect her. Now, with Nick gone, they think they can take her. Just like that."

"Where is she? We must do something."

"In the prison! It is in the middle of the town, you know, you walk past it on the way to the spice market."

"I've just come back from the spice market, I didn't know there was a jail there. They really put women in prison for having babies with no husband?"

"She says to the policeman, I hear her, but I have a husband, he is Muslim now, he went to the Imam. But they say, where is he then? The baby is here, you can see the baby. But where is the man? Invisible? And they laugh at her. They know it is Yann. They know what he is like, that he won't return."

"Oh, God. Where is the baby? They didn't take Souad too?"

"She is with Aisha's mother, in Sidi Kaouki. She is safe."

"Well, we must get Yann to come back," Sarah said.

"He will not return," said Sacha sadly. "I know this kind of man. He is all dreams. He has not—what do you say—feet on the ground. She did not choose wisely. But which of us can do this? This—" and she gestured to her pelvis—"this is too strong."

"Tell me about it. But, Sacha, why did you cry?"

"Why I cry? It is this country. It is my country and it is terrible for women, and it makes me afraid, and Aisha is a woman too. They don't come for me, these men, but who will be next, Sarah? You, me? Anything is possible."

She sat down at the desk in reception and looked suddenly businesslike. "We must think. We must think what to do, no?"

"We could call Nick."

Sarah called Nick's number in London and left a message, as he was out. Then she called his number in Los Angeles and left another one. Both times, the voice on the machine was Nick's, but in London it was polite and clipped, in California, drawling and relaxed. Two more of Nick's personas greeted her down the line. "The old ham. Slippery as an eel. But he has to be somewhere."

"He does not care, he is gone, he is like all men," Sacha said.

"No, I think if he knew, he would care. He would do something." Minimize the damage: that was the phrase.

She called his two numbers several times during the rest of the day. Omar and Jake came in together in the late morning and Sacha told them what had happened. Omar sat down silently with tears in his eyes; his whole self was lax with gloom. Jake exploded into anger again and thumped the table; he glared at Sacha.

"Jake, it is not my fault, really. I try to stop them. I tell them, she works here, she is good, she has done nothing. They say she is a whore, that she has always been a whore, that now she has a baby to prove it."

"It's fucking terrible! It's fucking insane!" He began to swear in Spanish, a chant of obscenities, as far as Sarah could tell.

Omar said, "If somebody is already in jail here, he will never come out."

"Not never, Omar. They don't die in there."

"Some do. I know it. They go in and they never come out. Or they come out old, with white hair; they are almost dead. Or crazy. They come out crazy."

"Can we get her a lawyer?" Anything, Sarah thought, to dispel

Omar's contagious hopelessness; the vision of Aisha rotting away
in there for ever, with long white hair like the people let out of the
Bastille.

"No lawyer here will disobey the Imam. This is a religious
law."

"Unbelievable. But you aren't fundamentalists. Anyway, what
about the king? He has several wives, doesn't he?"

"Many wives is not the same as woman with no husband,"
Omar said sadly. "Many wives is just for king, for rich men. They
can do what they like. For Aisha, it is disgrace. She disgraces her
family. Her mother, she looks after the baby, she says nothing; but
the others, they don't want her, she has disgraced them."

"But they got on with Yann, didn't they? He used to go to Sidi
Kaouki to see them?"

He said, "They think he will marry her. To have a baby before
the marriage is one thing. That is not serious. But when the man goes,
and there is the baby, that is another thing."

Against the wall, there was still the sign that Nick had had
painted. A man, a woman and no baby. Now, Sarah thought, they
should paint in the baby and paint out the man. What makes a family?
What makes one thing right and another wrong? Aisha with Souad
wrapped in her cloak coming in that winter's night to sit before the
fire. Yann with the baby dancing on his knees. "She could have had
an abortion." Nick's comment, "She told him she was too old." Aisha
saying, "My little Berber princess. *Embrasse* papa, baby." Yann on the
roof: "I am going to see my daughter." How could the existence of
Souad sentence anybody to a life in jail?

What could any of them do without Nick? Nick had the
money; Nick had the ear of all the officials in town, even the mayor,
since he had given in about the sign. He spoke Arabic and had given
out enough sweet pastry in all directions, he had planted enough palm
trees and drunk enough glasses of tea and spent enough time listening
to people's anxieties. He had the time, the wit, the knowledge, and
above all he had the money and the open-handedness that does not
generally go with wealth. He knew that if he lost it all, he could eas-

ily make some more. Sarah thought: What would Nick do? Use his contacts, flatter, cajole, pay, issue veiled threats, spend the morning on the phone and the afternoon drinking slow glasses of tea, tease the mayor into laughter, butter up the Imam, walk into the jail and simply get her released, by showing his Californian driving licence or something equally ridiculous.

She thought then of President Roosevelt and Mohammed v., meeting in 1943. The promise of independence, given from among the trappings of what must have seemed, even to a king, ultimate power.

"Well, I'm off." Jake stood up.

"Where are you going? You aren't leaving now, *nom de Dieu!*" Sacha shouted.

"I'm going to see the Chief of Police."

He turned his hands to show them handfuls of worn dirham notes, tens and twenties. Some fluttered to the table, and he stuffed them back into his pockets.

"It's what Nick would do. So—see you later. Don't ask me where I got it, Sacha, because I'm not telling and it isn't your business. I'm not leaving Aisha in there another minute." His voice shook. He rubbed a tear away with his knuckles. He was a boy moving rockily into manhood.

"I'll come with you," Sarah said.

"No, thanks all the same. She's my family. I'll go alone." His thin shoulders hunched high, he left the room. They heard him slop downstairs in Yann's old slippers.

Omar said, "She is like his mother, Aisha. Yann is his father."

"You know that for sure?"

"I know. Yann is now with his mother, in Spain. He is the child of Nick's sister and Yann. Nick tells me this. I know. But Jake, he has two mothers. Aisha is his other mother. That is why he must go. It is his honour, you understand."

Chapter twenty-five
Pathways of Desire

Where there was no explanation and no obvious course of action, perhaps healing was possible. That afternoon, Sarah went to the *hammam*, because that was what Aisha had told her to do. It is for cleaning yourself, but not just outside. After it, you can start your life again. She stood inside the door of the *hammam* with a towel and a bar of soap. A very large naked woman sat behind the counter and sipped a glass of tea. It was dark inside after the brightness of the day. She combed back her long wet hair.

"Take off your clothes, Madame. You put them there."

Sarah took off her clothes, rolled them into a bundle and put them in the locker. She stood naked, bare feet on the damp, tiled floor. This must surely be as far from her life in America as she was ever going to get, naked on this filthy floor, being examined by this vast woman.

"You have shampoo? No? I will lend you mine. Here. You have a towel?" She smiled and her huge breasts with their dark nipples lolled sideways upon her stomach. She had a full, fine face, her hair was perfectly straight and black, her fat arms tapered to slim wrists and small hands. Sarah took the shampoo and towel, which felt like small talismans of protection. She held them in front of her.

"You go with this woman, yes?"

The second woman was dressed but wore her skirts rolled up the way Aisha rolled hers when she washed the floor. She pushed Sarah ahead of her into a large, dark, vaulted space full of naked women, who sat and splashed water over themselves, giggled and stared. Sarah stood there uncertainly and looked back at the laughing faces, the slippery streaming flesh. Her own body felt thin and insubstantial among the abundance of them all, the spreading thighs and breasts, the mammoth backs, the long slicked-back hair. She wasn't, could never be, enough. Everything that had protected her in her life had fallen away. Here, you had no passports, money, possessions, career, even clothes. No identity, but that give-away, the body. The woman with her pointed to a patch of floor and set down a bucket of hot water. Again, she pointed and gave her a little push. Sarah sat down on the tiles in running water and the woman knelt beside her and began to scrub her all over. She scrubbed her back, ears, head, neck, breasts, buttocks, legs. She threw buckets of hot water over her and rubbed shampoo into her head with strongly massaging hands. Sarah sat beneath the hot streams and shrank, back into babyhood, into the very earliest time of being washed, the indignity and the peace, the giving up all control. The scratchy cloth found its way into ears, nose and armpits. The woman lifted her breasts and washed beneath them. Then she pointed to her patch of pubic hair. All the women laughed and pointed too. She realized she was to wash her genitals herself, and did this among general laughter. Then the next scalding bucketful came. She squatted and gasped under drowning streams. The woman pushed her down on the hard floor and began pummelling her back and shoulders with hard direct blows until she felt bones and muscles flinch and re-align. Then she turned her over and did the other side. Strong fingers raked her stomach, feeling for all the organs under the skin. She pressed her shoulders back to the floor and slapped her breasts with light little blows. She forced her legs apart and pushed her hips back to the ground. Sarah sat up in the runnels of water, battered and pummelled and scrubbed and released into a simple state of well being. When else had she felt this way? A memory came of sitting naked, sloshing water about, of being wet and small and bare and guileless, a simple creature made by the hands of others.

All around her there were women washing themselves and each other, scrubbing, intimate with each other's nakedness, matter-of-fact about it. She followed the woman who had washed her back into the outer room, away from the steam and darkness into another vaulted place where all the benches round the walls were covered with seated women: naked women. There were women with towels around their waists, old women, young women, girls with no breasts, beautiful teenagers with bodies like budding trees, huge women, skinny women, women drinking tea and combing their long wet tails of hair, women dressing layer by layer, putting back the garments that would cover them completely. They looked and smiled as she came in. She sat among them holding her towel, naked and suddenly at ease. Her body was her own; she was physically real, as they were. She was Sarah, just Sarah. Nobody, nothing else. Zahrah, they laughed with her. They were ordinary, all of them; them, she, us. All of these bodies sweated and menstruated and came to fiery life with the bodies of men. All of them grew and aged and died. All were beautiful. All these breasts that gave pleasure and fed children and were carried through life like antennae, sensing everything. All these vaginas, these secrets, pathways of desire. She sat down on her towel and accepted a glass of tea. All the hair on her body sprang back to dry and curly life. She thought of Aziz and how they had been together. The curious Christian doctrine of the separation of body and soul and how unlikely that seemed. The Islamic belief that sexual joy is a foretaste of paradise. Then she thought back to the schools that she'd been to, the summer camps where girls had undressed under their clothes, ashamed for no reason. Women's bodies in America, both hidden and on view. And she thought again of Aisha.

The woman who had loaned her shampoo slopped across in slippers with a towel at her waist. Her vast breasts shook and gleamed. She existed in the naked beauty of the very fat.

"*Ça va, c'etait bien?* It was good?"

"Very good. Here is your shampoo, thank you. I've never felt so clean in all my life."

"That is good. Clean is good."

Nor so free, so light, so absolved of everything. With these others now she could smile and laugh at it, the small hidden tragic joke of life. The women of Morocco. Women came out through the door dressed from head to toe in the white of the haik.

"*Salut, au revoir, bonsoir, b'slama.*" They greeted her with casual ease. They were no longer just eyes above veils, invisible beings. Their world was no longer unknown. Sarah put on dark glasses against the sun. They all wore these disguises and underneath them, all were as naked as the day they were born.

* * *

She was there at the house when Jake came back, with Aisha.

"Aisha! Oh, how are you?"

Aisha turned away, would not meet her eye. She seemed small, battered, her fierce fire diminished.

Jake said, "She's going back to her family, I'm taking her there."

"What happened? How did you do it?"

"Avenged my honour. If a man's honour is at stake, they can't keep her. She is my mother, I tell them, and they are insulting her. They have to let her go."

Chapter twenty-six

The Language of Silence

The last of her dreams mixed with the call of the muezzin across the city. The sky was just beginning to lighten behind the white curtains. It was time to go down and find Abdel Jadid, if that was truly who he was. In a few minutes she was dressed and moving out through the quiet house, into the narrow street between the house and the Medina wall. Walking through the gateway in the red wall, down towards the sea.

He was there, where she'd last seen him on the day of the *Fête*. She came up to him from behind as he stooped to take scraps from his sack, then reached to throw them into the wind, his arm swinging in a generous arc—that gesture again, of a man sowing seed. The gulls came down scrapping and clamouring. She came level, and stood beside him at the sea wall. The tide was coming in with its choppy splash at the wall and the moon was still up, a faint face over the ocean, although the sun was rising and would flood them in a moment with light.

"*Bonjour, Monsieur. Vous êtes Monsieur Abdel Jadid?*"

He moved, startled. She'd addressed him in French, not Arabic. Maybe nobody spoke to him in French any more.

Yes, that face could be the ruined version of the one she knew from the photograph, that half-face turned towards the young woman and the light, its right side dark in shadow. She saw the curve of the nose, the set of the eyes. Or not. There was always the possibility of a mistake.

He began bundling up his sack, to depart. She laid a hand on his sleeve and spoke again. "*Menfedlik.* Please."

He paused, looked down at her.

Summoning Arabic to the best of her ability, she said to him, "*Smehli.* Excuse me I don't want anything. I am a friend."

He might walk away, shake her off. But no, he stayed. She took the small photograph out of her pocket and gave it to him. He looked at it, at her, at it again. She passed a hand over her hair, pushed it back behind her ears, the way Aziz had sometimes, when he caressed her face. The way Marion had worn it, the day that picture was taken. He stared at the photograph and then turned it over and looked at the back, where the date was pencilled, 1936.

What was memory? The thin string that attached one to the rest of the world. A well, her mother had said; but you can lose the rope. Without memory, there was no identity. Unless, like a baby, you lived from minute to minute, at sea in time. He said at last, "*Américaine?*"

"*Oui.* I am her daughter. *La fille de Marianne. L'Anglaise. Vous comprenez?*"

Silence, in which nothing happened. Sarah thought, I could have misunderstood from the very beginning. What was it Aziz had said, "Sarah, a man looks at a woman a thousand times in a life."

Then he let go his bag and put his arms around her. Strong arms, gripping her tight. He stroked her head and crooned, Marianne, Marianne.

"I am Sarah. Sarah, her daughter. *Sa fille.*"

"*Zahrah.*"

His cheek on her head, he rocked her back and forth. He smelled of fish and unwashed cloth, but she stayed, holding her breath, in his embrace for as long as she could. It could be that he was just repeating what she said, a name, any name, out of the confusion of his mind.

"I know your story. I know what happened." Hoping that the French language would not bring back the terror: the cell, the beating, whatever they had done.

But he rocked her and murmured, "*Ma'a lesh.* So it goes. *Ça, c'est l'histoire.*"

It's history. How glibly that phrase was used, these days, meaning, it's over. While real history is never over, but carries its dire effects, its damage, into the present time.

A man who remembers is not crazy. Crazy is the word we give to the unforgivable sin of having forgotten. But what did he remember? A prison cell, perhaps. A woman, perhaps. A foreign woman. His life, locked inside him, was not hers to decipher. Only the brief physical contact, the touching, this moment, now; and the hermetic truth of that contact, hand-to-hand, eye to eye.

The sun was up, a red egg. The strange waiting period of before-dawn was over for another day. People were beginning to walk through the city gates and down towards the port and the Riad; the town was waking up. She stood, quite visible, with the man who fed seagulls, and he still had hold of her hand.

"I have to go. Keep this."

The photograph was in his hand; it might be all the memory he had, the shred or nerve that responded to that faded image. Or it might be meaningless, a message he could not decode. In his ruin of a face, she imagined a young man's eyes. Intelligence flickered like light from a lamp burning low. It was just a moment, but it was there. A light flickering in darkness, in the time before death.

"Bless you, *binti.*"

He could have been speaking to anyone, but the language and

the tenderness were there, that could have rusted away with disuse. He put out a hand to caress her head, to let his hand remember. Then he picked up his bag and the gulls came swarming back, their little red eyes and sharp beaks very close and urgent to be fed.

* * *

I have forgotten many things that have happened since.

It was long ago. In Mogador.

The things one does not really forget are the things that happen just once. There is no repetition. It is a first and only time. Those things have a taste, a smell.

The chalk we put on the floor, to dance. A face half in sunlight, half in shade. The strangeness of language. The smell of cold stone.

I was young. It was long ago. In the place they called Mogador.

* * *

In a nursing home in Boston, her mother had struggled with her to get a hand back on the rope; pull up the water that smelled of cold stone. Then she had let go. This man, on a windy street in Essaouira, could be making the same huge effort with whatever had been left to him of his brain. He looked at her as her mother had done. She couldn't know what he remembered, only that he'd seen her, in a moment that was already now the past. They had made their human connection. *Binti Marianne*, he had said. Perhaps, she thought, we are the children of our parents' desires. Whatever the outcome, the desire was there, and we take it in with our first breath without even knowing. Whatever this man and her mother had been to each other, in those few months in that distant year, she was here in Morocco now because of it. It was what had brought her to this place.

There were the ones who left, and those who never got away. The people who didn't have passports, who became the scapegoats: Aisha, Abdel Jadid. She thought, we're the ones who just leave memories behind us wherever we go, scraps of memory, a touch, a photograph, a word in our own language: Marion, Nick, Yann, even

I, myself. We can all just get up and go. We can say: I was once in a house in Morocco. Once, a long time ago, I lived in a house in Morocco. It becomes a story; it isn't the rest of our lives. Until we realize what brought us here, and that it is what informs the rest of our lives, whether we know it or not. Like a song played invisibly in the next room.

*   *   *

He had been waiting for her. He'd seen her move about the town, week after week, sometimes with the young man from the windsurf base. He'd noticed her, from her first day. Sometimes she came close to him, greeted him and then moved away. He let her move away from him as he let the birds fly up, knowing that they would return. Something, some turn of events would bring her to him, would let her know him, he was sure.

Silence had become his language. He was, since those days, a poet of silence. People had stopped speaking to him because they thought he did not understand them; perhaps that he had no tongue, even, perhaps that they had taken that. He knew the stories: of how he had been seduced on the ramparts by Aisha Gandisha, how she had spoiled his brains and left him senseless. The truth was always less than the myth, and more. He never spoke, except to the birds. Nobody touched him these days; only the flutter of gulls' wings about his head spoke to him, and the grip of their claws on his arm. It was better this way. History such as his was best forgotten by others. Yet, only he did not forget. In his silence, he was made of memory. In his withdrawal from all human touch and speech, he kept the mark of that time scalding in his flesh. The attentions they had paid him were enough for all time; he wanted no approach from any human being.

The eyes of the town had seen the woman come, though, and he was one of the town's eyes. Nothing that went on here escaped him. He had seen the death of the fat man on the fishermen's quay, and the police who came to Sadia's house to arrest Aisha the cook. Not speaking, he was able to see everything; he had become all gaze. Once people thought you were crazy, they hardly noticed your presence.

So like the other, she was. Marianne, the woman from England, still a girl when he was hardly more than a boy. Nothing had been erased from his memory. He had been touched, wrecked on the outside, but they had not come in. He saw the house in Rabat, its polished wood floors, the drinks cabinet, and the gramophone as they called it, the black polished discs of its music. The shy young woman with the hair brushed back like a boy's behind her ears, her eager eyes. The French consul with his pursed-up wife. The veranda, where he first spoke to her; where he dared to ask her to dance.

When you faced torture in order to hold on to information that others wanted, you kept what was precious to you deep inside. It was the best way to remember: to decide, deep inside you, never to tell anything. You could not tell a part, and have the whole survive. Once they had started unravelling you, you came undone.

He'd followed in his mind, the journey back to this town where he'd lived. Over and over. The borrowed car in which he had driven her. The scarf wrapping her head. The house to which he took her, in the Rue Oujda, up behind the spice market. The squeak of the opening door. He had told the servant to light a fire in the fireplace, because she was cold. Details were what saved you. He had held her hands, both of them wrapped in his. Memory was inside him, a locked box, to open and explore again and again when the attentions they had given him became too strong.

He'd been in Fez, when she left. He'd not known that she was going, had not had time to say anything, even goodbye. He came back to find her and she had gone. Her uncle, that good man, told him, "Abdel, I am sorry, I had to send her home. The consequences were going to be too difficult, you understand?"

It was then he'd known he was already a marked man, with whom nobody must associate. After that, he'd given himself entirely to Al Fassi and the cause of Independence. The first task was to feed people where they were starving. This he had done. Now, he fed birds. They looked for him, waited for him at the sea wall, rose in a cloud about him. It was his alibi. As being thought crazy was; it gave you time to live, and think. When she gave him the photograph, he hardly needed it; he still knew her face so well.

*   *   *

"Aisha?"

"Good morning Sarah."

"How are you? Are you all right?"

"Me, of course. I am Berber. I stay here, this is my house. With Jake here, all will be well. He is a good boy, Jake. My son, you know that? Everybody knows this now."

Aisha was back in the kitchen, brewing coffee on the little stove, a *tajine* already cooking on the burning charcoal. She took Sarah into a brief embrace. The grey, crushed look she had had yesterday was gone, but she still had dark circles under her eyes and she was pale. "You take care, Sarah. You take care."

There were questions—What happened to you?—that Sarah could have asked. But Aisha's whole slight body told her: No.

There was no way to know what had happened, or when it would happen again, once she had no man to protect her.

*   *   *

It rained, the day before she left. Wet wheels on the street were the only sound in a town where all the shops were closed. She dashed through the straight rain to Driss' patisserie. The blue doors of the carpet and jewellery shops were closed and bolted, the narrow streets filled with water. In the back room at Driss' shop, a few men sat at tables with glasses of coffee and pastries in front of them. A few people ran down the street in *d'jellabas* with newspapers or briefcases on their heads and dashed inside, shaking raindrops from their sleeves, their faces sluiced with rain. Inside it was green as an aquarium, with the yellow canary singing at its heart.

Driss himself brought coffee and croissants. He stayed to talk for a moment as she picked the warm croissants apart and dipped pieces into her coffee.

"You are leaving?"

"Yes."

"But you will not forget us?"

"Never."

To be remembered, not to be forgotten, is a passport. Out of the present and into the future. Across the boundaries of geographical space. To have a life, elsewhere.

"You see, Madame Sarah, there are places people must come to, and they pass through. Many, many people pass through this place. There are other places like this in the world. You do not know why you must go to them, but you must. They are the needles through which passes the thread of life. You go through, and then you go on. Somewhere else will call you. Again, you will not know why. But for us who must stay, who cannot go, it is important that you remember, *Ouacha*? That you do not forget."

The canary sang and the rain still poured down outside and Driss, whose ancestors had been making pastry here for generations, held her gaze.

"I won't forget," she said, as Marion, more than fifty years ago, might well have said to this man's father. As Roosevelt probably said to Mohammed v. Only we do, she knew. To remember is more than not forgetting. It is to decide what matters. It is a promise. At the end of a life, what's left? Only what you have decided to remember: what speaks to you, from the photograph you took, the odour you inhaled, the moment you took to pause, to let the world in, let it inhabit you in its strangeness and beauty. Only that tug from an outer reality which has made you its own.

When the rain cleared, the sea was red. The mud from the rivers had churned its way down to the estuaries all down the coast and stained the ocean as far as the eye could see. She looked for one last time down the whole expanse of the empty rain washed beach, past the Chalet de la Plage with its furled umbrellas and soaked terraces, along to the closed and shuttered windsurf base, and beyond it to the dunes that had been carved hard and different by the rain. The red tide came in fast. At the end of the beach the ruined fortress showed at the edge of the sea, eaten away by the centuries-long movement of waves, but clear and sharp in outline as the mist lifted. Beyond it was the old summer palace of the Sultans of Morocco, and the beach that stretched all the way to Sidi Kaouki, unmarked where Aziz and she had galloped their horses and left hoof prints deeply, briefly incised in wet sand.

Epilogue

Aziz wrote to her, a letter she opened on the Long Island Railroad one day when she was travelling to spend the weekend with a friend. She had it in her pocket for several hours, unopened. She was afraid to read things, these days. The papers screamed their headlines, everything screamed, there was nothing quiet to be opened in private, read to oneself. Somehow his letter in her pocket was more of a comfort unopened. She could imagine it containing anything, nothing, a message she needed uniquely to hear. She could not bear it, after this time, to be banal. So she crossed Manhattan and took the train from Penn Station. It was a Saturday morning in January. A year exactly. She slit the blue envelope with her thumb. It meant he had not forgotten. But what had he not forgotten? Of what might she be accused?

"*Habibti.*"

He called her that still. "*I am at home and I have to write to you. This is a bad time in France. This war makes me afraid. Everybody is wanting to buy guns—and for what? To arm themselves against Arabs. My neighbourhood is full of slogans written upon walls, of insults to my* race. *My daughter, who can read now, is afraid because her father is an Arab. My Felicité, who knew no fear. Do you know what that means? She, who is French, who was born in France. Nobody even remembers that in Saudi Arabia there are thirty thousand Moroccan soldiers with the French, British and American allies. I read that they bake their own bread and carry Kalashnikovs. But they are there! The King has decided: we are Europeans, we are civilized, so we go to fight other Arabs, we fight with the whites, with the Westerners. But in the countries of Europe we are insulted just the same.*

Sarah, I am full of bitterness. In my bitterness I reach out to remember you. Our true memories are our shield against lies, against bitterness. I remember that you are an American woman and you crossed the ocean, you came to love me, our bodies were close as our souls, not in lust alone but in true companionship. You are one person in a whole world and you have made a difference in my life. I want not just to thank you for this—that would be false. I know that it also mattered for you, you did this for you, not just for me. I think you loved me. I think you came to me with your hands open, in surrender. Remembering this, I can survive better in this time of war, in which every Arab man, every brown man with black hair even, must know that he is hated for his very existence. Remember me well, Sarah. Je t'embrasse. Aziz."

She sat and she read in a train full of other Americans, each one reading the crude headlines of war. The television images were in their heads, every one of them. You could not avoid them. Yesterday a bunker in Iraq had been bombed. Hundreds of people had been inside it. The news people decided what happened and how it was interpreted. Among them, Bill Jackson, who had been her lover, was on the front line for CNN, having been to the right embassy parties and learned a little Arabic in time. He was getting the war he wanted, he was there. You could only be where you were: Bill in Kuwait, or in Saudi or wherever he was; Aziz in France, she herself here on a train going through the snowy suburbs of Long Island with their bare trees, a letter in her pocket that linked her to the rest of the world. In Morocco, there was the war. The hotels emptied, tourists shipped home, the economy falling apart, drought burning the pastures dry. No work, no harvest, no windsurfing, no innocent playing with the Atlantic, no hoof prints carved on a sloping beach.

That night in her friend's quiet house in Great Neck, she dreamed of Sidi Kaouki. The saint's house was locked and silent, proof against the invasions of both tourism and war. She and Aziz stood outside it where the beach curved around and the water came in from the Atlantic on a strong tide, the criss-cross of the current drawing its patterns on the sand. In France, Aziz woke his daughter because it was time for school. In America, she slept and dreamed. In Sidi Kaouki, where the Atlantic tide came in and went out again, there was no one to see it turn.

Acknowledgments

I would like to thank the following for their help with various aspects of this book: Andrew Greig for the journey; James Waley of the Hurricane Hotel, Tarifa, for the house; Lahbib and Marie el Omari for my introduction to Morocco; Delia Morris for sending me information, music and encouragement; Allen Meece, my husband, for living with both author and book for the years it took; Ann and Ellen McLaughlin and Robin Orlandi for reading and re-reading; Margit Bisztray, Theresa Foley and J.T. Eggers for their support of the project and myself; Markham McGill for constant computer help; Madeleine and Stephan Strobel for our long friendship and for generously providing me with a room in their house in which to work. Particular thanks to Matthew Miller of Toby Press for believing in this book and to Aloma Halter, my editor, for her inspired and patient thinking.

About the author

Rosalind Brackenbury

Rosalind Brackenbury was born in London, in 1942, grew up in the south of England, has lived in Scotland and France and now lives in Key West, Florida, with her American husband. She has published ten novels and four collections of poetry. She has worked variously as a parent, teacher, writer in residence, newspaper columnist and deck hand on a schooner.

The fonts used in this book are from the Garamond family